FLYING FINISH

Also published in Large Print
from G.K. Hall by Dick Francis:

Enquiry
Whip Hand
In the Frame
Forfeit
Decider
Dead Cert
Comeback
Longshot
Blood Sport
Odds Against
Straight
The Edge

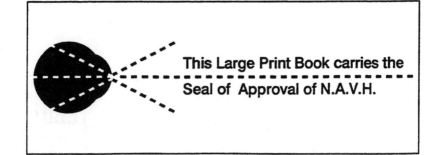

This Large Print Book carries the
Seal of Approval of N.A.V.H.

FLYING FINISH

Dick Francis

G. K. Hall & Co.
Thorndike, Maine

Copyright © 1966 by Dick Francis

All rights reserved.

Published in 1995 by arrangement with
HarperCollins Publishers, Inc.

G.K. Hall Large Print Mystery Collection.

The text of this Large Print edition is unabridged.
Other aspects of the book may vary from the original edition.

Set in 16 pt. News Plantin by Rick Gundberg.

Printed in the United States on permanent paper.

Library of Congress Cataloging in Publication Data

Francis, Dick.
  Flying finish / Dick Francis.
      p.   cm.
    ISBN 0-7838-1141-1 (lg. print : hc)
    1. Large type books. I. Title.
  [PR6056.R27F56 1995]
  823'.914—dc20   94-40718

With my thanks to

THE BRITISH BLOODSTOCK AGENCY

BRUCE DAGLISH
OF LEP TRANSPORT

PETER PALMER,
AIRLINE CAPTAIN

JOHN MERCER
OF C.S.E. AVIATION,
OXFORD AIRPORT

**I assure them that everyone
in this book is imaginary.**

1

"You're a spoiled, bad-tempered bastard," my sister said, and jolted me into a course I nearly died of.

I carried her furious, unattractive face down to the station and into the steamed-up compartment of Monday gloom and half-done crosswords and all across London to my unloved office.

Bastard I was not; not with parents joined by bishop with half Debrett and Burke in the pews. And if spoiled, it was their doing, their legacy to an heir born accidentally at the last possible minute when earlier intended pregnancies had produced five daughters. My frail eighty-six-year-old father in his second childhood saw me chiefly as the means whereby a much hated cousin was to be done out of an earldom he had coveted; my father delighted in my existence and I remained to him a symbol.

My mother had been forty-seven at my birth and was now seventy-three. With a mind which had to all intents stopped developing round about Armistice Day 1918, she had been for as long as I could remember completely batty. Eccentric, her acquaintances more kindly said. Anyway, one of the first things I ever learned was that age had nothing to do with wisdom.

Too old to want a young child around them, they had brought me up and educated me at arm's length — nursemaids, prep school and Eton — and in my hearing had regretted the length of the school holidays. Our relationship was one of politeness and duty, but not of affection. They didn't even seem to expect me to love them, and I didn't. I didn't love anyone. I hadn't had any practice.

I was first at the office as usual. I collected the key from the caretaker's cubbyhole, walked unhurriedly down the long, echoing hall, up the gritty stone staircase, down a narrow, dark corridor, and at the far end of it unlocked the heavily brown varnished front door of the Anglia Bloodstock Agency. Inside, typical of the old London warren-type blocks of offices, comfort took over from barracks. The several rooms opening right and left from the passage were close carpeted, white painted, each with the occupant's name in neat black on the door. The desks ran to extravagances like tooled leather tops, and there were sporting prints on the wall. I had not yet, however, risen to this success bracket.

The room where I had worked, on and off, for nearly six years lay at the far end, past the reference room and the pantry. "Transport" it said on the half-open door. I pushed it wide.

Nothing had changed from Friday. The three desks looked the same as usual: Christopher's, with thick uneven piles of papers held down by cricket balls; Maggie's, with the typewriter cover askew, carbons screwed up beside it, and a vase of dead chrysanthemums dropping petals into a scummy teacup; and mine, bare.

I hung up my coat, sat down, opened my desk drawers one by one and uselessly straightened the already tidy contents. I checked that it was precisely eight minutes to nine by my accurate watch, which made the office clock two minutes slow. After this activity I stared straight ahead unseeingly at the calendar on the pale green wall.

A spoiled, bad-tempered bastard, my sister said.

I didn't like it. I was not bad-tempered, I assured myself defensively. I was not. But my thoughts carried no conviction. I decided to break with tradition and refrain from reminding Maggie that I found her slovenly habits irritating.

Christopher and Maggie arrived together, laughing, at ten past nine.

"Hullo," said Christopher cheerfully, hanging up his coat. "I see you lost on Saturday."

"Yes," I agreed.

"Better luck next time," said Maggie automatically, blowing the sodden petals out of the cup on to the floor. I bit my tongue to keep it still. Maggie picked up the vase and made for the pantry, scattering petals as she went. Presently she came back with the vase, fumbled it, and left a dripping trail of Friday's tea across my desk.

9

In silence I took some white blotting paper from the drawer, mopped up the spots, and threw the blotting paper in the wastebasket. Christopher watched in sardonic amusement, pale eyes crinkling behind thick spectacles.

"A short head, I believe?" he said, lifting one of the cricket balls and going through the motions of bowling it through the window.

"A short head," I agreed. All the same if it had been ten lengths, I thought sourly. You got no present for losing, whatever the margin.

"My uncle had a fiver on you."

"I'm sorry," I said formally.

Christopher pivoted on one toe and let go. The cricket ball crashed into the wall, leaving a mark. He saw me frowning at it and laughed. He had come straight into the office from Cambridge two months before, robbed of a cricket blue through deteriorating eyesight and having failed his finals into the bargain. He remained always in better spirits than I, who had suffered no similar reverses. We tolerated each other. I found it difficult, as always, to make friends, and he had given up trying.

Maggie came back from the pantry, sat down at her desk, took her nail varnish out of the stationery drawer and began brushing on the silvery pink. She was a large, assured girl from Surbiton with a naturally unkind tongue and a suspect talent for registering remorse immediately after the barbs were securely in.

The cricket ball slipped out of Christopher's

hand and rolled across Maggie's desk. Lunging after it, he brushed one of his heaps of letters into a fluttering muddle on the floor, and the ball knocked over Maggie's bottle of varnish, which scattered pretty pink viscous blobs all over the "We have received yours of the fourteenth ult."

"Goddamn," said Christopher with feeling.

Old Cooper, who dealt with insurance, came into the room at his doddery pace and looked at the mess with cross disgust and pinched nostrils. He held out to me the sheaf of papers he had brought.

"Your pigeon, Henry. Fix it up for the earliest possible."

"Right."

As he turned to go he said to Christopher and Maggie in a complaining voice certain to annoy them, "Why can't you two be as efficient as Henry? He's never late, he's never untidy, his work is always correct and he's always done on time. Why don't you try to be more like him?"

I winced inwardly and waited for Maggie's inevitable retaliation. She would be in good form; it was Monday morning.

"I wouldn't want to be like Henry in a thousand years," she said sharply. "He's a prim, dim, sexless *nothing*. He's not alive."

Not my day, definitely.

"He rides those races, though," said Christopher in mild defense.

"And if he fell off and broke both his legs,

11

all he'd care about would be seeing they got the bandages straight."

"The bones," I said.

"What?"

"The bones straight."

Christopher blinked and laughed. "Well, well, what do you know? The still waters of Henry might just possibly be running deep."

"Deep, nothing," said Maggie. "A stagnant pond, more like."

"Slimy and smelly?" I suggested.

"No . . . oh dear . . . I mean, I'm sorry. . . ."

"Never mind," I said. "Never mind." I looked at the paper in my hand and picked up the telephone.

"Henry . . ." said Maggie desperately. "I didn't mean it."

Old Cooper tut-tutted and doddered away along the passage, and Christopher began sorting his varnished letters. I got through to Yardman Transport and asked for Simon Searle. "Four yearlings from the Newmarket sales to go to Buenos Aires as soon as possible," I said.

"There might be a delay."

"Why?"

"We've lost Peters."

"Careless," I remarked.

"Oh, ha-ha."

"Has he left?"

Simon hesitated perceptibly. "It looks like it."

"How do you mean?"

"He didn't come back from one of the trips.

Last Monday. Just never turned up for the flight back, and hasn't been seen or heard of since."

"Hospitals?" I said.

"We checked those, of course. And the morgue, and the jail. Nothing. He just vanished. And as he hasn't done anything wrong the police aren't interested in finding him. No police would be; it isn't criminal to leave your job without notice. They say he fell for a girl, very likely, and decided not to go home."

"Is he married?"

"No." He sighed. "Well, I'll get on with your yearlings, but I can't give you even an approximate date."

"Simon," I said slowly. "Didn't something like this happen before?"

"Er . . . do you mean Ballard?"

"One of your liaison men," I said.

"Yes. Well . . . I suppose so."

"In Italy?" I suggested gently.

There was a short silence at the other end. "I hadn't thought of it," he said. "Funny coincidence. Well . . . I'll let you know about the yearlings."

"I'll have to get on to Clarksons if you can't manage it."

He sighed. "I'll do my best. I'll ring you back tomorrow."

I put down the receiver and started on a large batch of Customs declarations, and the long morning disintegrated toward the lunch house. Maggie and I said nothing at all to each other and Chris-

13

topher cursed steadily over his letters. At one sharp I beat even Maggie in the rush to the door.

Outside, the December sun was shining. On impulse I jumped onto a passing bus, got off at Marble Arch, and walked slowly through the park to the Serpentine. I was still there, sitting on a bench, watching the sun ripple on the water, when the hands on my watch read two o'clock. I was still there at half past. At a quarter of three I threw some stones with force into the lake, and a park keeper told me not to.

A spoiled, bad-tempered bastard. It wouldn't have been so bad if she had been used to saying things like that, but she was a gentle, see-no-evil person who had been made to wash her mouth out with soap for swearing as a child and had never taken the risk again. She was my youngest sister, fifteen years my elder, unmarried, plain, and quietly intelligent. She had reversed roles with our parents: she ran the house and managed them as her children. She also to a great extent managed me, and always had.

A repressed, quiet, "good" little boy I had been, and a quiet, withdrawn, secretive man I had become. I was almost pathologically tidy and methodical, early for every appointment, controlled alike in behavior, handwriting and sex. A prim dim nothing, as Maggie said. The fact that for some months now I had not felt in the least like that inside was confusing, and getting more so.

I looked up into the blue, gold-washed sky.

Only there, I thought with a fleeting inward smile, only there am I my own man. And perhaps in steeplechases. Perhaps there too, sometimes.

She had been waiting for me as usual at breakfast, her face fresh from her early walk with the dogs. I had seen little of her over the weekend. I'd been racing on Saturday, and on Sunday I'd left home before breakfast and gone back late.

"Where did you go yesterday?" she asked.

I poured some coffee and didn't answer. She was used to that, however.

"Mother wanted to speak to you."

"What about?"

"She has asked the Filyhoughs to lunch next Sunday."

I tidily ate my bacon and egg. I said calmly, "That coy spotty Angela. It's a waste of time. I won't be here anyway."

"Angela will inherit half a million," she said earnestly.

"And we have beetles in the roof," I agreed dryly.

"Mother wants to see you married."

"Only to a very rich girl."

My sister acknowledged that this was true, but saw nothing particularly wrong in it. The family fortunes were waning. As my parents saw it, the swap of a future title for a future fortune was a suitable bargain. They didn't seem to realize that a rich girl nowadays had more sense than to hand over her wealth to her husband, and could leave with it intact if she felt like it.

15

"Mother told Angela you would be here."

"That was silly of her."

"Henry!"

"I do not like Angela," I said coldly. "I do not intend to be here next Sunday. Is that quite clear?"

"But you must. . . . You can't leave me to deal with them all alone."

"You'll just have to restrain Mother from issuing these stupid invitations. Angela is the umpteenth unattractive heiress she's invited this year. I'm fed up with it."

"We need. . . ."

"I am not," I said stiffly, "a prostitute."

She stood up, bitterly offended. "That's unkind."

"And while we are at it, I wish the beetles good luck. This damp decaying pile of a house eats up every penny we've got and if it fell down tomorrow we'd all be far better off."

"It's our home," she said, as if that was the final word.

When it was mine, I would get rid of it; but I didn't say that, and encouraged by my silence she tried persuasion. "Henry, please be here for the Filyhoughs."

"No," I said forcefully. "I won't. I want to do something else next Sunday. You can count me right out."

She suddenly and completely lost her temper. Shaking, she said, "I cannot stand much more of your damned autistic behavior. You're a spoiled, bad-tempered *bastard*. . . ."

Hell, I thought by the Serpentine, was I really? And if so, why?

At three, with the air growing cold, I got up and left the park, but the office I went to was not the elegant suite of Anglia Bloodstock in Hanover Square. There, I thought, they could go on wondering why the ever-punctual Henry hadn't returned from lunch. I went instead by taxi to a small, dilapidated, rubbish-strewn wharf down in the Pool, where the smell of Thames mud at low tide rose earthily into my nostrils as I paid the fare.

At one end of the wharf, on an old bombed site, a small square concrete building had been thrown up shortly after the war and shoddily maintained ever since. Its drab walls, striped by rust from leaking gutters, badly needed a coat of "Snowcem"; its rectangular metal windows were grimed and flaking, and no one had polished the brass door fittings since my previous visit six months ago. There was no need here to put on a plushy front for the customers; the customers were not expected to come.

I walked up the uncarpeted stairs, across the eight foot square of linoleumed landing and through the open door of Simon Searle's room. He looked up from some complicated doodling on a memo pad, lumbered to his feet and greeted me with a huge handshake and a wide grin. As he was the only person who ever gave me this sort of welcome I came as near to unbending

17

with him as with anyone. But we had never done more than meet now and again on business and occasionally repair to a pub afterward. There he was inclined to lots of beer and bonhomie, and I to a single whisky, and that was that.

"You haven't trekked all the way down here about those yearlings?" he protested. "I told you . . ."

"No," I said, coming to the point abruptly. "I came to find out if Yardman would give me a job."

"*You*," said Simon, "want to work *here?*"

"That's right."

"Well, I'm damned." Simon sat down on the edge of his desk and his bulk settled and spread comfortably around him. He was a vast shambling man somewhere in the doldrums between thirty-five and forty-five, bald on top, Bohemian in dress and broad of mind.

"Why, for God's sake?" he said, looking me up and down. A more thorough contrast than me in my charcoal worsted to him in his baggy green corduroys would have been hard to find.

"I need a change."

"For the worse?" He was sardonic.

"Of course not. And I'd like the chance of a bit of globe-trotting now and then."

"You can afford to do that in comfort. You don't have to do it on a horse transport."

Like so many other people, he took it for granted that I had money. I hadn't. I had only my salary from Anglia, and what I could earn by being frankly, almost notoriously, a shamateur jockey. Every penny I got was earmarked. From my father I took only my food and the beetle-infested roof over my head, and neither expected nor asked for anything else.

"I imagine I would like a horse transport," I said equably. "What are the chances?"

"Oh," Simon laughed. "You've only to ask. I can't see him turning you down."

But Yardman very nearly did turn me down, because he couldn't believe I really meant it.

"My dear boy, now think carefully, I do beg you. Anglia Bloodstock is surely a better place for you? However well you might do here, there isn't any power or any prestige. . . . We must face facts, we must indeed."

"I don't particularly care for power and prestige."

He sighed deeply. "There speaks one to whom they come by birth. Others of us are not so fortunate as to be able to despise them."

"I don't despise them. Also I don't want them. Or not yet."

He lit a dark cigar with slow care. I watched him, taking him in. I hadn't met him before, and as he came from a different mold from the top men at Anglia I found that I didn't instinctively know how his mind worked. After years of being employed by people of my own sort of background, where much that was understood never needed to be stated, Yardman was a foreign country.

He was being heavily paternal, which somehow

came oddly from a thin man. He wore black-rimmed spectacles on a strong beaky nose. His cheeks were hollowed, and his mouth in consequence seemed to have to stretch to cover his teeth and gums. His lips curved downward strongly at the corners, giving him at times a disagreeable and at times a sad expression. He was bald on the crown of his head, which was not noticeable at first sight, and his skin looked unhealthy. But his voice and his fingers were strong, and as I grew to acknowledge, his will and character also.

He puffed slowly at the cigar, a slim, fierce-looking thing with an aroma to match. From behind the glasses his eyes considered me without haste. I hadn't a clue as to what he was thinking.

"All right," he said at last. "I'll take you on as an assistant to Searle, and we'll see how it goes."

"Well . . . thank you," I answered. "But what I really came to ask for was Peters's job."

"*Peters's* . . ." His mouth literally fell open, revealing a bottom row of regular false teeth. He shut it with a snap. "Don't be silly, my boy. You can't have Peters's job."

"Searle says he has left."

"I dare say, but that's not the point, is it?"

I said calmly, "I've been in the Transport Section of Anglia for more than five years, so I know all the technical side of it, and I've ridden horses all my life, so I know how to look after them. I agree that I haven't any practical experience, but I could learn very quickly."

"Lord Grey," he said, shaking his head. "I don't think you realize just what Peters's job was."

"Of course I do," I said. "He traveled on the planes with the horses and saw they arrived safely and well. He saw that they passed the Customs all right at both ends and that the correct people collected them, and where necessary saw that another load of horses was brought safely back again. It is a responsible job and it entails a lot of traveling and I am seriously applying for it."

"You don't understand," he said with some impatience. "Peters was a traveling head groom."

"I know."

He smoked, inscrutable. Three puffs. I waited, quiet and still.

"You're not . . . er . . . in any trouble at Anglia?"

"No. I've grown tired of a desk job, that's all." I had been tired of it from the day I started, to be exact.

"How about racing?"

"I have Saturdays off at Anglia, and I take my three weeks annual holiday in separate days during the winter and spring. And they have been very considerate about extra half-days."

"Worth it to them in terms of trade, I dare say." He tapped off the ash absentmindedly into the inkwell. "Are you thinking of giving it up?"

"No."

"Mm . . . if you work for me, would I get any increase in business from your racing connections?"

21

"I'd see you did," I said.

He turned his head away and looked out of the window. The river tide was sluggishly at the ebb, and away over on the other side a row of cranes stood like red meccano toys in the beginnings of dusk. I couldn't even guess then at the calculations clicking away at high speed in Yardman's nimble brain, though I've often thought about those few minutes since.

"I think you are being unwise, my dear boy. Youth . . . youth. . . ." He sighed, straightened his shoulders and turned the beaky nose back in my direction. His shadowed greenish eyes regarded me steadily from deep sockets, and he told me what Peters had been earning; fifteen pounds a trip plus three pounds expenses for each overnight stop. He clearly thought that that would deter me, and it nearly did.

"How many trips a week?" I asked, frowning.

"It depends on the time of year. You know that, of course. After the yearling sales, and when the brood mares come over, it might be three trips. To France, perhaps even four. Usually two, sometimes none."

There was a pause. We looked at each other. I learned nothing.

"All right," I said abruptly. "Can I have the job?"

His lips twisted in a curious expression which I later came to recognize as an ironic smile.

"You can try it," he said. "If you like."

2

A job is what you make it. Three weeks later, after Christmas, I flew to Buenos Aires with twelve yearlings, the four from Anglia and eight more from different bloodstock agencies, all mustered together at five o'clock on a cold Tuesday morning at Gatwick. Simon Searle had organized their arrival and booked their passage with a charter company; I took charge of them when they unloaded from their various horseboxes, installed them in the plane, checked their papers through the Customs, and presently flew away.

With me went two of Yardman's traveling grooms, both of them fiercely resenting that I had been given Peters's job over their heads. Each of them had coveted the promotion, and in terms of human relationships the trip was a frostbitten failure. Otherwise, it went well enough. We arrived in Argentina four hours late, but the new owners' horseboxes had all turned up to collect the cargo. Again I cleared the horses and papers through the Customs, and made sure that each of the five new owners had got the right horses and the certificates to go with them. The following day the plane picked up a load of crated furs for the return journey, and we flew back to Gatwick, arriving on Friday.

On Saturday I had a fall and a winner at Sandown Races, Sunday I spent in my usual way, and Monday I flew with some circus ponies to Germany. After a fortnight of it I was dying from exhaustion; after a month I acclimatized. My body got used to long hours, irregular food, nonstop coffee, and sleeping sitting upright on bales of hay ten thousand feet up in the sky. The two grooms, Timmie and Conker, gradually got over the worst of their anger, and we developed into a quick, efficient, laconic team.

My family were predictably horrified by my change of occupation and did their best to pry me away from it. My sister anxiously retracted the words I knew I'd earned, my father foresaw the earldom going to the cousin after all, airplanes being entirely against nature and usually fatal, and my mother had hysterics over what her friends would say.

"It's a laborer's job," she wailed.

"A job is what you make it."

"What will the Filyhoughs think?"

"Who the hell cares what they think?"

"It isn't a *suitable* job for you." She wrung her hands.

"It's a job I like. It suits me, therefore it is suitable."

"You know that isn't what I mean."

"I know exactly what you mean, Mother, and

24

I profoundly disagree with you. People should do work they like doing; that's all that should decide them. Whether it is socially O.K. or not shouldn't come into it."

"But it does," she cried desperately.

"It has for me for nearly six years," I admitted, "but not any more. And ideas change. What I am doing now may be the top thing next year. If I don't look out half the men I know will be muscling in on the act. Anyway, it's right for me, and I'm going on with it."

All the same she couldn't be won over, and could only face her own elderly convention-bound circle by pretending my job was "for the experience, you know," and by treating it as a joke.

It was a joke to Simon Searle too, at first.

"You won't stick it, Henry," he said confidently. "Not you and all that dirt. You with your spotless dark suits and your snowy-white shirts and not a hair out of place. One trip will be enough."

After a month, looking exactly the same, I turned up for my pay packet late on Friday afternoon, and we sauntered along to his favorite pub, a tatty place with stained glass doors and a chronic smell of fog. He oozed on to a bar stool, his bulk drooping around him. A pint for him, he said. I bought it, and a half for me, and he drank most of his off with one much practiced swallow.

"How's the globe-trotting, then?" He ran his tongue over his upper lip for the froth.

"I like it."

"I'll grant you," he said, smiling amicably, "that you haven't made a mess of it yet."

"Thanks."

"Though of course since I do all the spade work for you at both ends, you bloody well shouldn't."

"No," I agreed. He was, in truth, an excellent organizer, which was mainly why Anglia often dealt with Yardman Transport instead of Clarkson Carriers, a much bigger and better known firm. Simon's arrangements were clear, simple, and always twice confirmed: agencies, owners and airlines alike knew exactly where they stood and at what hours they were expected to be where. No one else in the business, that I had come across at any rate, was as consistently reliable. Being so precise myself, I admired his work almost as a work of art.

He looked me over, privately amused. "You don't go on trips dressed like that?"

"I do, yes, more or less."

"What does more or less mean?"

"I wear a sweater instead of my jacket, in and around the aircraft."

"And hang up your jacket on a hanger for when you land?"

"Yes, I do."

He laughed, but without mockery. "You're a rum sort of chap, Henry." He ordered more beer, shrugged when I refused, and drank deep again. "Why are you so methodical?"

"It's safer."

"Safer." He choked on his beer, coughing and laughing. "I suppose it doesn't strike you that to many people steeplechasing and air transport might not seem especially safe?"

"That wasn't what I mean."

"What, then?"

But I shook my head, and didn't explain.

"Tell me about Yardman," I said.

"What about him?"

"Well, where he came from . . . anything."

Simon hunched his great shoulders protectively around his pint, and pursed his lips.

"He joined the firm after the war, when he left the army. He was a sergeant in an infantry regiment, I think. Don't know any details; never asked. Anyway he worked his way up through the business. It wasn't called Yardman Transport then, of course. Belonged to a family, the May-hews, but they were dying out . . . nephews weren't interested, that sort of thing. Yardman had taken it over by the time I got there; don't know how really, come to think of it, but he's a bright lad, there's no doubt of that. Take switching to air, for instance. That was him. He was pressing the advantages of air travel for horses while all the other transport agencies were going entirely by sea."

"Even though the office itself is on a wharf," I remarked.

"Yes. Very handy once. It isn't used much at all now since they clamped down on exporting horses to the Continent for meat."

"Yardman was in that?"

"Shipping agent," he nodded. "There's a big warehouse down the other end of the wharf where we used to collect them. They'd start being brought in three days before the ship came. Once a fortnight, on average. I can't say I'm sorry it's finished. It was a lot of work and a lot of mess and noise, and not much profit, Yardman said."

"It didn't worry you, though, that they were going to be slaughtered?"

"No more than cattle or pigs." He finished his beer. "Why should it? Everything dies sometime." He smiled cheerfully and gestured to the glasses. "Another?"

He had one, I didn't.

"Has anyone heard any more of Peters?" I asked.

He shook his head. "Not a murmur."

"How about his cards?"

"Still in the office, as far as I know."

"It's a bit odd, isn't it?"

Simon shrugged. "You never know, he might have wanted to duck someone, and did it thoroughly."

"But did anyone ever come looking for him?"

"Nope. No police, no unpaid bookies, no rampaging females, no one."

"He just went to Italy and didn't come back?"

"That's the size of it," Simon agreed. "He went with some brood mares to Milan and he should have come back the same day. But there was some trouble over an engine or something, and

28

the pilot ran out of time and said he'd be in dead trouble if he worked too many hours. So they stayed there overnight and in the morning Peters didn't turn up. They waited nearly all day, then they came back without him."

"And that's all?"

"That's the lot," he agreed. "Just one of life's little mysteries. What's the matter, are you afraid Peters will reappear and take back his job?"

"Something like that."

"He was an awkward bastard," he said thoughtfully. "Stood on his rights. Always arguing; that sort of chap. Belligerent. Never stood any nonsense from foreign customs officers." He grinned. "I'll bet they're quite glad to see you instead."

"I dare say I'll be just as cussed in a year or two."

"A year or two?" He looked surprised. "Henry, it's all very well you taking Peters's job for a bit of a giggle but you surely can't mean to go on with it permanently?"

"You think it would be more suitable if I was sitting behind a nice solid desk at Anglia?" I asked ironically.

"Yes," he said seriously. "Of course it would."

I sighed. "Not you too. I thought you at least might understand. . . ." I stopped wryly.

"Understand what?"

"Well . . . that who one's father is has nothing to do with the sort of work one is best suited for. And I am not fitted for sitting behind a desk. I came to that conclusion my first week at Anglia, but I stayed there because I'd kicked up a fuss and insisted on getting an ordinary job, and I wasn't going to admit I'd made a mistake with it. I tried to like it. At any rate I got used to it, but now . . . now . . . I don't think I could face that nine-to-five routine ever again."

"Your father's in his eighties, isn't he?" Simon said thoughtfully.

I nodded.

"And do you think that when he dies you will be allowed to go on carting horses round the world? And for how long *could* you do it without becoming an eccentric nut? Like it or not, Henry, it's easy enough to go up the social scale, but damn difficult to go down. And still be respected, that is."

"And I could be respected sitting behind a desk at Anglia, transferring horses from owner to owner on paper, but not if I move about and do it on airplanes?"

He laughed. "Exactly."

"The world is mad," I said.

"You're a romantic. But time will cure that." He looked at me in a large tolerant friendship, finished his beer, and flowed down from the stool like a green corduroy amoeba.

"Come on," he said, "there's time for another along the road at the Saracen's Head."

At Newbury Races the following afternoon I watched five races from the stands and rode in one.

This inactivity was not mine by choice, but

30

thrust upon me by the Stewards. They had, by the time I was twenty, presented me with their usual ultimatum to regular amateur riders: either turn professional, or ride in only fifty open races each season. In other words, don't undercut the trade; stop taking the bread and butter out of the professionals' mouths. (As if jockeys ate much bread and butter, to start with.)

I hadn't turned professional when I was twenty because I had been both too conventional and not really good enough. I was still not good enough to be a top rank professional, but I had long been a fully employed amateur. A big fish in a small pond. In the new-found freedom of my Yardman's job I regretted that I hadn't been bolder at twenty. I liked steeplechasing enormously, and with fulltime professional application I might just have made a decent success. Earthbound on the stands at Newbury I painfully accepted that my sister had brought me to my senses a lot too late.

The one horse I did ride was in the "amateurs only" race. As there were no restrictions on the number of amateur events I could ride in, few were run without me. I rode regularly for many owners who grudged paying professional jockeys' fees, for some who reckoned their horses stood more chance in amateur races, and for a few who genuinely liked my work.

All of them knew very well that if I won either amateur or open races I expected ten per cent of the prize. The word had got around. Henry

Grey rode for money, not love. Henry Grey was the shamateur to end all shamateurs. Because I was silent and discreet and they could trust my tongue, I had even been given cash presents by stewards; and solely because my father was the Earl of Creggan, my amateur permit survived.

In the changing room that afternoon I found that however different I might feel, I could not alter my long-set pattern. The easy bantering chat flowed round me and as usual it was impossible to join in. No one expected me to. They were used to me. Half of them took my aloofness to be arrogant snobbery, and the rest shrugged it off as "just Henry's way." No one was actively hostile, and it was I, I, who had failed to belong. I changed slowly into my racing clothes and listened to the jokes and the warm earthy language, and I could think of nothing, not one single thing, to say.

I won the race. The well-pleased owner gave me a public clap on the shoulder and a drink in the members' bar, and surreptitiously, round a private corner, forty pounds.

On the following day, Sunday, I spent the lot.

I started my little Herald in the garage in the pre-dawn dark, and as quietly as possible opened the doors and drifted away down the drive. Mother had invited yet another well-heeled presumptive virgin for the weekend, together with her slightly forbidding parents, and having dutifully escorted them all to Newbury Races the day before and tipped them a winner — my own — I felt I had done quite enough. They would be gone, I thought coolly, before I got back late that evening, and with a bit of luck my bad manners in disappearing would have discouraged them forever.

A steady two and a half hours driving northward found me at shortly before ten o'clock turning in through some inconspicuously signposted gates in Lincolnshire. I parked the car at the end of the row of others, climbed out, stretched, and looked up into the sky. It was a cold, clear morning with maximum visibility. Not a cloud in sight. Smiling contentedly I strolled over to the row of white painted buildings and pushed open the glass door into the main hall of the Fenland Flying Club.

The hall was a big room with several passages leading off it and a double door on the far side opening to the airfield itself. Round the walls hung framed charts, Air Ministry regulations, a large map of the surrounding area, do's and don't for visiting pilots, a thumbtacked weather report, and a list of people wanting to enter for a ping-pong tournament. There were several small wooden tables and hard chairs at one end, half occupied, and across the whole width of the other end stretched the reception-cum-operations-cum-everything-else desk. Yawning behind it and scratching between his shoulder blades stood a plump sleepy man of about my own age, sporting a thick sloppy sweater and a fair-sized hangover.

He held a cup of strong coffee and a cigarette in his free hand, and he was talking lethargically to a gay young spark who had turned up with a girl friend he wanted to impress.

"I've told you, old chap, you should have given us a ring. All the planes are booked today. I'm sorry, no can do. You can hang about if you like, in case someone doesn't turn up. . . ."

He turned toward me, casually.

"Morning, Harry," he said. "How's things?"

"Very O.K.," I said. "And you?"

"Ouch," he grinned, "don't cut me. The gin would run out." He turned round and consulted the vast timetable charts covering most of the wall behind him. "You've got Kilo November today, it's out by the petrol pumps, I think. Cross country again; is that right?"

"Uh-huh," I nodded.

"Nice day for it." He put a tick on his chart where it said H. Grey, solo cross.

"Couldn't be better."

The girl said moodily, "How about this afternoon, then?"

"No dice. All booked. And it gets dark so early. . . . There'll be plenty of planes tomorrow."

I strolled away, out of the door to the airfield and round to the petrol pumps.

There were six single-engined aircraft lined up there in two rows of three, with a tall man in white overalls filling one up through the opening on the upper surface of the port wing. He waved when he saw me coming, and grinned.

"Just doing yours next, Harry. The boys have tuned her up special. They say you couldn't have done it better yourself."

"I'm delighted to hear it," I said, smiling.

He screwed on the cap and jumped down.

"Lovely day," he said, looking up. There were already two little planes in the air, and four more stood ready in front of the control tower. "Going far?" he asked.

"Scotland," I said.

"That's cheating." He swung the hose away and began to drag it along to the next aircraft. "The navigation's too easy. You only have to go west till you hit the A.1 and then fly up it."

"I'm going to Islay," I smiled. "No roads, I promise."

"Islay. That's different."

"I'll land there for lunch and bring you back a bit of heather."

"How far is it?"

"Two seventy nautical miles, about."

"You'll be coming back in the dark." It was a statement, not a question. He unscrewed the cap of Kilo November and topped up the tanks.

"Most of the way, yes."

I did the routine checks all round the aircraft, fetched my padded jacket and my charts from the car, filed my flight plan, checked with the control tower for taxi clearance, and within a short while was up in the sky and away.

Air is curious stuff. One tends to think that because it is invisible it isn't there. What you

35

can't see doesn't exist, sort of thing. But air is tough, elastic and resistant; and the harder you dig into it the more solid it becomes. Air has currents stronger than tides and turbulences that would make Charybdis look like bath water running away.

When I first went flying I rationalized the invisibility thing by thinking of an aircraft being like a submarine; in both one went up and down and sideways in a medium one couldn't see but which was very palpably around. Then I considered that if human eyes had been constructed differently it might have been possible to see the mixture of nitrogen and oxygen we breathe as clearly as the hydrogen and oxygen we wash in. After that I took the air's positive plastic existence for granted, and thought no more about it.

The day I went to Islay was pure pleasure. I had flown so much by then that the handling of the little aircraft was as normal as driving a car, and with the perfect weather and my route carefully worked out and handy on the empty passenger seat behind me, there was nothing to do but enjoy myself. And that I did, because I liked being alone. Specifically I liked being alone in a tiny noisy efficient little capsule at 2,500 revs a minute, four thousand five hundred feet above sea level, speed over the ground one hundred and ten miles an hour, steady on a course 313 degrees, bound northwest toward the sea and a Scottish island.

I found Islay itself without trouble, and turned

my radio to the frequency — 118.5 — of Port Ellen Airfield.

I said, "Port Ellen tower, this is Golf Alpha Romeo Kilo November, do you read?"

A Scots accent crackled back, "Golf Kilo November, good afternoon, go ahead."

"Kilo November is approaching from the southeast, range fifteen miles, request joining instructions, over."

"Kilo November is cleared to join right base for runway zero four, QFE 998 millibars. Surface wind zero six zero, ten knots, call field in sight."

Following his instructions I flew in and round the little airfield on the circuit, cut the engine, turned into the wind, glided in at eighty, touched down, and taxied across to the control tower to report.

After eating in a snack bar, I went for a walk by the sea, breathing the soft Atlantic air, and forgot to look for some heather to take back with me. The island lay dozing in the sun, shut up close because it was Sunday. It was peaceful and distant, and slowed the pulse; soul's balm if you stayed three hours, devitalizing if you stayed for life.

The gold had already gone from the day when I started back, and I flew contentedly along in the dusk and the dark, navigating by compass and checking my direction by the radio beacons over which I passed. I dropped down briefly at Carlisle to refuel, and uneventfully returned to Lincolnshire, landing gently and regretfully on the well-known field.

As usual on Sundays the club room next to the main hall was bursting with amateur pilots like myself all talking at once about stalls and spins and ratings and side slips and allowances for deviations. I edged round the crowd to the bar and acquired some whisky and water, which tasted dry and fine on my tongue and reminded me of where I had been.

Turning round I found myself directly beside the reception-desk man and a red-haired boy he was talking to. Catching my eye he said to the boy, "Now here's someone you ought to have a word with. Our Harry here, he's dead quiet, but don't let that fool you. . . . He could fly the pants off most of that lot." He gestured round the room. "You ask Harry, now. He started just like you, knowing nothing at all, only three or four years ago."

"Four," I said.

"There you are, then. Four years. Now he's got a commercial license and enough ratings to fill a book and he can strip an engine down like a mechanic."

"That's enough," I interrupted mildly. The young man looked thoroughly unimpressed anyway, as he didn't understand what he was being told. "I suppose the point is that once you start, you go on," I said. "One thing leads to another."

"I had my first lesson today," he said eagerly, and gave me a rev by rev account of it for the next fifteen minutes. I ate two thick ham sandwiches while he got it off his chest, and finished the whisky. You couldn't really blame him, I thought, listening with half an ear; if you liked it, your first flight took you by the throat and you were hooked good and proper. It had happened to him. It had happened to me, one idle day when I passed the gates of the airfield and then turned back and went in, mildly interested in going up for a spin in a baby aircraft just to see what it was like.

I'd been to visit a dying great-aunt, and was depressed. "Certainly Mr. . . . ?" "Grey," I said. Certainly Mr. Grey could go up with an instructor, the air people said; and the instructor, who hadn't been told I only wanted a sight-seeing flip, began as a matter of course to teach me to fly. I stayed all day and spent a week's salary in fees; and the next Sunday I went back. Most of my Sundays and most of my money had gone the same way since.

The redhead was brought to a full stop by a burly tweed-suited man who said "Excuse me," pleasantly but very firmly, and planted himself between us.

"Harry, I've been waiting for you to come back."

"Have a drink?"

"Yes . . . all right, in a minute."

His name was Tom Wells. He owned and ran a small charter firm which was based on the airfield, and on Sundays, if they weren't out on jobs, he allowed the flying club to hire his planes.

It was one of his that I had flown to Islay.

"Have I done something wrong?" I asked.

"Wrong? Why should you, for God's sake? No, I'm in a spot and I thought you might be able to help me out."

"If I can, of course."

"I've overbooked next weekend and I'm going to be a pilot short. Will you do a flight for me next Sunday?"

"Yes," I said. I'd done it before, several times.

He laughed. "You never waste words, Harry boy. Well, thanks. When can I ring you to give you a briefing?"

I hesitated. "I'd better ring you, as usual."

"Saturday morning, then."

"Right."

We had a drink together, he talking discontentedly about the growing shortage of pilots and how it was now too expensive for a young man to take it up on his own account; it cost at least three thousand pounds to train a multiengine pilot, and only the airlines could afford it. They trained their own men and kept them, naturally. When the generation who had learned flying in the R.A.F. during the war got too old, the smaller charter firms were going to find themselves in very sticky straits.

"You now," he said, and it was obviously what he'd been working round to all along. "You're an oddity. You've got a commercial license and all the rest, and you hardly use it. Why not? Why don't you give up that boring old desk job and come and work for me?"

I looked at him for a long, long moment. It was almost too tempting, but apart from everything else, it would mean giving up steeplechasing, and I wasn't prepared to do that. I shook my head slowly, and said not for a few years yet.

Driving home I enjoyed the irony of the situation. Tom Wells didn't know what my desk job was, only that I worked in an office. I hadn't got around to telling him that I no longer did, and I wasn't going to. He didn't know where I came from or anything about my life away from the airfield. No one there did, and I liked it that way. I was just Harry who turned up on Sundays and flew if he had any money and worked on the engines in the hangars if he hadn't.

Tom Wells had offered me a job on my own account, not, like Yardman, because of my father, and that pleased me very much. It was rare for me to be sure of the motive behind things which were offered to me. But if I took the job my anonymity on the airfield would vanish pretty soon, and all the old problems would crowd in, and Tom Wells might very well retract, and I would be left with nowhere to escape to on óne day a week to be myself.

My family did not know I was a pilot. I hadn't told them I had been flying that first day because by the time I got home my great-aunt had died and I was ashamed of having enjoyed myself while she did it. I hadn't told them afterward because I was afraid that they would make a fuss and

41

stop me. Soon after that I realized what a release it was to lead two lives and I deliberately kept them separate. It was quite easy, as I had always been untalkative; I just didn't answer when asked where I went on Sundays, and I kept my books and charts, slide rules and computers securely locked up in my bedroom. And that was that.

3

It was on the day after I went to Islay that I first met Billy.

With Conker and Timmie, once they had bitten down their resentment at my pinching their promotion, I had arrived at a truce. On trips they chatted exclusively to each other, not to me, but that was as usual my fault; and we had got as far as sharing things like sandwiches and chocolate — and the work — on a taken-for-granted level basis.

Billy at once indicated that with him it would be quite, quite different. For Billy the class war existed as a bloody battlefield upon which he was the most active and tireless warrior alive. Within five seconds of our first meeting he was sharpening his claws.

It was at Cambridge airport at five in the morning. We were to take two consignments of recently sold racehorses from Newmarket to Chantilly near Paris, and with all the loading and unloading at each end it would be a long day. Locking my car in the car park I was just thinking how quickly Conker and Timmie and I were getting to be

43

able to do things when Yardman himself drove up alongside in a dark Jaguar Mark 10. There were two other men in the car, a large indistinct shape in the back, and in front, Billy.

Yardman stepped out of his car, yawned, stretched, looked up at the sky, and finally turned to me.

"Good morning, my dear boy," he said with great affability. "A nice day for flying."

"Very," I agreed. I was surprised to see him; he was not given to early rising or to waving us bon voyage. Simon Searle occasionally came if there were some difficulty with papers, but not Yardman himself. Yet here he was with his black suit hanging loosely on his too thin frame and the cold early-morning light making uncomplimentary shadows on his stretched coarsely pitted skin. The black-framed spectacles as always hid the expression in his deep-set eyes. After a month in his employ, seeing him at the wharf building two or three times a week on my visits for instructions, reports and pay, I knew him no better than on that first afternoon. In their own way his defense barriers were as good as mine.

He told me between small shut-mouthed yawns that Timmie and Conker weren't coming, they were due for a few days' leave. He had brought two men who obligingly substituted on such occasions and he was sure I would do a good job with them instead. He had brought them, he explained, because public transport wasn't geared to five o'clock rendezvous at Cambridge airport.

While he spoke the front passenger climbed out of his car.

"Billy Watkins," Yardman said casually, nodding between us.

"Good morning, Lord Grey," Billy said. He was about nineteen, very slender, with round cold blue eyes.

"Henry," I said automatically. The job was impossible on any other terms and these were in any case what I preferred.

Billy looked at me with eyes wide, blank and insolent. He spaced his words, bit them out and hammered them down.

"Good . . . morning . . . Lord . . . Grey."

"Good morning then, Mr. Watkins."

His eyes flickered sharply and went back to their wide stare. If he expected any placatory soft soaping from me, he could think again.

Yardman saw the instant antagonism and it annoyed him.

"I warned you, Billy," he began swiftly, and then as quickly stopped. "You won't, I am sure, my dear boy," he said to me gently, "allow any personal . . . er . . . clash of temperaments to interfere with the safe passage of your valuable cargo."

"No," I agreed.

He smiled, showing his grayish regular dentures back to the molars. I wondered idly why, if he could afford such a car, he didn't invest in more natural-looking teeth. It would have improved his unprepossessing appearance one hundred per cent.

"Right then," he said in brisk satisfaction. "Let's get on."

The third man levered himself laboriously out of the car. His trouble stemmed from a paunch which would have done a pregnant mother of twins proud. About him flapped a brown storeman's overall which wouldn't do up by six inches, and under that some bright red braces. over a checked shirt did a load-bearing job on some plain dark trousers. He was about fifty, going bald, and looked tired, unshaven and sullen, and he did not then or at any time meet my eyes.

What a crew, I thought resignedly, looking from him to Billy and back. So much for a day of speed and efficiency. The fat man, in fact, proved to be even more useless than he looked, and treated the horses with the sort of roughness which is the product of fear. Yardman gave him the job of loading them from their own horseboxes up the long matting-covered sidewalled ramp into the aircraft, while Billy and I inside fastened them into their stalls.

John, as Yardman called him, was either too fat or too scared of having his feet trodden on to walk side by side with each horse up the ramp; he backed up it, pulling the horse after him, stretching its head forward uncomfortably. Not surprisingly they all stuck their toes in hard and refused to budge. Yardman advanced on them

46

from behind, shouting and waving a pitchfork, and prodded them forward again. The net result was some thoroughly upset and frightened animals in no state to be taken flying.

After three of them had arrived in the plane sweating, rolling their eyes and kicking out, I went down the ramp and protested.

"Let John help Billy, and I'll lead the horses," I said to Yardman. "I don't suppose you'll want them to arrive in such an unnerved state that their owners won't use the firm again? Always supposing that they don't actually kick the aircraft to bits en route."

He knew very well that this had really happened once or twice in the history of bloodstock transport. There was always the risk that a horse would go berserk in the air at the best of times. Taking off with a whole planeload of het-up thoroughbreds would be a fair way to commit suicide.

He hesitated only a moment, then nodded.

"All right. Change over."

The loading continued with less fuss but no more speed. John was as useless at installing the horses as he was at leading them.

Cargo on airplanes has to be distributed with even more care than on ships. If the center of gravity isn't kept to within fairly close specific limits the plane won't fly at all, just race at high speed to the end of the runway and turn into scrap metal. If the cargo shifts radically in mid-air it keels the plane over exactly as it would a ship, but with less time to put it right, and no lifeboats handy as a last resort.

From the gravity point of view, the horses had to be stowed down the center of the plane, where for their own comfort and balance they had to face forward. This meant, in a medium-sized aircraft such as Yardman's usually chartered, four pairs of horses standing behind each other. From the balance point of view, the horses had to be fairly immobile, and they also had to be accessible, as one had to be able to hold their heads and soothe them at take-off and landing. Each pair was therefore boxed separately, like four little islands down the center of the plane. There were narrow gangways between the boxes and up both sides the whole length of the aircraft so that one could easily walk round and reach every individual horse to look after him.

The horses stood on large trays of peat which were bolted to the floor. The boxes of half-inch-thick wood panels had to be built up round the horses when each pair was loaded; one erected the forward end wall and the two sides, led in the horses and tied them up, added the back wall, and made the whole thing solid with metal bars banding the finished box. The bars were joined at each corner by lynch pins. There were three bars, at the top, center and bottom. To prevent the boxes from collapsing inward, each side of each box had to be separately fixed to the floor with chains acting as guy ropes. When the loading was complete, the result looked like four huge packing cases chained down, with the horses' backs and heads showing at the open tops.

As one couldn't afford to have a box fall apart in the air, the making of them, though not difficult, demanded attention and thoroughness. John conspicuously lacked both. He was also unbelievably clumsy at hooking on and tightening the guy chains, and he dropped two lynch pins which we couldn't find again. We had to use wire instead, which wouldn't hold if a strong-minded horse started kicking. By the end Billy and I were doing the boxes alone, while John stood sullenly by and watched; and Billy throughout made my share as difficult as he could.

It all took such a time that at least the three frightened horses had calmed down again before the pilot climbed aboard and started the engines. I closed the first of the big double doors we had loaded the horses through, and had a final view of Yardman on the tarmac, the slipstream from the propellers blowing his scanty hair up round the bald patch like a black sea anemone. The light made silver window panes of his glasses. He lifted his hand without moving his elbow, an awkward little gesture of farewell. I put my own hand up in acknowledgment and reply, and fastened the second door as the plane began to move.

As usual there was a crew of three flying the aircraft, pilot, copilot and engineer. The engineer, on all the trips I had so far made, was the one who got landed with brewing the coffee and who could also reasonably be asked to hold a pair of horses' heads during takeoff. This one did so with far more familiarity than John.

The trip was a relatively short one and there was a helpful following wind, but we were over an hour late at the French end. When we had landed the airport staff rolled another ramp up to the doors and I opened them from inside. The first people through them were three unsmiling businesslike Customs officials. With great thoroughness they compared the horses we had brought against our list and their own. On the papers for each horse were details of its physical characteristics and color. The Customs men checked carefully every star, blaze and sock, guarding against the possibility that some poorer animal had been switched for the good one bought. France proved more hard to satisfy and more suspicious than most other countries.

Content at length that no swindle had been pulled this time, the chief Customs man politely gave me back the papers and said that the unloading could begin.

Four horseboxes from French racing stables had turned up to collect the new purchases. The drivers, phlegmatically resigned to all delays, were engaged in digging round their mouths with toothpicks in a solid little group. I went down the ramp and across to them and told them in which order the horses would be unloaded. My French vocabulary, which was shaky on many subjects, covered at least all horse jargon and was fairly idiomatic when it came to racing or bloodstock.

At Anglia I had done quite a bit of work on French horses, and after six years I knew my way round the French stud book as well as I did the British.

The drivers nodded, sucked their teeth and drove up the boxes in the right order. The first horse off (the last loaded at Cambridge) was a nondescript brown filly who was led into the waiting horsebox by the driver himself. He took her casually from my hand, slapped her rump in a friendly fashion, and by the time I led out the second horse he had already loaded her up and was on his way.

The other drivers had, more usually, brought one or two grooms with them, as they were to collect more than one horse. Billy took over leading the horses from the ramp, and I dismantled the boxes with John. This very nearly meant, in effect, doing it by myself. He dropped the bars, tripped over the anchorages on the floor, caught his fingers in the chains, and because of the paunch could do nothing which entailed bending down. Why Yardman employed him at all, I thought in irritation, was an unfathomable mystery.

We were supposed to be taking four horses back on the return trip, but by the time the last of our cargo had departed, not one of the four had turned up. When they were more than half an hour overdue, I walked over to the port buildings and rang up one of the trainers concerned. Certainly he was sending two horses today he

51

said, two four-year-old hurdlers which he had sold to an English stable, but they were not due at the airport until three o'clock. Fifteen hundred hours, it was typed clearly on his notice from Yardman Transport. A second trainer, consulted, said the same, and although I had no phone number for the third, I took it for granted that his notice had been identical. Either Simon, or more likely his typist, had written five instead of nought on all three. It was a bore, as it meant unloading at the end of the last trip when we would all be tired.

The day's troubles, however, had barely warmed up. On my way back to the plane I saw Billy and John standing beside it engaged in a furious argument, but they broke off before I was close enough to hear what they were saying. John turned his back and kicked moodily at the bottom of the ramp and Billy gave me his best insulting stare.

"What's the matter?" I said.

Billy pursed his lips into an expression which said clearly that it was none of my business, but after a visible inner struggle he did answer.

"He's got a headache," he said, nodding at John. "From the noise."

A headache. That hardly explained the fat man's hopeless inefficiency, his sullenness, his shifty manner or his row with Billy. Nor, I realized in some surprise, did it explain why he hadn't spoken a single word to me the whole trip. But as repeating the question was unlikely to get a more fruitful answer, I shrugged and didn't bother.

"Get on board," I said instead. "We're going back empty. There's been a mix-up and we'll have to take the French horses back next time."

"——" said Billy calmly. He used a word so obscene that I wondered what he used for when he was annoyed.

"I dare say," I said dryly. "Let's not waste any more time."

John lumbered unwillingly and morosely up the ramp. Billy followed him after a pause, and I too let Billy get well ahead before I started after him. The spaces between us, I thought sardonically, were symbolic.

The airport staff removed the ramp, the plane's crew returned from their coffee break, and we proceeded back to Cambridge. On the way we sat on three separate bales of straw along the length of the aircraft and didn't even look at each other. John put his elbows on his knees and held his head in his hands, and Billy looked steadily and sightlessly at the cloud-dotted sky.

With all the sides of the boxes lying flat and strapped down on the peat trays the body of the aircraft seemed large and empty. In that state it echoed and was much noisier than usual, and I had some small sympathy for John's head. The plane was adapted, by the charter company who owned it, for any purpose that was required. The regularly spaced anchorages on the floor were as often used for fastening passenger seats as boxes

53

for animals, and the airline would fly sixty people on a coach tour type holiday to Europe one day and a load of pigs or cattle the next. In between they merely bolted or unbolted the rows of seats and swept out the relevant debris, either farmyard manure and straw or cigarette packets and bags full of vomit.

One was not allowed to sweep out manure onto foreign soil. The whole lot had to be solemnly carted back to England to comply with quarantine regulations. The odd thing was, I reflected again, that the peat trays never seemed to smell. Not even now that there was no live horse smell to mask it. Of course this plane was unpressurized, so that fresh air continually found its way in, but all the same it smelled less than an ordinary stable, even after a whole day in a hot climate.

The first person on the plane at Cambridge was a cheerful underworked bareheaded excise officer who had come there especially to clear the horses. He bounced in as soon as the cockpit ladder was in position, made a loud rude comment to the pilot and came back through the galley into the main cabin.

"What have you done with then, then?" he said, looking round at the emptiness. "Dumped them in the Channel?"

I explained the situation.

"Damn," he said. "I wanted to get off early. Well, did any of you buy anything in France?"

John didn't answer. I shook my head. Billy said offensively, "We weren't given a sodding minute to get off the sodding plane."

The Customs man in his navy blue suit glanced at me sideways in amusement. I gathered that he had met Billy before.

"O.K.," he said. "See you this afternoon, then."

He opened the big double doors, beckoned to the men outside who were wheeling up the ramp, and as soon as it was in position walked jauntily down it and back across the tarmac toward the airport building. As we were now more or less up to schedule through not having to load and unload the French hurdlers, John and Billy and I followed him in order to have lunch. I sat at one table and Billy and John ostentatiously moved to another as far away as they could get. But if Billy thought he could distress me in that way, he was wrong. I felt relieved to be alone, not shunned.

By one o'clock the horseboxes bringing the next consignment had arrived, and we started loading all over again. This time I got the groom who had brought the horses to lead them up to the plane. Billy and I made the boxes, and John belched and got in the way.

When I had finished I went into the airport building, checked the horses' export papers with the Customs man and persuaded the pilot away from his fourth cup of coffee. Up we went again into the clear wintry sky, across the gray sea, and down again in France. The same French Customs men came on board, checked every horse as meticulously as before, and as politely let it go. We took down the boxes, led out the horses, saw them loaded into their horse boxes, and watched them depart.

This time the French hurdlers for the return journey had already arrived and without a pause we began getting them on board. As there were only four we had only two boxes to set up, which by that point I found quite enough. John's sole contribution toward the fourth journey was to refill and hang the haynets for the hurdlers to pick from on their way, and even at that he was clumsy and slow.

With the horses at length unconcernedly munching in their boxes we went across to the airport buildings, Billy and John ahead, I following. The only word I heard pass between them as they left down the ramp was "beer."

There was a technical delay over papers in one of the airport offices. One of the things I had grown to expect in the racehorse export business was technical delays. A journey without one of some sort was a gift. With up to twenty horses sometimes carried on one airplane there only had to be a small query about a single animal for the whole load to be kept waiting for hours. Occasionally it was nothing to do with the horses themselves but with whether the airlines owed the airport dues for another plane or another trip, in which case the airport wouldn't clear the horse plane to leave until the dues were paid. Sometimes the quibbling was enough to get one near to jumping out of the window. I was growing very good indeed at keeping my temper when all around were losing theirs and blaming it on me. Kipling would have been proud.

This time it was some question of insurance which I could do nothing to smooth out as it involved the owner of one of the hurdlers, who was fighting a contested claim on a road accident it had been slightly hurt in. The insurance company didn't want the horse to leave France. I said it was a bit late, the horse was sold, and did the insurance company have the right to stop it anyway. No one was quite sure about that. A great deal of telephoning began.

I was annoyed, mainly because the horse in question was in the forward of the two boxes; if we had to take it off the plane it meant dismantling the rear box and unloading the back pair first in order to reach it, and then reloading those two again once we had got it off. And with Billy and John full of all the beer they were having plenty of time to ship, this was likely to be a sticky maneuver. The horses' own grooms and motor boxes had long gone home. The hurdlers were each worth thousands. Who, I wondered gloomily, was I going to trust not to let go of them if we had to have them standing about on the tarmac.

The pilot ran me to earth and said that if we didn't take off soon we would be staying all night as after six o'clock he was out of time. We had to be able to be back at Cambridge at six, or he couldn't start at all.

I relayed this information to the arguing officials. It produced nothing but some heavy Gallic shrugs. The pilot swore and told me that until twenty to five I would find him having coffee and after that he'd be en route for Paris. And I would have to get another pilot as he had worked the maximum hours for a long spell and was legally obliged now to have forty-eight hours' rest.

Looking morosely out of the window across to where the plane with its expensive cargo sat deserted on the apron, I reflected that this was the sort of situation I could do without. And if we had to stay all night, I was going to have to sleep with those horses. A delightful new experience every day, I thought in wry amusement. Join Yardman Transport and see the world, every discomfort thrown in.

With minutes to spare, the insurance company relented. The hurdler could go. I grabbed the papers, murmuring profuse thanks, raced to dig out the pilot, and ran Billy to earth behind a large frosty glass. It was clearly far from his first.

"Get John," I said shortly. "We've got to be off within ten minutes."

"Get him yourself," he said with sneering satisfaction. "If you can."

"Where is he?"

"Halfway to Paris." He drank unconcernedly. "He's got some whore there. He said he'd come back tomorrow on a regular airline. There isn't a sodding thing you can do about it, so put that in your pipe and smoke it."

John's presence, workwise, made little difference one way or another. I really cared not a bent sou if he wanted to pay his own fare back. He was free enough. He had his passport in his pocket, as we all did. Mine was already dog-eared and soft from constant use. We had to produce them whenever asked, though they were seldom stamped, as we rarely went into the passengers' immigration section of airports. We showed them more like casual passes than weighty official documents, and most countries were so tolerant of people employed on aircraft that one pilot told me he had left his passport in a hotel bedroom in Madrid and had been going unhindered round the world for three weeks without it while he tried to get it back.

"Ten minutes," I said calmly to Billy. "Fifteen, and you'll be paying your own fare back too."

Billy gave me his wide-eyed stare. He picked up his glass of beer and poured it over my foot. The yellow liquid ran away in a pool over the glossy stone floor, froth bubbles popping round the edges.

"What a waste," I said, unmoving. "Are you coming?"

He didn't answer. It was too much to expect him to get up meekly while I waited, and as I wanted to avoid too decisive a clash with him if I could I turned away and went back alone, squelching slightly, to the aircraft. He came as I had thought he would, but with less than two minutes in hand to emphasize his independence.

The engines were already running when he climbed aboard, and we were moving as soon as the doors were shut.

As usual during take-off and landing, Billy stood holding the heads of two horses and I of the other two. After that, with so much space on the half-loaded aircraft, I expected him to keep as far from me as he could, as he had done all day. But Billy by then was eleven hours away from Yardman's restraining influence and well afloat on airport beer. The crew were all up forward in the cockpit, and fat useless John was sex-bent for Paris.

Billy had me alone, all to himself.

Billy intended to make the most of it.

4

"Your kind ought not to be allowed," he said with charming directness. He had to say it very loudly, also, on account of the noise of the aircraft.

I sat on a hay bale with my back against the rear wall of the cabin and looked at him as he stood ten feet in front of me with his legs apart for balance.

"Your kind, of course," I shouted back, "are the salt of the earth."

He took a step forward and the plane bumped hard in an air pocket. It lurched him completely off his balance and he fell rolling onto his side. With sizzling fury, though it wasn't I who had pushed him, he raised himself up on one knee and thrust his face close to mine.

"—— you," he said.

At close quarters I could see how very young he was. His skin was still smooth like a child's and he had long thick eyelashes round those vast pale blue-gray searchlight eyes. His hair, a fairish brown, curled softly close to his head and down the back of his neck, cut short and in the shape of a helmet. He had a soft, full-lipped mouth and a strong straight nose. A curiously sexless face. Too unlined to be clearly male, too heavily boned to be female.

He wasn't so much a man, not even so much a person, as a force. A wild, elemental, poltergeist force trapped barely controllably in a vigorous steel-spring body. You couldn't look into Billy's cold eyes from inches away and not know it. I felt a weird unexpected primitive tingle away down somewhere in my gut, and at the same time realized on a conscious level that friendliness and reason couldn't help, that there would be no winning over, ever, of Billy.

He began mildly enough.

"Your sort," he yelled. "You think you own the bloody earth. You soft lot of out-of-date nincompoops, you and your lah-di-dah bloody Eton."

I didn't answer. He put his sneering face even nearer.

"Think yourself something special, don't you? You and your sodding ancestors."

"They aren't very usual," I yelled in his ear.

"What aren't?"

"Sodding ancestors."

He had no sense of humor. He looked blank.

"You didn't spring from an acorn," I said resignedly. "You've had as many ancestors as I have."

He stood up and took a step back. "Bloody typical," he shouted, "making fun of people you look down on."

I shook my head, got to my feet, and went along the plane to check the horses. I didn't care for useless arguments at the best of times, let alone those which strained the larynx. All four hurdlers were standing quiet in the boxes, picking peacefully at the haynets, untroubled by the noise. I patted their heads, made sure everything was secure, hesitated about going forward to the galley and cockpit for more friendly company, and had the matter settled for me by Billy.

"Hey," he shouted. "Look at this." He was pointing downward with one arm and beckoning me with sweeps of the other. There was anxiety on his face.

I walked back between the last box and the side wall of the aircraft, into the open space at the back, and across to Billy. As soon as I got near enough to see what he was pointing at, the anxiety on his face changed to spite.

"Look at this," he shouted again, and jabbed his clenched fist straight at my stomach.

The only flicker of talent I had shown in a thoroughly mediocre and undistinguished career at Eton had been for boxing. I hadn't kept it up afterward, but all the same the defense reflex was still there even after eight years. Billy's unexpected blow landed on a twisting target and my head did not go forward to meet a punch on the jaw. Or more likely in this case, I thought fleetingly, a chop on the back of the neck. Instead, I gave him back as good as I got, a short hard jolt to the lower ribs. He was surprised, but it

63

didn't stop him. Just the reverse. He seemed pleased.

There are better places for fighting than the back of an aircraft. The floor of that one was banded by the rows of seat anchorages, so that it was only a matter of time before one of us caught his foot in them and overbalanced, and it happened to be me, dodging away from a hand stretched at my throat. I went down flat on my back, unable to stop myself.

Billy fell deliberately and heavily on top of me, grinning fiercely with his own private pleasure, stabbing his elbows sharply into my chest and pressing me down hard on to the rigid anchorages. It hurt, and he meant it to. I kicked and rolled over, trying to get him underneath for a taste of it, but he was off like a cat at the crucial point and already aiming his boot as I stood up. I took that on the thigh and lunged accurately in return at his head. He just shook it briefly and went on punching, hard, quick, and with no respect for convention; but the pleasure left his face when he continued to get everything back with interest.

Thankful at least that he had produced no flick knife or bicycle chain I battled on, knowing in a cold detached part of my brain that I would gain nothing even if I won. Billy's resentment would be greater, not less, for being slogged by what he despised.

I did win in the end, if anyone did, but only because he had a belly full of beer and I hadn't.

We were both very near to a standstill. I hit him finally very hard just below the navel, my fist sinking in deep, and he fell against the aft box retching and clutching himself and sliding down onto his knees. I caught hold of one of his wrists and twisted his arm up and across his back.

"Now you listen, Billy," I said loudly in his ear, panting to get enough breath, "I don't see any point in fighting you, but I will if you make me. You can forget I'm an earl's son, Billy, and take me as I am, and this is what I am. . . ." I jerked his arm. "Hard, Billy, not soft. As tough as necessary. Remember it."

He didn't answer, perhaps because he was showing signs of being sick. I yanked him to his feet, pushed him across to the lavatory compartment in the tail, opened the door for him, and shoved him through. As the only lock was on the inside I couldn't make sure he stayed there, but from the sounds which presently issued from the open door, he was in no state to leave.

My own body ached from head to foot from his punches and kicks and from brisk contact with many sharp and knobbed edges, not the least those spaced regularly on the floor. I sat down weakly on a straw bale and rubbed at a few places which didn't do much good, and was suddenly struck by something very odd indeed.

My face was completely unmarked.

I had bashed my head against one of the metal bars on the rear box and there was a tender swelling a little above my right ear. But Billy, I remembered distinctly, had not once even aimed at my face; not at any point higher than my throat.

For someone in the grip of obsessive fury, surely that was extraordinary, I thought. The usual impulse in such a case was to "smash his face in." Billy had actually taken pains not to. I didn't understand why. I thought about it all the way to Cambridge.

It was dark when we landed and the cabin lights were on. The cheerful Customs man made his way through the plane, raised his eyebrows, and asked where my two mates were.

"Billy is in there," I nodded toward the lavatory, "and John stayed in France. He said he was coming back tomorrow."

"O.K." He checked through the horses' papers perfunctorily. "All clear," he said, and as an afterthought, "Buy anything?"

I shook my head, and he grinned, helped me open the double doors, and whistled away down the ramp as soon as it was in position.

Billy had locked himself into the lavatory and refused to come out, so I had to get one of the box drivers who had arrived to collect the cargo to help me unload the horses. Unloading was always quicker and easier than loading, but I had begun to stiffen up all over with bruises, and I was glad when it was done. The helpful box driver led out the last horse, an undistinguished brown mare, and before turning back to tidy up I watched them step and slither down the ramp.

That mare, I thought idly, was very like the one we had taken across in the morning, though the rug she wore might be misleading. But it couldn't of course be the same. No one would ship a horse out in the morning and back in the afternoon.

I turned away and began slowly to stack the box sides and the bars, wished painfully that Billy hadn't been quite so rough, and forgot about it.

The following day I went down to the wharf building and hooked Simon out for a liquid lunch. We shambled down the road to the usual hideous pub and he buried his face in a pint like a camel at an oasis.

"That's better," he said, sighing, when a scant inch remained. "How did yesterday's trip go?"

"All right."

His eyes considered me thoughtfully. "Did you have a fall on Saturday?"

"No. A winner. Why?"

"You're moving a bit carefully, that's all."

I grinned suddenly. "You should see the other fellow."

His face melted in comprehension and he laughed. "I imagine I have," he said. "Billy has a sunset of a black eye."

"You've seen him?" I was surprised.

Simon nodded. "He was in the office this morning, talking to Yardman."

"Getting his version in first, I suppose."

"What happened?" he asked interestedly.

"Billy picked a fight," I shrugged. "He resents

67

my existence. It's ridiculous. No one can help what his father is. You can't choose your birth."

"You feel strongly about it," Simon observed, ordering another pint. I shook my head to his invitation.

"So would you, if you had to live with it. I mostly get treated as a villain or a nit or a desirable match, and not much else." I was exaggerating, but not unduly.

"That last doesn't sound too bad," he grinned.

"You haven't had half the debs' mums in London trying to net you for their daughters," I said gloomily, "with your own mother egging them on."

"It sounds a wow." He had no sympathy for such a fate.

"It isn't me they want," I pointed out. "It's only my name. Which is no fun at all. And on the other end from the wedding ring I get bashed around for exactly the same reason."

"Very few can feel as strongly as Billy."

I looked at him. "There were the French in seventeen eighty-nine, remember? And the Russians in nineteen-seventeen. They all felt as strongly as Billy."

"The English like their aristocrats."

"Don't you believe it. They don't mind them from the social point of view because titles make the scandal sheets juicier. But they make damn sure they have no effective power. They say we are a joke, an anachronism, out-of-date, and weak and silly. They pretend we are these things so that we are kept harmless, so that no one will take us seriously. Think of the modern attitude to the House of Lords, for example. And you — you still think it funny that I want this sort of job, but you wouldn't think so if my father was a . . . a farmer, or a pubkeeper, or a schoolmaster. But I'm me, here and now, a man of now, not of some dim glorious past. I am not an anachronism. I'm Henry Grey, conceived and born like everyone else, into this present world. Well, I insist on living in it. I am not going to be shoved off into an unreal playboy existence where my only function is to sire the next in line, which is what my parents want."

"You could renounce your title, when you get it," Simon pointed out calmly. He spotted a pin on the bar counter and absentmindedly tucked it into his lapel. It was such a habit with him that he sported a whole row of them, like a dressmaker.

"I could," I said, "but I won't. The only good reason for doing that is to stay in the House of Commons, and I'll never be a politician. I'm not the type. Renouncing for any other reason would be just a retreat. What I want is for people to acknowledge that an earl is as good as the next man, and give him an equal chance."

"But if you get on, they say it's because of your title, not because you have talent."

"You are so right. But there's a prince or two, a few dukes' sons, and some others like me, all in the same boat just now, and I reckon that our generation, if we try hard enough, might in the end be treated on our own terms. Have some more beer."

He laughed and agreed.

"I've never heard you say so much," he said, smiling.

"It's Billy's fault. Forget it."

"I don't think I will."

"You know something odd? I'm covered with bruises, and there isn't a single one on my face."

He considered, drinking.

"He'd have got into trouble if he'd marked you for all to see."

"I suppose so."

"I gather you haven't told Yardman?"

"No."

"Why not?"

I shrugged. "I think he expected it, or something like it. He was ironic when he gave me the job. He must have known that sooner or later I would come up against Billy. And yesterday, he knew Billy would be after me. He warned me, in his way."

"What are you going to do about it?"

"Nothing."

"But if you find yourself on another trip with Billy? I mean, you're bound to, sometime."

"Yes, I know. Well, it's up to him entirely. I wouldn't start anything. I didn't yesterday. But I did tell him plainly that I'd fight back any time. And I am not, repeat *not* leaving here because of him."

"And you look so quiet and mild." He smiled one-sidedly, looking down into his again empty glass. "I think," he said slowly, almost it seemed to me sadly, "that one or two people in Yardman Transport have miscalculated about you, Henry."

But when I pressed him to explain, he wouldn't.

With no more export trips to be flown until Thursday, I went the next day, Wednesday, to the races. Someone offered me a spare ride in the novice chase and for some reason it fretted me more than ever to have to refuse. "I can't," I said, explaining thoroughly so that he wouldn't think I was being rude. "I'm only allowed to ride in fifty open races a season, and I'm already over the forty mark, and I've got mounts booked for Cheltenham and the Whitbread and so on. And if I ride too much now I'll be out of those, but thank you very much for asking me."

He nodded understandingly and hurried off to find someone else, and in irritation two hours later I watched his horse canter home to a ten lengths win. It was some consolation, however, when immediately afterward I was buttonholed by a large shrewd-faced man I knew very slightly, the father of another well-occupied amateur jockey. Between them, father and son owned and trained half a dozen good hunter 'chasers which they ran only in amateur events with notoriously satisfactory results. But on this particular afternoon Mr. Thackery, a large-scale farmer from Shropshire, showed signs both of worry and indecision.

71

"Look," he said, "I'll not beat about the bush, I'm a blunt man, so I'm told. Now, what do you say to riding all my horses until the end of the season?"

I was astonished. "But surely Julian . . . I mean, he hasn't had a bad fall or anything, has he?"

He shook his head. The worry stayed in place. "Not a fall. He's got jaundice. Got it pretty badly, poor chap. He won't be fit again for weeks. But we've a grand lot of horses this year and he won't hear of them not running just because he can't ride them. He told me to ask you, it's his idea."

"It's very good of him," I said sincerely. "And thank you, I'd like to ride for you very much, whenever I can."

"Good, then." He hesitated, and added, "Er . . . Julian told me to tell you, to ask you, if ten per cent of the prize money would be in order?"

"Thank you," I said. "That will be fine."

He smiled suddenly, his heavy face lightening into wrinkles which made him look ten years younger. "I wasn't sure about asking you, I'll tell you that, only Julian insisted on it. There's no nonsense about Henry, he said, and I can see he's right. He said Henry don't drink much, don't talk much, gets on with the job and expects to be paid for it. A pro at heart, he says you are. Do you want expenses?"

I shook my head. "Ten per cent for winning. Nothing else."

"Fair enough." He thrust out his hand and I shook it.

"I'm sorry about Julian's jaundice," I said.

Mr. Thackery's lip twitched. "He said if you said that, that he hoped for the sake of our horses you were being hypocritical."

"Oh, subtle stuff." I pondered. "Tell him to get up too soon and have a relapse."

The next afternoon I went on a flight to New York. With Billy.

The ice between us was as cold as the rarefied air outside the pressurized stratocruiser which took us. Yardman, I reflected, wasn't showing much sense in pushing us off together so soon, and on a two-day journey at that.

The wide cold stare was somewhat marred by the blackish streaks and yellow smudges left by my fist, and Billy was distinctly warier than he had been on the French journeys. There were no elementary taunts this time; but at the end of everything he said to me he tacked on the words "Lord Grey," and made them sound like an insult.

He tried nothing so crude as punching to make my trip memorable; instead he smashed down one of the metal bars as I was fixing a guy chain during the loading. I looked up angrily, squeezing four squashed right fingers in my left hand, and met his watchful waiting eyes. He was looking down at me with interest, with faintly sneering calculation, to see what I would do.

If anyone else had dropped the bar, I would have known it was accidental. With Billy, apart from the force with which it had landed, I knew it wasn't. But the day had barely begun, and the cargo was much too valuable to jeopardize for personal reasons, which I dare say he was counting on. When he saw that I was not going to retaliate, or at least not instantly, he nodded in satisfaction, picked up the bar with a small cold private smile, and calmly began putting it into place.

The loading was finished and the plane took off. There were thick dark red marks across my fingers an inch below the nails, and they throbbed all the way to America.

With us on that trip, looking after a full load of twelve horses, we took two other grooms, an elderly deaf one supplied by Yardman, and another man traveling privately with one particular horse. Owners occasionally sent their own grooms instead of entrusting their valued or difficult animals entirely to Yardman's, and far from resenting it I had learned from Timmie and Conker to be glad of the extra help.

The horse involved on this occasion had come from Norway, stayed in England overnight, and was bound for a racing stable in Virginia. The new owner had asked for the Norwegian groom to go all the way, at his expense, so that the horse should have continuous care on the journey. It didn't look worth it, I reflected, looking over at it idly while I checked the horses in the next box. A weak-necked listless chestnut, it had a straggle of hair round the fetlocks which suggested there had been a cart horse not far enough back in its ancestry, and the acute-angled hocks didn't have the best conformation for speed. Norway was hardly famed for the quality of its racing any more, even though it was possibly the Vikings who had invented the whole sport. They placed heaps of valued objects (the prizes) at varying distances from the starting point, then all the competitors lined up, and with wild whoops the race began. The prizes nearest the start were the smallest, the farthest away the richest, so each rider had to decide what suited his mount best, a quick sprint or a shot at stamina. Choosing wrong meant getting no prize at all. Twelve hundred years ago fast sturdy racing horses had been literally worth a fortune in Norway, but the smooth-skinned long-legged descendants of those tough shaggy ponies didn't count for much in the modern thoroughbred industry. It was sentiment, I supposed, which caused an American to pay for such an inferior looking animal to travel so far from home.

I asked the middle-aged Norwegian groom if he had everything he wanted, and he said, in halting, heavily accented English, that he was content. I left him sitting on his hay bale staring mindlessly into space, and went on with my rounds. The horses were all traveling quietly, munching peacefully at their haynets, oblivious to rocketing round the world at six hundred miles an hour. There is no sensation of speed if you can't see an environment rushing past.

We arrived without incident at Kennedy Airport, where a gumchewing Customs man came on aboard with three helpers. He spoke slowly, every second word an "uh," but he was sharply thorough with the horses. All their papers were in order, however, and we began the unloading without more ado. There was the extra job of leading all the horses through a tray of disinfectant before they could set foot on American soil, and while I was seeing to it I heard the Customs man asking the Norwegian groom about a work permit, and the halting reply that he was staying for a fortnight only, for a holiday, the kindness of the man who owned the horse.

It was the first time I too had been to the States, and I envied him his fortnight. Owing to the five hours' time difference, it was only six in the evening, local time, when we landed at Kennedy, and we were due to leave again at six next morning; which gave me about nine free hours in which to see New York. Although to my body mechanism it was already bedtime, I didn't waste any of them in sleeping.

The only snag to this was having to start another full day's work with eyes requiring matchsticks. Billy yawned over making the boxes as much as I did and only the third member of the team, the deaf elderly Alf, had had any rest. Since even if one shouted he could hear very little, the three of us worked in complete silence like robots, iso-

lated in our own thoughts, with gaps as unbridge-
able between us as between like poles of magnets.
Unlike poles attract, like poles repel. Billy and
I were a couple of cold Norths.

There was a full load going back again, as was
usual on Yardman trips from one continent to
another. He hated wasting space, and was accustomed to telephone around the studs when a
long flight was on the books, to find out if they
had anything to send or collect. The customers
all liked it, for on full long distance loads Yardman
made a reduction in the fares. Timmie and Conker
had less cheerful views of this practice, and I
now saw why. One's body didn't approve of tricks
with the clock. But at the point of no return
way out over the Atlantic I shed my drowsiness
in one leaping heartbeat, and with horror had
my first introduction to a horse going berserk
in mid-air.

Old Alf shook my shoulder, and the fright in
his face brought me instantly to my feet. I went
where he pointed, up toward the nose of the aircraft.

In the second to front box a solidly-muscled
three-year-old colt had pulled his head collar to
pieces and was standing free and untied in the
small wooden square. He had his head down,
his forelegs straddled, and he was kicking out
with his hind feet in a fixed, fearful rhythm. White
foamy sweat stood out all over him, and he was
squealing. The companion beside him was trying
in a terrified way to escape, his eyes rolling and

his body pushing hard against the wooden side of the box.

The colt's hooves thudded against the back wall of the box like battering rams. The wooden panels shook and rattled and began to splinter. The metal bars banding the sides together strained at the corner lynch pins, and it only needed one to break for the whole thing to start disintegrating.

I found the copilot at my elbow, yelling urgently.

"Captain says how do you expect him to fly the aircraft with all this thumping going on. He says to keep that horse still, it's affecting the balance."

"How?" I asked.

"That's your affair," he pointed out. "And for God's sake do something about it quickly."

The back wall of the colt's box cracked from top to bottom. The pieces were still held in place by the guy chains, but at the present rate they wouldn't hold more than another minute, and then we should have on our hands a maddened animal loose in a pressurized aircraft with certain death to us all if he got a hoof through a window.

"Have you got a humane killer on board?" I said.

"No. This is usually a passenger craft. Why don't you bring your own?"

There were no rules to say one had to take a humane killer in animal transport. There should be. But it was too late to regret it.

"We've got drugs in the first-aid kit," the co-pilot suggested.

I shook my head. "They're unpredictable. Just as likely to make him worse." It might even have been a tranquilizer which started him off, I thought fleetingly. They often backfired with horses. And it would be quite impossible in any case to inject even a safe drug through a fine needle designed for humans into a horse as wild as this.

"Get a carving knife or something from the galley," I said. "Anything long and sharp. And quick."

He turned away, stumbling in his haste. The colt's hind feet smashed one broken half of the back wall clean out. He turned round balefully, thrust his head between the top and center banding bars, and tried to scramble through. The panic in his eyes was pitiful.

From inside his jerkin Billy calmly produced a large pistol and pointed it toward the colt's thrashing head.

"Don't be a bloody fool," I shouted. "We're thirty thousand feet up."

The copilot came back with a white-handled saw-edged bread knife, saw the gun, and nearly fainted.

"D . . . don't," he stuttered. "D . . . d . . . don't."

Billy's eyes were very wide. He was looking fixedly at the heaving colt and hardly seemed to hear. All his mind seemed to be concentrated on aiming the gun that could kill us all.

The colt smashed the first of the lynch pins and lunged forward, bursting out of the remains of the box like flood water from a dam. I snatched the knife from the copilot and as the horse surged toward me stuck the blade into the only place available, the angle where the head joined the neck.

I hit by some miracle the carotid artery. But I couldn't get out of his way afterwards. The colt came down solidly on top of me, pouring blood, flailing his legs and rolling desperately in his attempts to stand up again.

His mane fell in my mouth and across my eyes, and his heaving weight crushed the breath in and out of my lungs like some nightmare form of artificial respiration. He couldn't right himself over my body, and as his struggles weakened he eventually got himself firmly wedged between the remains of his own box and the one directly aft of it. The copilot bent down and put his hands under my armpits and in jerks dragged me out from underneath.

The blood went on pouring out, hot sticky gallons of it, spreading down the gangways in scarlet streams. Alf cut open one of the hay bales and began covering it up, and it soaked the hay into a sodden crimson-brown mess. I don't know how many pints of blood there should be in a horse; the colt bled to death and his heart pumped out nearly every drop.

My clothes were soaked in it, and the sweet

smell made me feel sick. I stumbled down the plane into the lavatory compartment and stripped to the skin, and washed myself with hands I found to be helplessly trembling. The door opened without ceremony, and the copilot thrust a pair of trousers and a sweater into my arms. His overnight civvies.

"Here," he said. "Compliments of the house."

I nodded my thanks, put them on, and went back up the plane, soothing the restive frightened cargo on the way.

The copilot was arguing with Billy about whether Billy would really have pulled the trigger and Billy was saying a bullet from a revolver wouldn't make a hole in a metal aircraft. The copilot cursed, said you couldn't risk it, and mentioned ricochets and glass windows. But what I wanted to know, though I didn't ask, was what was Billy doing carrying a loaded pistol round with him in an underarm holster as casually as a wallet.

5

I slept like the dead when I finally got home, and woke with scant time the next morning to reach Kempton for the amateurs' chase. After such a mangling week I thought it highly probable I would crown the lot by falling off the rickety animal I had in a weak moment promised to ride. But though I misjudged where it was intending to take off at the last open ditch and practically went over the fence before it while it put in an unexpected short one, I did in fact cling sideways like a limpet to the saddle, through sheer disinclination to hit the ground.

Though I scrambled back on top, my mount, who wouldn't have won anyway, had lost all interest, and I trotted him back and apologized to his cantankerous owner, who considered I had spoiled his day and was churlish enough to say so. As he outranked my father by several strawberry leaves he clearly felt he had the right to be as caustic as he chose. I listened to him saying I couldn't ride in a cart with a pig-net over it and wondered how he treated the professionals.

Julian Thackery's father caught the tail end of

these remarks as he was passing, and looked amused; and when I came out of the weighing room after changing he was leaning against the rails waiting for me. He had brought the list of entries of his horses, and at his suggestion we adjourned to the bar to discuss them. He bought me some lemon squash without a quiver, and we sat down at a small table on which he spread out several sheets of paper. I realized, hearing him discussing his plans and prospects, that the year by year success of his horses was no accident; he was a very able man.

"Why don't you take out a public license?" I said finally.

"Too much worry," he smiled. "This way it's a hobby. If I make mistakes, I have no one on my conscience. No one to apologize to or smooth down. No need to worry about owners whisking their horses away at an hour's notice. No risk of them not paying my fees for months on end."

"You know the snags," I agreed dryly.

"There's no profit in training," he said. "I break even most years, maybe finish a little ahead. But I work the stable in with the farm, you see. A lot of the overheads come into the farm accounts. I don't see how half these public trainers stay in business, do you? They either have to be rich to start with, or farmers like me, or else they have to bet, if they want a profit."

"But they don't give it up," I pointed out mildly. "And they all drive large cars. They can't do too badly."

He shook his head and finished his whisky. "They're good actors, some of them. They put on a smiling not-a-care-in-the-world expression at the races when they've got the bank manager camping on their doorstep back home. Well, now," he shuffled the papers together, folded them, and tucked them into a pocket, "you think you can get next Thursday off to go to Stratford?"

"I'm pretty sure of it, yes."

"Right. I'll see you there, then."

I nodded and we stood up to go. Someone had left an *Evening Standard* on the next table, and I glanced at it casually as we passed. Then I stopped and went back for a closer look. A paragraph on the bottom of the front page started "Derby Hope Dead," and told in a few bald words that Okinawa, entered for the Derby, had died on the flight from the United States and was consequently scratched from all engagements.

I smiled inwardly. From the lack of detail or excitement, it was clear the report had come from someone like the trainer to whom Okinawa had been traveling, not from the airport reporters sniffing a sensational story. No journalist who had seen or even been told of the shambles on that plane could have written so starkly. But the horse had been disposed of now, and I had helped wash out the plane myself, and there was nothing to see any more. Okinawa had been well insured, a vet had certified that destroying him was essential, and I had noticed that my name on the crew list was spelled wrongly: H. Gray. With a bit of luck, and if Yardman himself had his way, that was the end of it. "My dear boy," he'd said in agitation when hurriedly summoned to the airport, "it does business no good to have horses go crazy on our flights. We will not broadcast it, will we?"

"We will not," I agreed firmly, more for my sake than for his.

"It was unfortunate. . . ." he sighed, and shrugged, obviously relieved.

"We should have a humane killer," I said, striking the hot iron.

"Yes. Certainly. All right. I'll get one."

I would hold him to that, I thought. Standing peacefully in the bar at Kempton I could almost feel the weight of Okinawa and the wetness of his blood, the twenty-four hour old memory of lying under a dying horse still much too vivid for comfort. I shook myself firmly back into the present and went out with Julian's father to watch a disliked rival ride a brilliant finish.

Saturday night I did my level best to be civil to Mother's youngest female weekend guest, while avoiding all determined maneuvers to leave me alone with her, and Sunday morning I slid away before dawn northward to Lincolnshire.

Tom Wells was out on the apron when I arrived, giving his planes a personal check. He had assigned me, as I had learned on the telephone the previous morning, to fly three men to Glasglow for a round of golf. I was to take them

85

in an Aztec and do exactly what they wanted. They were good customers. Tom didn't want to lose them.

"Good morning, Harry," he said as I reached him. "I've given you Quebec Bravo. You planned your route?"

I nodded.

"I've put scotch and champagne on board, in case they forgot to bring any," he said. "You're fetching them from Coventry — you know that — and taking them back there. They may keep you late at Gleneagles until after dinner. I'm sorry about that."

"Expensive game of golf," I commented.

"Hm," he said shortly. "That's an alibi. They are theee tycoons who like to compare notes in private. They stipulate a pilot who won't rat what he hears, and I reckon you fit that bill, Harry my lad, because you've been coming here for four years and if a word of gossip has passed your lips in that time I'm a second-class gas fitter's mate."

"Which you aren't."

"Which I'm not." He smiled, a pleasant solid sturdy man of forty plus, a pilot himself who knew chartering backward and ran his own little firm with the minimum of fuss. Ex-R.A.F., of course, as most flyers of his age were; trained on bombers, given a love for the air, and let down with a bang when the service chucked them out as redundant. There were too many pilots chasing too few jobs in the postwar years, but

Tom Wells had been good, persistent and lucky, and had converted a toe-hole copilot's job in a minor private airline into a seat on the board, and finally, backed by a firm of light aircraft manufacturers, had started his present company on his own.

"Give me a ring when you're leaving Gleneagles," he said, "I'll be up in the tower myself when you come back."

"I'll try not to keep you too late."

"You won't be the last." He shook his head. "Joe Wilkins is fetching three couples from a weekend in Le Touquet. A dawn job, that'll be, I shouldn't wonder. . . ."

I picked up the three impressive businessmen as scheduled and conveyed them to Scotland. On the way up they drank Tom Wells' Black and White and talked about dividend equalization reserves, unappropriated profits, and contingent liabilities, none of which I found in the least bit interesting. They moved on to exports and the opportunities available in the European market. There was some discussion about "whether the one and three-quarters was any positive inducement," which was the only point of their conversation I really understood.

The one and three-quarters, as I had learned at Anglia Bloodstock, was a percentage one could claim from the Government on anything one sold for export. The three tycoons were talking about machine tools and soft drinks, as far as I could gather, but the mechanism worked for bloodstock also. If a stud sold a horse abroad for say twenty thousand pounds, it received not only that sum from the buyer but also one and three-quarters per cent of it — three hundred and fifty pounds — from the Government. A carrot before the export donkey. A bonus. A pat on the head for helping the country's economy. In effect, it did influence some studs to prefer foreign buyers. But racehorses were simple to export; they needed no after sales service, follow-up campaign or multilingual advertising, which the tycoons variously argued were or were not worth the trouble. Then they moved on to taxation and I lost them again, the more so as there were some lowish clouds ahead over the Cheviots and at their request I was flying them below three thousand feet so that they could see the countryside.

I went up above the cloud into the quadrantal system operating above three thousand feet, where to avoid collision one had to fly on a steady regulated level according to the direction one was heading; in our case, going northwest, four thousand five hundred or six thousand five hundred or eight thousand five hundred, and so on up.

One of the passengers commented on the climb and asked the reason for it, and wanted to know my name.

"Grey."

"Well, Grey, where are we off to? Mars?"

I smiled. "High hills, low clouds."

"My God," said the weightiest and oldest tycoon, patting me heavily on the shoulder. "What wouldn't I give for such succinctness in my board-room."

They were in good form, enjoying their day as well as making serious use of it. The smell of whisky in the warm luxurious little cabin over-came even that of hot oil, and the expensive cigar smoke swirled huskily in my throat. I enjoyed the journey, and for Tom's sake as well as my own pride, knowing my passengers were con-noisseurs of private air travel, put them down on the Gleneagles strip like a whisper on a lake.

They played golf and drank and ate; and re-peated the program in the afternoon. I walked on the hills in the morning, had lunch, and in the late afternoon booked a room in the hotel, and went to sleep. I guess it was a satisfactory day all round.

It was half-past ten when the reception desk woke me by telephone and said my passengers were ready to leave, and eleven before we got away. I flew back on a double dog-leg, making for the St. Abbs radio beacon on the Northumber-land coast and setting a course of one sixty degrees south southeast from there on a one five two nautical mile straight course to Ottringham and then southwest across country to Conventry, com-ing in finally on their 122.70 homer signal.

The tycoons, replete, talked in mellow, rum-bling, satisfied voices, no longer about business but about their own lives. The heaviest was having trouble over currency regulations with regard to a villa he had bought on the Costa del Sol. The

Government had slapped a two-thousand pound ceiling on investment spending abroad, and two thousand would hardly buy the bath taps. . . .

The man sitting directly behind me asked about decent yachts available for charter in the Aegean, and the other two told him. The third said it was really time his wife came back from Gstaad, she had been there for two months, and they were due to go to Nassau for Easter. They made me feel poverty-stricken, listening to them.

We landed safely at Coventry, where they shook my hand, yawning, thanked me for a smooth trip, and ambled off to a waiting Rolls, shivering in the chilly air. I made the last small hop back to Fenland and found Tom, as good as his word, on duty in the control tower to help me down. He yelled out of the window to join him, and we drank coffee out of a thermos jug while he waited for his Le Touquet plane to come back. It was due in an hour, earlier than expected. Apparently the client had struck a losing streak and the party had fizzled out.

"Everything go all right with your lot?" Tom said.

"They seemed happy," I nodded, filling in the flight details on his record chart and copying them into my own logbook.

"I suppose you want your fee in flying hours, as usual?"

I grinned. "How did you guess?"

"I wish you'd change your mind and work for me permanently."

I put down the pen and stretched, lolling back on the wooden chair with my hands laced behind my head. "Not yet. Give it three or four years; perhaps then."

"I need you now."

Need. The word was sweet. "I don't know. . . . I'll think it over again, anyway."

"Well, that's something, I suppose." He ruffled his thinning light brown hair and rubbed his hands down over his face, his skin itching with tiredness. "Sandwich?"

"Thanks." I took one. Ham, with French mustard, made in their bungalow by Tom's capable wife Janie, not from the airport canteen. The ham was thick and juicy, homecooked in beer. We ate in silence and drank the hot strong coffee. Outside the glass-walled high-up square room the sky grew a thick matte black, with clouds drifting in to mask the stars. The wind was slowly backing, the atmospheric pressure falling. It was getting steadily colder. Bad weather on its way.

Tom checked his instruments, frowned, leaned back on his chair and twiddled his pencil. "The forecast was right," he said gloomily, "Snow tomorrow."

I grunted sympathetically. Snow grounded his planes and caused a hiatus in his income.

"Have to expect it in February, I suppose," he sighed.

I nodded in agreement. I wondered if Stratford Races would be snowed off on Thursday. I wondered if weather interfered much with Yardman's trips. I reflected that Janie Wells made good coffee, and that Tom was a sound sensible man. Untroubled, organized surface thoughts. And it was the last night I ever spent in my calm emotional deep-freeze.

The sky was a sullen orange-gray when we took off at eight the next morning from Gatwick, the as yet unshed snow hanging heavily as spawn in a frog's belly. We were carrying eight brood mares in an old unpressurized DC-4, flying away from the incoming storm, en route to Milan. Timmie and Conker were back, to my relief, but neither had had a scintillating holiday, by the sound of it. I overheard Conker, a much harassed small father of seven large hooligans, complaining as he loaded the cargo that he'd done nothing but cook and wash up while his wife curled up in bed with what was, in his opinion, opportunist malingering influenza. Timmie showed his sympathy in his usual way: a hearty gear-changing sniff. A thick-set black-haired square little Welshman, he suffered from interminable catarrh and everyone around him suffered also. It had been his sinuses, he unrepentantly said after one particularly repulsive spitting session, which had stopped him going down the mines like his pa. The February holiday, Timmie agreed, was not much cop.

"How many holidays do you have?" I asked, fixing chains.

"A week off every two months," Conker said.

"Blimey, mate, don't tell me you took this job without asking that."

"I'm afraid I did."

"You'll be exploited," Conker said seriously. "When you start a job, you want your terms cut and dried, wages, overtime, holidays with pay, bonuses, superannuation, the lot. If you don't stand up for your rights, no one else will, there isn't a union for us, you know, bar the agricultural workers, if you care for that which I don't. And old Yardman, he don't give nothing away you know. You want to make sure about your weeks off, mate, or you won't get any. I'm telling you."

"Well . . . thank you. I'll ask him."

"Aw, look, man," said Timmie in his soft Welsh voice, "we get other times off too. You don't want to work yourself to death. Mr. Yardman don't hold you to more than two trips a week, I'll say that for him. If you don't want to go, that is."

"I see," I said. "And if you don't go, Billy and Alf do?"

"That's about it," agreed Conker. "I reckon." He fitted the last lynch pin on the last box and rubbed his hands down the sides of his trousers.

I remembered Simon saying that my predecessor Peters had been a belligerent stand-on-your-rights man, and I supposed that Conker had caught his anti-exploitation attitude from him, because it seemed to me, from what they'd said, that Conker and Timmie both had free time positively lavished upon them. A day's return trip

93

certainly meant working a continuous stretch of twelve hours or more, but two of those in seven days wasn't exactly penal servitude. Out of interest I had added up my hours on duty some weeks, and even at the most they had never touched forty. They just don't know when they are well off, I thought mildly, and signaled to the airport staff to take the ramp away.

The DC-4 was noisy and very cramped. The gangways between and alongside the horses were too narrow for two people to pass, and in addition one had to go forward and backward along the length of the plane bent almost double. It was, as usual, normally a passenger ship, and it had low-hung luggage shelves along its length on both sides. There were catches to hold the racks up out of the way, but they were apt to shake open in flight and it was more prudent to start with all the racks down than have them fall on one's head. This, added to the angled guy chains cutting across at shin level, made walking about a tiresome process and provided the worst working conditions I had yet struck. But Conker, I was interested to notice, had no complaints. Peters, maybe, hadn't been with him on a DC-4.

After take-off, the horses all being quiet and well behaved, we went forward into the galley for the first cup of coffee. The engineer, a tall thin man with a habit of raising his right eyebrow five or six times rather fast when he asked a question, was already dispensing it into disposable mugs. Two full ones had names penciled on: Patrick and Bob. The engineer picked them up and took them forward to the pilot and copilot in the cockpit. Coming back, the engineer asked our names and wrote us each a mug.

"There aren't enough on board for us to throw them away every time," he explained, handing me "Henry." "Sugar?" He had a two-pound bag of granulated, and a red plastic spoon. "I know the way your lot drinks coffee. The skipper, too."

We drank the scalding brown liquid. It didn't taste of coffee, but if you thought of it as a separate unnamed thirst quencher, it wasn't too bad. In the galley the engine noise made it necessary to shout loudly to be heard, and the vibration shook concentric ripples in the coffee. The engineer sipped his gingerly over the scrawled word "Mike."

"You've got a right load there," he commented. "A ship full of expectant mums, aren't they?"

Conker, Timmie and I nodded in unison.

"Are they Italian?"

Together we shook our heads. Music hall stuff.

"What are they going for, then?"

"They are English mares going to be mated with Italian sires," explained Conker, who had once worked in a stud and would be positively happy if one of the mares foaled down prematurely on the flight.

"Pull the other one, it's got bells on," said the engineer.

"No, it's right," said Conker. "They have to have the foals they are carrying now in the stud

95

where their next mate is."

"Why?" The agile eyebrow worked overtime.

"Ah," said Conker seriously. "The gestation period for horses is eleven months, right? And a brood mare has a foal every twelve months, right? So there's only four weeks left between production and — er — reproduction, do you see? And in those four weeks the new foal isn't fit for traveling hundreds of miles in the freezing cold, so the mares have to have the foals in the stud of their next mate. Get?"

"I get," agreed the engineer. "I get indeed."

"That one," said Conker admiringly, pointing out in the foremost box an elegant brown silky head which owing to the general lack of space was almost in the galley, "that one's going to Molvedo."

"How do you know?" asked Timmie interestedly.

"Horsebox driver told me."

The copilot came back from the cockpit and said the skipper wanted a refill.

"Already? That man's a tank." The engineer poured into the Patrick mug.

"Here," said the copilot, handing it to me. "Take it to him, will you? I'm off to see a man about a dog." He brushed under Molvedo's future wife's inquisitive nose and bent down for the obstructed walk down to the john.

I took the steaming mug forward into the cockpit. The pilot, flying in whiter-than-white shirtsleeves despite the zero temperature outside, stretched out a languid hand and nodded his thanks. I stayed for a second look round at the banked instruments, and he glanced up at me and gestured to me to put my ear down to his mouth. The noise there made even ordinary shouting impossible.

"Are you the head chap with the horses?"

"Yes."

"Like to sit there for a bit?" He pointed to the empty copilot's seat.

"Yes, I would." He gestured permissively, and I edged sideways into the comfortable bucket seat beside him. The cockpit was tiny, considering how much had to be packed into it, and battered and dented with age. It was also, to me, very much my home.

I studied the instruments with interest. I had never flown a four-engined aircraft, only one and two, for the excellent reason that there were no four-engined planes at Fenland. As even small two-engined jobs like the Aztec I had taken to Gleneagles the day before cost nearly five pounds per flying hour to hire from Tom, I thought it unlikely I would ever raise enough cash for a course on the really big stuff, even if I could use the qualification once I got it. You couldn't just go up alone for an afternoon's jolly in an airliner; they simply weren't to be had. None of which stopped me for a moment being intent on learning everything I could.

The pilot, Patrick, indicated that I should put on the combined set of earphones and mouthpiece which was hanging over the semicircular wheel. I slid it on to my head, and through it he began to explain to me what all the switches and dials were for. He was the first pilot I'd flown with on Yardman's trips who had taken such trouble, and I listened and nodded and felt grateful, and didn't tell him I knew already most of what he was saying.

Patrick was a big striking-looking man of about thirty, with straight dark auburn hair cut a bit theatrically in duck tails, and light amber eyes like a cat's. His mouth turned naturally up at the corners so that even in repose he seemed to be smiling, as if everything in the world was delightful, with no evil to be found anywhere. Nor, I later proved, did the implication of that curve lie; he persisted in believing the best of everybody, even with villainy staring him in the face. He had the illogical faith in human goodness of a probation officer, though in that first half hour all I learned about him was that he was a gentle, careful, self-assured and eminently safe pilot.

He tuned in to the frequency of the radio beacon at Dieppe, explaining it to me as he went, and took a weather report there before turning on to the course to Paris.

"We'll go down to the Med and fly along the coast," he said. "There's too much cloud over the Alps to go straight across. Not being pressurized we ought not to go above ten thousand feet but fourteen thousand or so doesn't hurt unless you've got a bad heart. Even that doesn't give us enough in hand over the Alps in the present conditions, so I'm going the long way round."

I nodded, thoroughly approving.

He checked the de-icing equipment for a second time in ten minutes and said, "This bird won't fly with more than a quarter of a ton of ice on her, and the de-icers were U.S. last week." He grinned. "It's O.K., I've checked them six times since they were repaired, they're doing all right."

He peeled and ate one of a large bunch of bananas lying on the ledge over the instrument panel, then calmly unhinged the window beside him a few inches and threw the skin out. I laughed to myself in appreciation and began to like Patrick a good deal.

The copilot returned to claim his place, and I went back to the horses for the rest of the journey. Uneventfully we went down across France to Dijon, turned south down the Rhone valley, east at Saint-Tropez, and north again at Albenga, landing at Malpensa Airport, Milan, in exactly four hours from Gatwick.

Italy was cold. Shivering as the open doors let in air thirty degrees below the cabin temperature we watched about ten airport men in royal blue battle dress push the wide top-class ramp into position, and waited while three Customs men made their way over from the building. They came up the ramp, and the eldest of them said something in his own language.

"Non parlo italiano," I said apologetically, which useful sentence was all I knew.

"Non importa," he said. He took from me the mares' temporary import permits which had been made out in both English and Italian, and his two assistants began going from horse to horse calling out their descriptions.

All was in order. He gave me back the papers with a courteous nod of the head, and led his shadows away down the ramp. Again we went through the familiar routine of transferring the cargo from the plane to the waiting horse-boxes, Conker making a great fuss of the mare going to Molvedo.

With an hour to spare before we set about loading another cargo of mares bound in the opposite direction for the same reason, Conker, Timmie and I walked across a quarter of a mile of tarmac to the airport building to have lunch. We were met at the door by Patrick, looking very official with goldbraided shoulder tabs on his navy uniform jacket, and wearing an expression of resignation.

"We can't go back today," he said, "so you chaps don't need to hurry over your beer."

"What's up, then?" asked Timmie, sniffing loudly.

"A blizzard. Came down like a burst of eiderdown in a wind tunnel after we left this morning. It's raging all over the south and halfway across the channel, and snowing clear up to John O' Groats. The bottom's dropped out of the barometer and. . . . well, anyway, my instructions are not to go back."

"All that pasta," said Conker philosophically. "It does my tripes no good."

He and Timmie went off to the snack bar and Patrick showed me the telegraph office to send "no go" messages to Yardman and the expectant studs. After that we went back to the aircraft, where he collected his overnight bag and I turned homeward the arriving convoy of Italian mares. He waited for me to finish and helped me shut the big double doors from inside at the top of the ramp, and we walked forward across the flattened dismantled boxes, through the galley, and down the staircase which had been wheeled up to the door just behind the cockpit.

"Where will you stay?" he said.

"Hotel, I suppose," I said vaguely.

"If you like, you could come with me. There's a family in Milan I berth with while I'm stranded, and there's room for two."

I had a strong inclination, as usual, to be by myself, but principally because I couldn't even ask for a hotel room in Italian let alone find entertainment except looking at architecture for the rest of the day, I accepted his offer, and thanked him.

"You'll like them," he said.

We went two hundred yards in silence.

"Is it true," he said, "that you're a viscount?"

"No," I said casually. "A Boeing 707."

He chuckled. "A bleeding viscount, that little

Welshman said you were, to be precise."

"Would it make any difference to you if I were?"

"None whatever."

"That's all right, then."

"So you are?"

"On and off."

We went through the glass doors into the hall of the airport. It was spacious, airy, glass-walled, stone-floored. Along one side stretched a long gift counter with souvenir presents crowded in a row of display cases and stacked on shelves at the back. There were silk ties on a stand, and dolls in local dress scattered on the counter, and trays of paper-backed books and local view postcards. In charge of this display stood a tall dark-haired girl in a smooth black dress. She saw us coming and her coolly solemn face lit into a delicious smile.

"Patrick," she said. "Hullo, Patrick, come sta?"

He answered her in Italian, and as an afterthought waved his hand at me and said, "Gabriella, . . . Henry." He asked her a question, and she looked at me carefully and nodded.

"Si," she said. "Henry anche."

"That's fixed then," said Patrick cheerfully.

"You mean," I said incredulously, "that we are going to stay with — er — Gabriella?"

He stiffened. "Do you object?"

I looked at Gabriella, and she at me.

"I think," I said slowly, "that it is too good to be true."

102

It wasn't for another ten minutes, during which time she talked to Patrick while looking at me, that I realized that I spoke no Italian and the only English word that she knew was "Hullo."

6

You couldn't say it was reasonable, it was just electric. I found out between one heartbeat and the next what all the poets throughout the ages had been going on about. I understood at last why Roman Antony threw away his honor for Egyptian Cleopatra, why Trojan Paris caused a ten years' war abducting Greek Helen, why Leander drowned on one of his risky nightly swims across the Dardanelles to see Hero. The distance from home, the mystery, the unknownness, were a part of it; one couldn't feel like that for the girl next door. But that didn't explain why it hadn't happened before; why it should be this girl, this one alone who fizzed in my blood.

I stood on the cool stone airport floor and felt as if I'd been struck by lightning: the world had tilted, the air was crackling, the gray February day blazed with light, and all because of a perfectly ordinary girl who sold souvenirs to tourists.

The same thing, fantastically, had happened to her as well. Perhaps it had to be mutual, to happen at all. I don't know. But I watched the brightness grow in her eyes, the excitement and gaiety in her manner, and I knew that against all probability it was for me. Girls were seldom moved to any emotion by my brown-haired, tidy, unobtrusive self, and since I rarely set out to make an impression on them, I even more rarely did so. Even the ones who wanted to marry my title were apt to yawn in my face. Which made Gabriella's instant reaction doubly devastating.

"For God's sake," said Patrick in amusement, when she didn't answer a twice repeated question, "will you two stop gawping at each other?"

"Gabriella," I said.

"Si?"

"Gabriella. . . ."

Patrick laughed. "You're not going to get far like that."

"Parla francese?" she said anxiously.

Patrick translated. "Do you speak French."

"Yes." I laughed with relief. "Yes, more or less."

"E bene," she sighed, smiling. "E molto molto bene."

Perhaps because we were unburdened by having to observe any French proprieties and because we both knew already that we would need it later on, we began right away using the intimate form tu instead of vous, for "you." Patrick raised his eyebrows and laughed again and said in three languages that we were nuts.

I *was* nuts, there was no getting away from it. Patrick endured the whole afternoon sitting at a table in the snack bar drinking coffee and telling me about Gabriella and her family. We could see her from where we sat, moving quietly about behind her long counter, selling trinkets to departing travelers. She was made of curves, which after all the flat hips, flat stomachs, and more or less flat chests of the skinny debs at home, was as warming as a night watchman's fire on a snowy night. Her oval pale olive-skinned face reminded me of medieval Italian paintings, a type of bone structure which must have persisted through centuries, and her expression, except when she smiled, was so wholly calm as to be almost unfriendly.

It struck me after a while, when I had watched her make two or three self-conscious customers nervous by her detached manner, that selling wasn't really suited to her character, and I said so, idly, to Patrick.

"I agree," he said dryly. "But there are few places better for a smuggler to work than an airport."

"A . . . *smuggler?* I don't believe it." I was aghast.

Patrick enjoyed his effect. "Smuggler," he nodded. "Definitely."

"No," I said.

"So am I," he added, smiling.

I looked down at my coffee, very disturbed. "Neither of you is the type."

"You're wrong, Henry. I'm only one of many who brings . . . er . . . goods . . . in to Gabriella."

"What," I said slowly, fearing the answer, "are the goods?"

He put his hand into his jacket pocket, pulled out a flat bottle about five inches high, and handed it to me. A printed chemist's label on the front said "Two hundred aspirin tables B.P.," and the brown glass bottle was filled to the brim with them. I unscrewed the top, pulled out the twist of cotton wool, and shook a few out on to my hand.

"Don't take one," said Patrick, still smiling. "It wouldn't do you any good at all."

"They're not aspirins." I tipped them back into the bottle and screwed on the cap.

"No."

"Then what?"

"Birth control pills," he said.

"What?"

"Italy is a Roman Catholic country," he observed. "You can't buy these pills here. But that doesn't stop women wanting to avoid being in a constant state of baby production, does it? And the pills are marvelous for them, they can take them without the devoutest husbands knowing anything about it."

"Good God," I said.

"My brother's wife collects them at home from her friends and so on, and when she has a bottle full, I bring it to Gabriella and she passes them on at this end. I know for a fact that at least four other pilots do the same, not to mention a whole fleet of air hostesses, and she admitted to me once that a day seldom goes by without some supplies flying in."

"Do you . . . well . . . sell . . . them to Gabriella?"

He was quite shocked, which pleased me. "Of course not. She doesn't sell them, either. They are a gift, a service if you like, from the women of one country to the women of another. My sister-in-law and her friends are really keen on it; they don't see why any woman in the world should have to risk having a child if she doesn't want one."

"I've never thought about it," I said, fingering the bottle.

"You've never had a sister who's borne six children in six years and collapsed into a shattering nervous breakdown when she started the seventh."

"Gabriella's sister?"

He nodded. "That's why she got some pills, in the first place. And the demand just grew and grew."

I gave him back the bottle and he put it in his pocket. "Well?" he said, with a hint of challenge.

"She must be quite a girl," I said, "to do something like this."

His curving mouth curved wider. "If she smuggled the Crown Jewels you'd forgive her. Confess it."

"Whatever she did," I said slowly.

The amusement died right out of his face and he looked at me soberly. "I've heard of this sort of thing," he said. "But I've never seen it happen before. And you didn't even need to speak to each other. In fact, it's just damn lucky you can speak to each other. . . ."

Three times during the afternoon I made sure of that. She would get into trouble, she said, if she just talked to me when she should be working, so I bought presents separately, for my father, mother and sister, taking a long time over each choice. Each time she spoke and looked at me in a kaleidoscopic mixture of excitement, caution and surprise, as if she too found falling helplessly in love with a complete stranger an overwhelming and almost frightening business.

"I like that one."

"It costs six thousand lire."

"That is too dear."

"This one is cheaper."

"Show me some others."

We began like that, like school day textbooks, in careful stilted French, but by the end of the afternoon, when she locked the display cases and left with Patrick and me through the employees' entrance, we could talk with some ease. I perhaps knew the most French of the three of us, then Gabriella, then Patrick; but his Italian was excellent, so between us everything could in one language or another be understood.

We left the airport in a taxi, and as soon as we were on the move Patrick gave her the aspirin bottle. She thanked him with a flashing smile and asked him if they were all the same sort. He nodded, and explained they'd come from some

R.A.F. wives whose husbands were away on a three months overseas course.

From her large shoulder-sling bag of black leather she produced some of the bright striped wrapping paper from her airport gift shop and a large packet of sweets. The sweets and the aspirin bottle were expertly whisked into a ball-shaped parcel with four corners sticking up on top like leaves on a pineapple, and a scrap of sticky tape secured them.

The taxi stopped outside a dilapidated narrow terrace house in a poor-looking street. Gabriella climbed out of the taxi, but Patrick waved me back into my seat.

"She doesn't live here," he said. "She's just delivering the sweets."

She was already talking to a tired-looking young woman whose black dress accentuated the pallor of her skin, and whose varicose veins were the worst I had seen, like great dark blue knobbed worms networking just under the surface of her legs. Round her clung two small children with two or three more behind in the doorway, but she had a flat stomach in her skimpy dress and no baby in her arms. The look she gave Gabriella and her pretty present were all the reward that anyone would need. The children knew that there were sweets in the parcel. They were jumping up trying to reach it as their mother held it above their heads, and as we left she went indoors with them, and she was laughing.

"Now," said Patrick, turning away from the

window, "we had better show Henry Milan."

It was getting dark and was still cold, but not for us. I wouldn't have noticed if it had been raining ice. They began by marching me slowly around the Piazza del Duomo to see the great Gothic cathedral and the Palazzo Reale, and along the high glass arcade into the Piazza della Scala to gaze at the opera house, which Gabriella solemnly told me was the second-largest theater in Europe, and could hold three thousand six hundred people.

"Where is the largest?" said Patrick.

"In Naples," she said smiling. "It is ours too."

"I suppose Milan has the biggest cathedral, then," he teased her.

"No," she laughed, showing an unsuspected dimple, "Rome."

"An extravagant nation, the Italians."

"We were ruling the world while you were still painting yourselves blue."

"Hey, hey," said Patrick.

"Leonardo da Vinci lived in Milan," she said.

"Italy is undoubtedly the most beautiful country in the world and Milan is its pearl."

"Patrick, you are a great idiot," she said affectionately. But she was proud indeed of her native city, and before dinner that evening I learned that nearly a million and a half people lived there and that there were dozens of museums, and music and art schools, and that it was the best manufacturing town in the country, and the richest, and its factories made textiles and paper and railway engines and cars. And, in fact, airplanes.

We ate in a quiet warmly lit little restaurant which looked disconcertingly like Italian restaurants in London but smelled quite different, spicy and fragrant. I hardly noticed what I ate. Gabriella chose some sort of veal for us all, and it tasted fine, like everything else that evening. We drank two bottles of red local wine which fizzed slightly on the tongue, and unending little gold cups of black coffee. I knew even then that it was because we were all speaking a language not our own that I felt liberated from my usual self. It was so much easier to be uninhibited away from everything which had planted the inhibitions; another sky, another culture, a time out of time. But that only made the way simpler, it didn't make the object less real. It meant I didn't have chains on my tongue; but what I said wasn't said loosely, it was still rooted in some unchanging inner core. On that one evening in Milan I learned what it was like to be gay deep into the spirit, and if for nothing else I would thank Gabriella for that all my life.

We talked for hours, not profoundly, I dare say, but companionably; at first about the things we had done and seen that day, then of ourselves, our childhood. Then of Fellini's films, and a little about travel, and then, in ever-widening ripples, of religion, and our own hopes, and the state the world was in. There wasn't an ounce of natural reforming zeal among the three of us, as perhaps

112

there ought to have been when so much needed reforming; but faith didn't move mountains any more, it got bogged down by committees, Patrick said, and the saints of the past would be smeared as psychological misfits today.

"Could you imagine the modern French army allowing itself to be inspired and led into battle by a girl who saw visions?" he said. "You could not."

It was true. You could not.

"Psychology," Patrick said, with wine and candlelight in his yellow eyes, "is the death of courage."

"I don't understand," protested Gabriella.

"Not for girls," he said. "For men. It is now not considered sensible to take physical risks unless you can't avoid them. Ye gods, there's no quicker way to ruin a nation than to teach its young men it's foolish to take risks. Or worse than foolish, they would have you believe."

"What do you mean?" she said:

"Ask Henry. He'll cheerfully go out and risk his neck on a racehorse any day of the week. Ask him why."

"Why?" she said, half-serious, half-laughing, the glints of light in her dark eyes outpointing the stars.

"I like it," I said. "It's fun."

Patrick shook his red head. "You look out, pal, you mustn't go around admitting that sort of thing these days. You've got to say you do it only for the money, or you'll be labeled as a

113

masochistic guilt complex before you can say
. . . er . . . masochistic guilt complex."

"Oh yeah?" I said, laughing.

"Yeah, damn it, and it's not funny. It's deadly
serious. The knockers have had so much success
that now it's fashionable to say you're a coward.
You may not *be* one, mind, but you've got to
say so, just to prove you're normal. Historically,
it's fantastic. What other nation ever went around
saying on television and in the press and at parties
and things that cowardice is normal and courage
is disgusting? Nearly all nations used to have elab-
orate tests for young men to prove they were
brave. Now in England they are taught to settle
down and want security. But bravery is built in
somewhere in human nature and you can't stamp
it out any more than the sex urge. So if you
outlaw ordinary bravery it bursts out somewhere
else, and I reckon that's what the increase in
crime is due to. If you make enjoying danger
seem perverted, I don't see how you can complain
if it becomes so."

This was too much for his French; he said it
to me in hot English, and repeated it, when
Gabriella protested, in cooler Italian.

"But," she said wonderingly, "I do not like
a man to say he is a coward. Who wants that?
A man is for hunting and for defending, for keeping his wife safe."

"Back to the caves?" I said.

"Our instincts are still the same," agreed Patrick. "Basically good."

114

"And a man is for loving," Gabriella said.

"Yes, indeed," I agreed with enthusiasm.

"If you like to risk your neck, I like that. If you risk it for me, I like it better."

"You mustn't say so," said Patrick smiling. "There's probably some vile explanation for that too."

We all laughed, and some fresh coffee came, and the talk drifted away to what girls in Italy wanted of life as opposed to what they could have. Gabriella said the gap was narrowing fast, and that she was content, particularly as she was an orphan and had no parental pressure to deal with. We discussed for some time the pros and cons of having parents after adolescence, and all maintained that what we had was best; Gabriella her liberty, Patrick a widowed mother who spoiled him undemandingly, and I, free board and lodging. Patrick looked at me sharply when I said that, and opened his mouth to blow the gaff.

"Don't tell her," I said in English. "Please don't."

"She would like you even more."

"No."

He hesitated, but to my relief he left it, and when Gabriella asked, told her we had been arguing as to who should pay the bill. We shared it between us, but we didn't leave for some time after that. We talked, I remember, about loyalty; at first about personal loyalty, and then political.

Gabriella said that Milan had many Communists, and she thought that for a Roman Catholic

115

to be a Communist was like an Arab saying he wanted to be ruled by Israel.

"I wonder who they would be loyal to, if Russia invaded Italy?" Patrick said.

"That's a big if," I said smiling. "Pretty impossible with Germany, Austria and Switzerland in between, not to mention the Alps."

Gabriella shook her head. "Communists begin at Trieste."

I was startled and amused at the same time, hearing an echo of my die-hard father. "Wogs begin at Calais."

"Of course they do," Patrick said thoughtfully. "On your doorstep."

"But cheer up," she said laughing. "Yugoslavia also has mountains, and the Russians will not be arriving that way either."

"They won't invade any more countries with armies," I agreed mildly. "Only with money and technicians. Italian and French and British Communists can rely on never having to choose which side to shoot at."

"And can go on undermining their native land with a clear conscience," Patrick nodded, smiling.

"Let's not worry about it," I said, watching the moving shadows where Gabriella's smooth hair fell across her cheek. "Not tonight."

"It will never touch us, anyway," Patrick agreed. "And if we stay here much longer Gabriella's sister will lock us out."

Reluctantly we went out into the cold street. When we had gone ten paces Patrick exclaimed

116

that he had left his overnight bag behind, and went back for it, striding quickly.

I turned to Gabriella, and she to me. The street lights were reflected in her welcoming eyes, and the solemn mouth trembled on the edge of that transfiguring smile. There wasn't any need to say anything. We both knew. Although I stood with my body barely brushing hers and put my hands very gently on her arms just below the shoulders, she rocked as if I'd pushed her. It was the same for me. I felt physically shaken by a force so primitive and volcanic as to be frightening. How could just touching a girl, I thought confusedly, just touching a girl I'd been longing to touch all afternoon and all evening, sweep one headlong into such an uncivilized turbulence. And on a main street in Milan, where one could do nothing about it.

She let her head fall forward against my shoulder, and we were still standing like that, with my cheek on her hair, when Patrick came back with his bag. Without a word, smiling resignedly, he pulled her round, tucked her arm into his, and said briefly, "Come on. You'll get run in if you stay here much longer like that." She looked at him blindly for a moment, and then laughed shakily. "I don't understand why this has happened," she said.

"Struck by the gods," said Patrick ironically. "Or chemistry. Take your pick."

"It isn't sensible."

"You can say that again."

He began to walk down the road, pulling her with him. My feet unstuck themselves from the pavement and reattached themselves to my watery legs and I caught them up. Gabriella put her other arm through mine, and we strolled the mile and a half to where her sister lived, gradually losing the heavy awareness of passion and talking normally and laughing, and finally ending up on her doorstep in a fit of giggles.

Lisabetta, Gabriella's sister, was ten years older and a good deal fatter, though she had the same smooth olive skin and the same shaped fine dark eyes. Her husband, Giulio, a softly flabby man approaching forty, with a black mustache, bags under his eyes, and less hair than he'd once had, lumbered ungracefully out of his armchair when we went into his sitting room and gave us a moderately enthusiastic welcome.

Neither he nor Lisabetta spoke English or French so while the two girls made yet more coffee, and Patrick talked to Giulio, I looked around with some interest at Gabriella's home. Her sister had a comfortable four-bedroomed flat in a huge recently-built tower, and all the furnishings and fabrics were uncompromisingly modern. The floors were some sort of reconstituted stone heated from underneath and without carpet or rugs, and there were blinds, not curtains, to cover the windows. I thought the total effect rather stark, but reflected idly that Milan in midsummer must be an oven, and the flat had been planned for the heat.

Several children came and went, all indistinguishable to my eyes. Seven of them, there should be, I remembered. Four boys, three girls, Patrick had said. Although it was nearly midnight, none of them seemed to have gone to bed. They had all been waiting to see Patrick and tumbled about him like puppies.

When Lisabetta had poured the coffee and one of the children had handed it round Giulio asked Patrick a question, looking at me.

"He wants to know what your job is," Patrick said.

"Tell him I look after the horses."

"Nothing else?"

"Nothing else."

Giulio was unimpressed. He asked another question.

Smiling faintly, Patrick said, "He wants to know how much you earn?"

"My pay for a single trip to Milan is about one fifth of yours."

"He won't like that."

"Nor do I."

He laughed. When he translated Giulio scowled.

Patrick and I slept in a room which normally belonged to two of the boys, now doubling with the other two. Gabriella shared a third bedroom with the two elder girls, while the smallest was in with her parents. There were toys all over the place in our room, and small shoes kicked off and clothes dumped in heaps, and the unchanged sheets on the boys' beds were wrinkled like elephant skins from their restless little bodies. Patrick had from long globe-trotting habit come equipped with pajamas, slippers, washing things, and a clean shirt for the morning. I eyed this splendor with some envy, and slept in my underpants.

"Why," said Patrick in the dark, "won't you tell them you have a title?"

"It isn't important."

"It would be to Giulio."

"That's the best reason for not telling him."

"I don't see why you're so keen to keep it a secret."

"Well, you try telling everyone you're an earl's son, and see what happens."

"I'd love it. Everyone would be bowing and scraping in all directions. Priorities galore. Instant service. A welcome on every mat."

"And you'd never be sure if anyone liked you for yourself."

"Of course you would."

"How many head grooms have you brought here before?" I asked mildly.

He drew in a breath audibly and didn't answer.

"Would you have offered me this bed if Timmie had kept his big mouth shut?"

He was silent.

I said, "Remind me to kick your teeth in in the morning."

But the morning, I found, was a long way off. I simply couldn't sleep. Gabriella's bed was a foot away from me on the far side of the wall, and I lay and sweated for her with a desire I hadn't dreamed possible. My body literally ached. Cold, controlled Henry Grey, I thought helplessly. Grey by name and gray by nature. Cold, controlled Henry Grey lying in a child's bed in a foreign city biting his arm to stop himself crying out. You could laugh at such hunger; ridicule it away. I tried that, but it didn't work. It stayed with me hour after wretched hour, all the way to the dawn, and I would have been much happier if I'd been able to go to sleep and dream about her instead.

She had kissed me good night in the passage outside her door, lightly, gaily, with Patrick and Lisabetta and about six children approvingly looking on. And she had stopped and retreated right there because it was the same as in the street outside the restaurant; even the lightest touch could start an earthquake. There just wasn't room for an earthquake in that crowded flat.

Patrick lent me his razor without a word, when we got up.

"I'm sorry," I said.

"You were quite right. I would not have offered to take you with me if the Welshman hadn't said . . ."

"I know." I put on my shirt and buttoned the cuffs.

"All the same I still wouldn't have asked you if I hadn't thought you looked all right."

I turned toward him, surprised.

"What you need, Henry, is a bit more self-confidence. Why ever shouldn't people like you for yourself? Gabriella obviously does. So do I."

"People often don't." I pulled on my socks.

"You probably don't give them half a chance." With which devastatingly accurate shot he went out of the door, shrugging his arms into his authoritative captain's uniform.

Subdued by the raw steely morning, the three of us went back to the airport. Gabriella had dark shadows under her eyes and wouldn't look at me, though I could think of nothing I had done to offend her. She spoke only to Patrick, and in Italian, and he, smiling briefly, answered her in the same language. When we arrived at the airport, she asked me, hurriedly, not to come and talk to her at the gift counter, and almost ran away from me without saying good-by. I didn't try to stop her. It would be hours before we got the horses loaded, and regardless of what she asked, I intended to see her again before I left.

I hung around the airport all the morning with Conker and Timmie, and about twelve Patrick came and found me and with a wide grin said I was in luck, traffic at Gatwick was restricted because of deep snow, and unessential freight flights were suspended for another day.

"You'd better telephone the studs again, and tell them we are taking the mares to England tomorrow at eight," he said. "Weather permitting."

Gabriella received the news with such a flash

of delight that my spirits rose to the ionosphere. I hesitated over the next question, but she made it easy for me.

"Did you sleep well?" she asked gravely, studying my face.

"I didn't sleep at all."

She sighed, almost blushing, "Nor did I."

"Perhaps," I said tentatively, "if we spend the evening together, we could sleep tonight."

"Henry!" She was laughing. "Where?"

Where proved more difficult than I had imagined. She would not consider a hotel, as we must not sleep there, but go back to her sister's before midnight. One must not be shameless, she said. She could not stay out all night. We ended up, of all unlikely places, inside the DC-4, lying in a cozy nest hollowed in a heap of blankets stacked in the luggage bay alongside the galley.

There, where no one would ever find us, and with a good deal of the laughter of total happiness, we spent the whole of the evening in the age-old way, and were pleased and perhaps relieved to find that we suited each other perfectly.

Lying quietly cradled in my arms, she told me hesitantly that she had had a lover before, which I knew anyway by then, but that it was odd making love anywhere except in bed. She felt the flutter in my chest and lifted her head up to peer at my face in the dim reflected moonlight.

"Why are you laughing?" she said.

123

"It so happens that I have never made love in bed."

"Where then?"

"In the grass."

"Henry! Is that the custom in England?"

"Only at the end of parties in the summer."

She smiled and put her head down contentedly again, and I stroked her hair and thought how wholesome she was, and how dreadful in comparison seemed the half-drunk nymphs taken casually down the deb-dance garden path. I would never do that again, I thought. Never again.

"I was ashamed, this morning," she said, "of wanting this so much. Ashamed of what I had been thinking all night."

"There is no shame in it."

"Lust is one of the seven deadly sins."

"Love is a virtue."

"They get very mixed up. Are we this evening being virtuous or sinful?" She didn't sound too worried about it.

"Doing what comes naturally."

"Then it's probably sinful."

She twisted in my arms, turning so that her face was close to mine. Her eyes caught a sheen in the soft near-darkness. Her teeth rubbed gently against the bare skin on the point of my shoulder.

"You taste of salt," she said.

I moved my hand over her stomach and felt the deep muscles there contract. Nothing, I thought, shaken by an echoing ripple right down my spine, nothing was so impossibly potent as being wanted in return. I kissed her, and she gave a long soft murmuring sigh which ended oddly in a laugh.

"Sin," she said, with a smile in her voice, "is O.K."

We went back to her sister's and slept soundly on each side of the wall. Early in the morning, in her dressing gown, with tousled hair and dreaming eyes, she made coffee for Patrick and me before we set off for the airport.

"You'll come back?" she said almost casually, pouring my cup.

"As soon as I can."

She knew I meant it. She kissed me good-bye without clinging, and Patrick also. "For bringing him," she said.

In the taxi on the way to the airport Patrick said, "Why don't you just stay here with her? You easily could."

I didn't answer him until we were turning into the airport road.

"Would you? Stay, I mean?"

"No. But then, I need to keep my job."

"So do I. For different reasons, perhaps. But I need to keep it just the same."

"It's none of my business," he said, "but I'm glad."

We loaded the Italian mares and flew them to snowy England without another hitch. I soothed them on their way and thought about Gabriella, who seemed to have established herself as a warming knot somewhere under my diaphragm.

I thought about her with love and without even the conventional sort of anxiety, for she had said with a giggle, it would be a poor smuggler who couldn't swallow her own contraband.

7

Stratford Races were off because of snow, which was just as well as Yardman squeezed in an extra trip on that day at very short notice. Seven three-year-olds to France, he said; but at loading time there were eight.

I was held up on the way to Cambridge by a lorry which had skidded sideways and blocked the icy road, and when I reached the airport all the cargo had already arrived, with the box drivers stamping their feet to keep warm and cursing me fluently. Billy, and it was Billy again, not Conker and Timmie, stood about with his hands in his pockets and a sneer permanently fixed like epoxy resin, enjoying the disapproval I had brought on myself. He had not, naturally, thought of beginning the work before I arrived.

We loaded the horses, he, I, and deaf old Alf, whom Billy had brought with him, and we worked in uncompanionable silence. There was a fourth groom on the trip, a middle-aged characterless man with a large straggly mustache and a bad cold, but he had come with one particular horse from an upper crust stud, and he refrained from

offering to help with any others. Neither did he
lend a hand on the journey, but sat throughout
beside his own protégée, guarding it carefully
from no visible danger. Billy dropped a handful
of peat in my coffee and later poured his own,
which was half-full of sugar, over my head. I
spent the rest of the journey in the washroom,
awkwardly rinsing the stickiness out of my hair
and vowing to get even with Billy one day when
I hadn't thousands of pounds' worth of bloodstock
in my care.

During the unloading I looked closely at one
inconspicuous brown mare, trying to memorize
her thoroughly unmemorable appearance. She was
definitely not a three-year-old, like all the others
on the trip, and she was, I was sure, almost identical to the one we had taken to France the first
day I flew with Billy. And very like the one we
had brought back that afternoon on the second
trip. Three mares, all alike . . . well, it was not
impossible, especially as they had no distinct
markings between them, none at all.

The special groom left us in Paris, escorting
his own horse right through to its new home.
He had been engaged, he said, to bring another
horse back, a French stallion which his stud had
bought, and we would be collecting him again
the next week. We duly did collect him, the next
Tuesday, complete with the stallion, a tight-mus-
cled butty little horse with a fiery eye and a restless tail. He was squealing like a colt when we
stored him on board, and this time there was

some point in his straggly mustached keeper staying beside him all the way.

Among the cargo there was yet another undistinguished brown mare. I was leaning on the starboard side of her box, gazing over and down at her, not able to see her very clearly against the peat she stood on and the brown horse on her other side, when Billy crept up behind me and hit me savagely across the shoulders with a spare tethering chain. I turned faster than he expected and got in two hard quick kicks on his thigh. His lips went back with the pain and he furiously swung his arm, the short chain flickering and bending like an angry snake. I dodged it by ducking into one of the crossway alleys between the boxes, and the chain wrapped itself with a vicious clatter round the corner where I had been standing. Unhesitatingly I skipped through to the port side of the plane and went forward at top speed to the galley. Hiding figuratively under the engineer's skirts may not have been the noblest course, but in the circumstances by far the most prudent, and I stayed with him, drinking coffee, until we were on the final approach to Cambridge.

I did a good deal of hard thinking that night and I didn't like my thoughts.

In the morning I waited outside Yardman's office, and fell into step with Simon as he shambled out to lunch.

"Hullo," he said, beaming. "Where did you

spring from? Come and have a warmer up at the Angel."

I nodded and walked beside him, shuffling on the thawing remains of the previous week's snow. Our breaths shot out in small sharp clouds. The day was misty and overcast; the cold, raw, damp and penetrating, exactly matched my mood.

Simon pushed the stained glass and entered the fug; swam on to his accustomed stool, tugged free his disreputable corduroy jacket and hustled the willing barmaid into pouring hot water onto rum and lemon juice, a large glass each. There was a bright new modern electric fire straining at its kilowatts in the old brick fireplace, and the pulsating light from its imitation coal base lit warmly the big smiling face opposite me, and shone brightly on the friendliness in his eyes.

I had so few friends. So few.

"What's the matter then?" he said, sipping his steaming drink. "You're exceedingly quiet today, even for you."

I watched the fake flames for a while, but it couldn't be put off forever.

"I have found out," I said slowly, "about the brown mare."

He put down his glass with a steady hand but the smile drained completely away.

"What brown mare?"

I didn't answer. The silence lengthened hopelessly.

"What do you mean?" he said at last.

"I escorted a brown mare to France and back twice in a fortnight. The same brown mare every time."

"You must be mistaken."

"No."

There was a pause. Then he said again, but without conviction, "You are mistaken."

"I noticed her the day she went over in the morning and came back the same afternoon. I wondered when she went over again last Thursday . . . and I was certain it was the same horse yesterday, when she came back."

"You've been on several other trips. You couldn't remember one particular mare out of all those you dealt with. . . ."

"I know horses," I said.

"You're too quick," he said, almost to himself. "Too quick."

"No." I shook my head. "You were. You shouldn't have done it again so soon; then I might not have realized. . . ."

He shook himself suddenly, the bulk quivering in folds. "Done what?" he said more firmly. "What if a horse did go over and back twice? And what's it got to do with me?"

"There's no point in telling you what you already know."

"Henry." He leaned forward. "I know what I know, but I don't know what you think you know. You've got some damn-fool notion in your head and I want to hear what it is."

I watched the steam rise gently from my untouched drink and wished I hadn't come.

"Nice little fiddle," I sighed. "A sweet, neat little fraud. Easy as shelling peas. A few hundred quid every time you send the mare to France."

He looked at me without speaking, waiting, making me say it all straight out.

"All right then. You sell a horse — the brown mare — to an accomplice in France. He arranges for his bank to transfer the purchase price to England and the bank over here certifies that it has been received. You put in a claim to the Government that one thoroughbred has been exported for a thousand francs; part of the great bloodstock industry. The grateful Government pays you the bonus, the one and three-quarters per cent bonus on exports, and you put it in your pocket. Meanwhile you bring the horse back here and smuggle the money back as cash to France and you're ready to start again."

Simon sat like a stone, staring at me.

"All you really need is the working capital," I said. "A big enough sum to make the one and three-quarters per cent worth the trouble. Say twenty thousand pounds, for argument's sake. Three hundred and fifty pounds every time the mare goes across. If she went only once a month that would make an untaxed dividend of over 20 per cent on the year. Four thousand or more, tax free. You'd have a few expenses, of course, but even so . . ."

"Henry!" his voice was low and stunned.

"It's not a big fraud," I said. "Not big. But

132

pretty safe. And it had to be you, Simon, because it's all a matter of filling up the right forms, and you fill the forms at Yardman's. If anyone else, an outsider, tried it, he'd have to pay the horse's air passage each way, which would make the whole business unprofitable. No one would do it unless he could send the horse for nothing. You can send one for nothing, Simon. You just put one down on the flying list, but not on the office records. Every time there's room on a flight to France, you send the mare. Yardman told me himself there would be seven three-year-olds going over last Thursday, but we took eight horses, and the eighth wasn't a three-year-old, it was the brown mare.

"The day we did two trips, when we took her over in the morning and brought her back in the afternoon, that day it was no accident the return horses weren't at the airport to come back on the first trip. Not even you could risk unloading the mare and promptly loading her up again straight away. So you made a 'mistake' and put fifteen hundred hours on the trainers' traveling instructions instead of ten hundred hours, you, who never make such mistakes, whose accuracy is so phenomenal usually that no one queries or checks up on what you do . . ."

"How," he said dully. "How did you work it out?"

"I came from Anglia Bloodstock," I said gently. "Don't you remember? I used to fill up the same export forms as you do. I used to send them to you from the transport section. But I might not have remembered about the Government bonus if I hadn't heard three businessmen discussing it ten days ago, and last night while I was wondering how anyone could gain from shuffling that mare over and back, the whole thing just clicked."

"Clicked," he said gloomily.

I nodded. "No markings on the mare, either. You couldn't keep sending her in her own name, someone would have noticed at once. I would have, for a start. But all you had to do was go through the stud book, and choose other unmarked mares of approximately the same age and fill up the export forms accordingly. The Customs certify a brown mare was actually exported from here, and the French Customs certify it was imported there. No trouble at all. No one bothers to check with an owner that he has sold his horse. Why ever should they? And coming back, you go through the same process with the French stud book, only this time you have to be a bit careful your faked mare isn't too well bred because you can't spend more than two thousand in sterling abroad without searching inquiries, which you couldn't risk."

"Got it all buttoned up, haven't you?" he said bitterly.

"I was thinking about it nearly all night."

"Who are you going to tell?"

I glanced at him and away, uncomfortably.

"Yardman?" he asked.

I didn't answer.

"The police?"

I looked at the flickering fire. I wouldn't have told anyone had it not been for . . .

"Did you," I said painfully, "did you *have* to get Billy to knock me about?"

"Henry!" He looked shattered. "I didn't. How can you think I did that?"

I swallowed. "He's been on all the trips with the mare, and he's never given me a moment's peace on any of them, except perhaps the first. He's punched me and poured sirupy coffee on my hair, and yesterday when I was looking at the mare he hit me with a chain. He's not doing it because he dislikes me . . . or not only. It's a smoke screen to keep me away from looking too closely at the horses. That's why he didn't smash my face in . . . he was fighting for a purpose, not from real fury."

"Henry, I promise you, it isn't true." He seemed deeply distressed. "I wouldn't hurt you, for God's sake."

He put out his hand for his drink and took a long swallow. There was no more steam; drink and friendship were both cold.

"Don't look like that," he said, shivering. "Like an iceberg." He drank again. "All right, you've got it right about the mare. I'll admit that, but as God's my judge, I didn't put Billy on to you. I can't stand him. He's a young thug. Whatever he's been doing to you, it's from his own bloody nature. I promise you, Henry,

135

I promise you. . . ."

I looked at him searchingly, wanting very much to believe him, and feeling I'd merely be fooling myself if I did.

"Look," he said anxiously, leaning forward, "would you have sicked him on to me?"

"No."

"Well, then." He leaned back. "I didn't either."

There was a long, long pause.

"What do you do with the money?" I asked, shelving it.

He hesitated. "Pay my gambling debts."

I shook my head. "You don't gamble."

"I do."

"No."

"You don't know everything."

"I know that," I said tiredly. "I know that very well. You're not interested in racing. You never ask me for tips, never even ask me if I expect to win myself. And don't say you gamble at cards or something feeble like that . . . if you gambled enough to have to steal to pay your debts, you'd gamble on anything, horses as well. Compulsively."

He winced. "Steal is a hard word." He leaned forward, picked up my untasted drink, and swallowed the lot.

"There's no pension at Yardman's," he said.

I looked into his future, into his penurious retirement. I would have the remains of the Creggan fortune to keep me in cars and hot rums. He would have what he'd saved.

"You've banked it?"

"Only a third," he said. "A third is my cousin's. He's the one who keeps the mare on his small holding and drives her to the airport at this end. And a third goes to a chap with a horse-dealing business in France. He keeps the mare when she is over there, and drives her back and forth to the planes. They put up most of the stake, those two, when I thought of it. I hadn't anything like enough on my own."

"You really don't make much out of it, then, yourself, considering the risks."

"Double my salary," he observed dryly. "Tax free. And you underestimate us. We have two horses, and they each go about fifteen times a year."

"Have I seen the other one?"

"Yes," he nodded. "There and back."

"Once?"

"Once."

"And how do you get the money back to France?"

"Send it in magazines. Weeklies. The *Horse and Hound*, things like that."

"English money?"

"Yes. The chap in France has a contact who exchanges it."

"Risky, sending it by post."

"We've never lost any."

"How long have you been doing it?"

"Since they invented the bonus. Shortly after, anyway."

There was another long silence. Simon fiddled with his empty glass and didn't look like an embezzler. I wondered sadly if it was priggish to want one's friends to be honest, and found that I did still think of him as a friend, and could no longer believe that he had paid Billy to give me a bad time. Billy quite simply hated my pedigreed guts, and I could live with that.

"Well," he said in the end, "what are you going to do about it?"

He knew as well as I did that he'd have no chance in an investigation. Too many records of his transactions would still exist in various Government and banking files. If I started any inquiry he would very likely end up in jail. I stood up stiffly off the bar stool and shook my head.

"Nothing. . . ." I hesitated.

"Nothing . . . as long as we stop?"

"I don't know."

He gave me a twisted smile. "All right, Henry. We'll pack it in."

We went out of the pub and walked together through the slush back to the office, but it wasn't the same. There was no trust left. He must have been wondering whether I would keep my mouth shut permanently, and I knew, and hated the knowledge, that he could probably go on with his scheme in spite of saying he wouldn't. The brown mare wouldn't go again, but he could change her for another, and there was his second horse, which I hadn't even noticed. If he was careful, he could go on. And he was a careful man.

The travel schedules in the office, checked again, still showed no more trips to Milan till the Wednesday of the following week. Nor, as far as I could see, were there any flights at all before then; only a couple of sea passages booked for polo ponies, which weren't my concern. I knocked on Yardman's door, and went in and asked him if I could have the rest of the week off; my rights, Conker would have said.

"Milan next Wednesday," he repeated thoughtfully. "And there's nothing before that? Of course, my dear boy, of course you can have the time off. If you don't mind if I bring you back should an urgent trip crop up?"

"Of course not."

"That's good, that's good." The spectacles flashed as he glanced out of the window, the tight skin around his mouth lifting fleetingly into a skeletal smile. "You still like the job, then?"

"Yes, thank you," I said politely.

"Well, well, my dear boy, and I won't say that you're not good at it. I won't say that at all. Very reliable, yes, yes. I admire you for it, dear boy, I do indeed."

"Well . . . thank you, Mr. Yardman." I wasn't sure that underneath he wasn't laughing at me, and wondered how long it would be before he understood that I didn't look at my job as the great big joke everyone seemed to think it.

I wrote to Gabriella to tell her I would be coming back the following week, and drove moderately home, thinking alternately of her and Simon in an emotional seasaw.

There was a message for me at home to ring up Julian Thackery's father, which I did. The weather forecast was favorable, he said, and it looked as though there would be racing on Saturday. He was planning to send a good hunter 'chaser up to Wetherby, and could I go and ride it.

"I could," I said. "Yes."

"That's fine. She's a grand little mare, a real trier, with the shoulders of a champion and enough behind the saddle to take you over the best."

"Wetherby fences are pretty stiff," I commented.

"She'll eat them," he said with enthusiasm. "And she's ready. We gave her a mile gallop this morning, thinking she'd be backward after the snow, and she was pulling like a train at the end of it. Must thrive on being held up."

"Sounds good."

"A snip," he said. "I'll see you in the weighing room, just before the first. Right?"

I assured him I would be there, and was glad to be going, as I learned from a letter of acceptance lying beside the telephone that the Filyhoughs were again expected for the weekend. My sister Alice came along while I held the letter in my hand.

"I'm going up to Wetherby on Saturday," I said, forestalling her.

"Sunday . . ." she began.

"No, Alice dear, no. I have no intention whatsoever of marrying Angela Filyhough and there's no point in seeing her. I thought that we had agreed that Mother should stop this heiress hunting."

"But you must marry someone, Henry," she protested.

I thought of Gabriella, and smiled. Maybe her, once I was sure she'd be a friend for life, not just a rocket passion with no embers.

"I'll marry someone, don't you worry."

"Well," Alice said, "if you're going as far north as Wetherby you might as well go on and see Louise and cheer her up a bit."

"Cheer her up?" I said blankly. Louise was the sister just older than Alice. She lived in Scotland, nearly twice as far from Wetherby, as it happened, as Wetherby from home, but before I could point that out Alice replied.

"I told you yesterday evening," she said in exasperation. "Weren't you listening?"

"I'm afraid not." I'd been thinking about brown mares.

"Louise has had an operation. She goes home from hospital today and she'll be in bed for two or three weeks more."

"What's wrong with her?" But Alice either didn't know or wouldn't tell me, and though I hardly knew Louise in any deep sense I thought she would be far preferable to Angela Filyhough, and I agreed to go. Deciding, as I would be driving a long way after the races, to go up to Yorkshire on the Friday and spend the Saturday morning lazily, I set off northward at lunchtime and made a detour out of habit to Fenland.

"Hey, Harry, you're just the man I want. A miracle." Tom Wells grabbed my arm as I walked in. "Do me a short flight tomorrow? Two trainers and a jockey from Newmarket to Wetherby races."

I nearly laughed. "I'm awfully sorry. I can't, Tom. I really called in to cancel my booking for Sunday. I can't come then either. Got to go and visit a sick sister in Scotland. I'm on my way now."

"Blast," he said forcibly. "Couldn't you put it off?"

"Afraid not."

"You can have a plane to fly up, on Sunday." He was cunning, looking at me expectantly. "Free."

I did laugh then. "I can't."

"I'll have to tell the trainers I can't fix them up."

"I'm really sorry."

"Yeah. Damn it all. Well, come and have a cup of coffee."

We sat in the canteen for an hour and talked about aircraft, and I continued my journey to Wetherby thinking in amusement that my life was getting more and more like a juggling act, and that it would need skill to keep the racing, flying, horse-ferrying and Gabriella all spinning round safely in separate orbits.

At Wetherby the struggling sunshine lost to a fierce east wind, but the going was perfect, a surprise after the snow. Mr. Thackery's mare was all that he had promised, a tough workmanlike little chestnut with a heart as big as a barn, a true racer who didn't agree with giving up. She took me over the first two fences carefully, as she'd not been on the course before, but then with confidence, attacked the rest. I'd seldom had a more solid feeling ride and enjoyed it thoroughly, finding she needed the barest amount of help when meeting a fence wrong and was not too pigheaded to accept it. Coming round the last bend into the straight she was as full of running as when she started, and with only a flicker of encouragement from me she began working her way up smoothly past the four horses ahead of us. She reached the leader coming into the last, pecked a bit on landing, recovered without breaking up her stride, and went after the only horse in sight with enviable determination. We caught him in time, and soared past the winning post with the pleasure of winning coursing like wine in the blood.

"Not bad," said Julian's father, beaming. "Not bad at all," and he gave me a sealed envelope he'd had the faith to prepare in advance.

With about three hundred and fifty miles to go I left soon after the race, and on the empty northern roads made good time to Scotland. My sister Louise lived in a baronial hall near Elgin,

143

a house almost as big as ours at home and just as inadequately heated. She had pleased our parents by marrying for money, and hadn't discovered her husband's fanatical tightfistedness until afterward. For all she'd ever had to spend since, she'd have been better off in a semidetached in Peckham. Her Christmas gifts to me as a child had been Everyman editions of the classics. I got none at all now.

Even so, when I went in to see her in the morning, having arrived after she was sleeping the night before, it was clear that some of her spirit had survived. We looked at each other as at strangers. She, after a seven-year gap, was much older looking than I remembered, older than forty-three, and pale with illness, but her eyes were bright and her smile truly pleased.

"Henry, my little brother, I'm so glad you've come. . . ."

One had to believe her. I was glad too, and suddenly the visit was no longer a chore. I spent all day with her, looking at old photographs and playing Chinese checkers, which she had taught me as a child, and listening to her chat about the three sons away at boarding school, and how poor the grouse had been this winter and how much she would like to see London again, it was ten years since she had been down. She asked me to do various little jobs for her, explaining that "dear James" was apt to be irritated, and the maids had too much else to do, poor things. I fetched things for her, packed up a parcel, tidied

144

her room, filled her hot water bottle and found her some more toothpaste. After that she wondered if we couldn't perhaps turn out her medicine drawer while we had the opportunity.

The medicine drawer could have stocked a dispensary. Half of them, she said with relief, she would no longer need. "Throw them away." She sorted the bottles and boxes into two heaps. "Put all those in the wastepaper basket." Obediently I picked up a handful. One was labeled "Conovid," with some explanatory words underneath, and it took several seconds before the message got through. I picked that box out of the rubbish and looked inside. There was a strip of foil containing pills, each packed separately. I tore one square open and picked out the small pink tablet.

"Don't you want these?" I asked.

"Of course not. I don't need them any more, after the operation."

"Oh . . . I see. No, of course not. Then may I have them?"

"What on earth for?"

"Don't be so naïve, Louise."

She laughed. "You've got a girl friend at last? Of course you can have them. There's a full box lying around somewhere too, I think. In my top drawer, perhaps? Maybe some in the bathroom too."

I collected altogether enough birth control pills to fill a bottle nearly as big as the one Patrick had given Gabriella, a square-cornered brown bottle four inches high, which had held a prescription for penicillin sirup for curing the boys' throat infections. Louise watched with amusement while I rinsed it out, baked it dry in front of her electric fire, and filled it up, stuffing the neck with cotton wool before screwing on the black cap.

"Marriage?" she said. As bad as Alice.

"I don't know." I put the drawer she had tidied back into the bedside table. "And don't tell Mother."

Wednesday seemed a long time coming, and I was waiting at Gatwick a good hour before the first horses turned up. Not even the arrival of Billy and Alf could damp my spirits, and we loaded the horses without incident and faster than usual, as two of the studs had sent their own grooms as well, and for once they were willing.

It was one of the mornings that Simon came with last minute papers, and he gave them to me warily in the charter airline office when the plane was ready to leave.

"Good morning, Henry."

"Good morning."

One couldn't patch up a friendship at seven-thirty in the morning in front of yawning pilots and office staff. I took the papers with a nod, hesitated, and went out across the tarmac, bound for the aircraft and Milan.

There were running steps behind me and a hand on my arm.

"Lord Grey? You're wanted on the telephone.

146

They say it's urgent."

I picked up the receiver and listened, said "All right," and slowly put it down again. I was not, after all, going to see Gabriella. I could feel my face contract into lines of pain.

"What is it?" Simon said.

"My father . . . my father has died . . . sometime during the night. They have just found him . . . he was very tired, yesterday evening . . ."

There was a shocked silence in the office. Simon looked at me with great understanding, for he knew how little I wanted this day.

"I'm sorry," he said, his voice thick with sincerity.

I spoke to him immediately, without thinking, in the old familiar way. "I've got to go home."

"Yes, of course."

"But the horses are all loaded, and there's only Billy. . . ."

"That's easy, I'll go myself," he fished in his brief case and produced his passport.

It was the best solution. I gave him back the papers and took the brown bottle of pills out of my pocket. With a black ballpoint I wrote on the label, "Gabriella Barzini, Souvenir Shop, Malpensa Airport."

"Will you give this to the girl at the gift counter, and tell her why I couldn't come, and say I'll write?"

He nodded.

"You won't forget?" I said anxiously.

"No, Henry." He smiled as he used to. "I'll

147

see she gets it, and the message, I promise."

We shook hands, and after a detour through the passport office he shambled across the tarmac and climbed up the ramp into the plane. I watched the doors shut. I watched the aircraft fly away, taking my job, my friend and my gift, but not me.

Simon Searle went to Italy instead of me, and he didn't come back.

8

It was over a week before I found out. I went straight up to his room when I reached the wharf, and it was empty and much too tidy.

The dim teen-age secretary next door, in answer to my questions, agreed that Mr. Searle wasn't in today, and that no one seemed to know when he would be in at all . . . or whether.

"What do you mean?"

"He hasn't been in for a week. We don't know where he's got to."

Disturbed, I went downstairs and knocked on Yardman's door.

"Come in."

I went in. He was standing by the open window, watching colliers' tugs pulling heavy barges up the river. A Finnish freighter, come up on the flood, was maneuvering alongside across the river under the vulture-like meccano cranes. The air was alive with hooter signals and the bang and clatter of dock work, and the tide was carrying the garbage from the lower docks steadily upstream to the Palace of Westminster. Yardman turned, saw me, carefully closed the window, and

came across the room with both hands out-
stretched.

"My dear boy," he said, squeezing one of mine.
"My condolences on your sad loss, my sincere
condolences."

"Thank you," I said awkwardly. "You are very
kind. Do you . . . er . . . know where Simon
Searle is?"

"Mr. Searle?" He raised his eyebrows so that
they showed above the black spectacle frames.

"He hasn't been in for a week, the girl says."

"No . . ." He frowned. "Mr. Searle, for reasons
best known to himself, chose not to return to
this country. Apparently he decided to stay in
Italy, the day he went to Milan in your place."

"But why?" I said.

"I really have no idea. It is very inconvenient.
Very. I am having to do his work until we hear
from him."

He shook his head. "Well, my dear boy, I suppose our troubles no longer concern you. You'd
better have your cards, though I don't expect
you'll be needing them." He smiled the twisted
ironic smile and stretched out his hand to the
inter-office phone.

"You're giving me the sack, then?" I said
bluntly.

He paused, his hand in mid-air. "My dear boy,"
he protested. "My dear boy. It simply hadn't
occurred to me that you would want to stay on."

"I do."

He hesitated, and then sighed. "It's against my

150

better judgment, it is indeed. But with Searle and you both away, the agency has had to refuse business, and we can't afford much of that. No, we certainly can't. No, we certainly can't. Very well then, if you'll see us through at least until I hear from Searle, or find someone to replace him, I shall be very grateful, very grateful indeed."

If that was how he felt, I thought I might as well take advantage of it. "Can I have three days off for Cheltenham races in a fortnight? I've got a ride in the Gold Cup."

He nodded calmly. "Let me have the exact dates, and I'll avoid them."

I gave them to him then and there, and went back to Simon's room thinking that Yardman was an exceptionally easy employer, for all that I basically understood him as little as on our first meeting. The list of trips on Simon's wall showed that the next one scheduled was for the following Tuesday, to New York. Three during the past and present week had been crossed out, which as Yardman had said, was very bad for business. The firm was too small to stand much loss of its regular customers.

Yardman confirmed on the intercom that the Tuesday trip was still on, and he sounded so pleased that I guessed that he had been on the point of canceling it when I turned up. I confirmed that I would fetch the relevant papers from the office on Monday afternoon, and be at Gatwick on the dot on Tuesday morning. This gave me

151

a long weekend free and unbeatable ideas on how to fill it. With some relief the next day I drove determinedly away from the gloomy gathering of relations at home, sent a cable, picked up a stand-by afternoon seat with Alitalia, and flew to Milan to see Gabriella.

Three weeks and three days apart had changed nothing. I had forgotten the details of her face, shortened her nose in my imagination and lessened the natural solemnity of her expression, but the sight of her again instantly did its levitation act. She looked momentarily anxious that I wouldn't feel the same, and then smiled with breathtaking brilliance when she saw that I did.

"I got your cable," she said. "One of the girls has changed her free day with me, and now I don't have to keep the shop tomorrow or Sunday."

"That's marvelous."

She hesitated, almost blushing. "And I went home at lunch time to pack some clothes, and I have told my sister I am going to stay for two days with a girl friend near Genoa."

"Gabriella!"

"Is that all right?" she asked anxiously.

"It's a miracle," I said fervently, having expected only snatched unsatisfactory moments by day, and nights spent each side of a wall. "It's unbelievable."

When she had finished for the day we went to the station and caught a train, and on the principle of not telling more lies than could be helped, we did in fact go to Genoa. We booked separately into a large impersonal hotel full of incurious businessmen, and found our rooms were only four doors apart.

Over dinner in a warm obscure little restaurant she said, "I'm sorry about your father, Henry."

"Yes. . . ." Her sympathy made me feel a fraud. I had tried to grieve for him, and had recognized that my only strong emotion was an aversion to being called by his name. I wished to remain myself. Relations and family solicitors clearly took it for granted, however, that having sown a few wild oats I would now settle down into his pattern of life. His death, if I wasn't careful, would be my destruction.

"I was pleased to get your letter," Gabriella said, "because it was awful when you didn't come with the horses. I thought you had changed your mind about me."

"But surely Simon explained?"

"Who is Simon?"

"The big fat bald man who went instead of me. He promised to tell you why I couldn't come, and to give you a bottle . . ." I grinned, "a bottle of pills."

"So they were from you!"

"Simon gave them to you. I suppose he couldn't explain why I hadn't come, because he doesn't know Italian. I forgot to tell him to speak French."

She shook her head.

"One of the crew gave them to me. He said he'd found them in the toilet compartment just

153

after they had landed, and he brought them across to see if I had lost them. He is a tall man, in uniform. I've seen him often. It was not your bald, fat Simon."

"And Simon didn't try to talk to you at all?"

"No." She shook her head. "I don't think so. I see hundreds of bald fat travelers, but no one tried to speak to me about you."

"A friendly big man, with kind eyes," I said. "He was wearing a frightful old green corduroy jacket, with a row of pins in one lapel. He has a habit of picking them up."

She shook her head again. "I didn't see him."

Simon had promised to give her my message and the bottle. He had done neither, and he had disappeared. I hadn't liked to press Yardman too hard to find out where Simon had got to because there was always the chance that too energetic spadework would turn up the export bonus fraud, and I had vaguely assumed that it was because of the fraud that Simon had chosen not to come back. But even if he had decided on the spur of the moment to duck out, he would certainly have kept his promise to see Gabriella. Or didn't a resuscitated friendship stretch that far?

"What's the matter?" Gabriella asked.

I explained.

"You are worried about him?"

"He's old enough to decide for himself. . . ." But I was remembering like a cold douche that my predecessor Peters hadn't come back from Milan, and before him the liaison man Ballard.

154

"Tomorrow morning," she said firmly, "you will go back to Milan and find him."

"I can't speak Italian."

"Undoubtedly you will need an interpreter," she nodded. "Me."

"The best," I agreed, smiling.

We walked companionably back to the hotel.

"Were the pills all right?" I asked.

"Perfect, thank you very much. I gave them to the wife of our baker. . . . She works in the bakery normally, but when she gets pregnant she's always sick for months, and can't stand the sight of dough, and he gets bad-tempered because he has to pay a man to help him instead. He is not a good Catholic." She laughed. "He makes me an enormous cake oozing with cream when I take the pills."

No one took the slightest notice of us in the hotel. I went along an empty passage in my dressing gown and knocked on her door, and she opened it in hers to let me in. I locked it behind me.

"If my sister could see us," she said smiling, "she'd have a fit."

"I'll go away . . . if you like."

"Could you?" She put her arms round my neck.

"Very difficult."

"I don't ask it."

I kissed her. "It would be impossible to go now," I said.

She sighed happily. "I absolutely agree. We will just have to make the best of it."

We did.

155

We went back to Milan in the morning sitting side by side in the railway carriage and holding hands surreptitiously under her coat, as if by this tiny area of skin contact we could keep alive the total union of the night. I had never wanted to hold hands with anyone before; never realized it could feel like being plugged into a small electric current, warm, comforting, and vibrant, all at the same time.

Apart from being together, it was a depressing day. No one had seen Simon.

"He couldn't just vanish," I said in exasperation, standing late in the afternoon in a chilly wind outside the last of the hospitals. We had drawn a blank there as everywhere else, though they had gone to some trouble to make sure for us. No man of his description had been admitted for any illness or treated for any accident during the past ten days.

"Where else can we look?" she said, the tiredness showing in her voice and in the droop of her rounded body. She had been splendid all day, asking questions unendingly from me and translating the replies, calm and businesslike and effective. It wasn't her fault the answers had all been negative. Police, Government departments, undertakers, we had tried them all. We had rung up every hotel in Milan and asked for him; he had stayed in none.

"I suppose we could ask the taxi drivers at the airport," I said finally.

"There are so many . . . and who would re-member one passenger after so long?"

"He had no luggage," I said as I'd said a dozen times before. "He didn't know he was coming here until fifteen minutes before he took off. He couldn't have made any plans. He doesn't speak Italian. He hadn't any Italian money. Where did he go? What did he do?"

She shook her head dispiritedly. There was no answer. We took a tram back to the station and with half an hour to wait made a few last inquiries from the station staff. They didn't remember him. It was hopeless.

Over dinner at midnight at the same café as the night before we gradually forgot the day's frustration; but the fruitless grind, though it hadn't dug up a trace of Simon, had planted foundations beneath Gabriella and me.

She drooped against me going back to the hotel and I saw with remorse how exhausted she was. "I've tired you too much."

She smiled at the anxiety in my voice. "You don't realize how much energy you have."

"Energy?" I repeated in surprise.

"Yes. It must be that."

"What do you mean?"

"You don't look energetic. You're quiet, and you move like machinery, oiled and smooth. No effort. No jerks. No awkwardness. And inside somewhere is a dynamo. It doesn't run down. I can feel its power. All day I've felt it."

I laughed. "You're too fanciful."

"No. I'm right."

I shook my head. There were no dynamos ticking away inside me. I was a perfectly ordinary and not too successful man, and the smoothness she saw was only tidiness.

She was already in bed and half asleep when I went along to her room. I locked the door and climbed in beside her, and she made a great effort to wake up for my sake.

"Go to sleep," I said, kissing her lightly. "There is always the morning."

She smiled contentedly and snuggled into my arms, and I lay there cradling her sweet soft body, her head on my chest and her hair against my mouth, and felt almost choked by the intensity with which I wanted to protect her and share with her everything I had. Henry Grey, I thought in surprise in the dark, was suddenly more than halfway down the untried track to honest-to-goodness love.

Sunday morning we strolled aimlessly round the city, talking and looking at the mountains of leatherwork in the shops in the arcades; Sunday afternoon we went improbably to a football match, an unexpected passion of Gabriella's; and Sunday night we went to bed early because, as she said with her innocent giggle, we would have to be up at six to get her back to start work in the shop on time. But there was something desperate in the way she clung to me during the night, as if it were our last forever instead of only a week or two, and when I kissed her there were tears on her cheeks.

"Why are you crying?" I said, wiping them away with my fingers. "Don't cry."

"I don't know why." She sniffed, half laughing. "The world is a sad place. Beauty bursts you. An explosion inside. It can only come out as tears."

I was impossibly moved. I didn't deserve her tears. I kissed them away in humility and understood why people said love was painful, why Cupid was invented with arrows. Love did pierce the heart, truly.

It wasn't until we were on the early train to Milan the next morning that she said anything about money, and from her hesitation in beginning I saw that she didn't want to offend me.

"I will repay you what you lent me for my bill," she said matter-of-factly, but a bit breathlessly. I had pushed the notes into her hand on the way downstairs, as she hadn't wanted me to pay for her publicly, and she hadn't enough with her to do it herself.

"Of course not," I said.

"It was a much more expensive place than I'd thought of. . . ."

"Big hotels ignore you better."

She laughed. "All the same . . ."

"No."

"But you don't earn much. You can't possibly afford it all. The hotel and the train fares, and the dinners."

159

"I earned some money winning a race."

"Enough?"

"I'll win another race . . . then it will be enough."

"Giulio doesn't like it that you work with horses." She laughed. "He says that if you were good enough to be a jockey you'd do it all the time instead of being a groom."

"What does Giulio do?"

"He works for the Government in the taxation office."

"Ah," I said, smiling. "Would it help if you told him my father has left me some money? Enough to come to see you, anyway, when I get it."

"I'm not sure I'll tell him. He judges people too much by how much money they've got."

"Do you want to marry a rich man?"

"Not to please Giulio."

"To please yourself?"

"Not rich necessarily. But not too poor. I don't want to worry about how to afford shoes for the children."

I smoothed her fingers with my own.

"I think I will have to learn Italian," I said.

She gave me the flashing smile. "Is English very difficult?"

"You can practice on me."

"If you come back often enough. If your father's money should not be saved for the future."

"I think," I said slowly, smiling into her dark eyes, "that there will be enough left. Enough to buy the children's shoes."

160

I went to New York with the horses the following day in the teeth of furious opposition from the family. Several relatives were still staying in the house, including my three sharp-tongued eldest sisters, none of whom showed much reserve in airing their views. I sat through a depressing lunch, condemned from all sides. The general opinion was, it seemed, that my unexplained absence over the weekend was disgraceful enough, but that continuing with my job was scandalous. Mother cried hysterical tears and Alice was bitterly reproving.

"Consider your *position*," they all wailed, more or less in chorus.

I considered my position and left for Yardman's and Gatwick three hours after returning from Milan.

Mother had again brought up the subject of my early marriage to a suitable heiress. I refrained from telling her I was more or less engaged to a comparatively penniless Italian girl who worked in a gift shop, smuggled birth control pills, and couldn't speak English. It wasn't exactly the moment.

The outward trip went without a hitch. Timmie and Conker were along, together with a pair of grooms with four Anglia Bloodstock horses, and in consequence the work went quickly and easily. We were held up for thirty-six hours in New York by an engine fault, and when I rang up Yardman to report our safe return on the Friday

161

morning he asked me to stay at Gatwick, as another bunch of brood mares was to leave that
afternoon.

"Where for?"

"New York again," he said briskly. "I'll come
down with the papers myself, early in the afternoon. You can send Timms and Chestnut
home. I'm bringing Billy and two others to replace
them."

"Mr. Yardman. . . ." I said.

"Yes?"

"If Billy tries to pick a fight, or molests me
at all on the way, my employment with you ceases
the instant we touch down in New York, and
I will not help unload the horses or accept any
responsibility for them."

There was a short shocked silence. He couldn't
afford to have me do what I threatened, in the
present sticky state of the business.

"My dear boy . . ." he protested sighing. "I
don't want you to have troubles. I'll speak to
Billy. He's a thoughtless boy. I'll tell him not
everyone is happy about his little practical
jokes."

"I'd appreciate it," I said with irony at his
view of Billy's behavior.

Whatever Yardman said to him worked. Billy
was sullen, unhelpful, and calculatingly offensive,
but for once I completed a return trip with him
without a bruise to show for it.

On the way over I sat for a time on a hay
bale beside Alf and asked him about Simon's last

162

trip to Milan. It was hard going, as the old man's deafness was as impenetrable as seven-eighths cloud.

"Mr. Searle," I shouted. "Did he say where he was going?"

"Eh?"

After about ten shouts the message got through, and he nodded.

"He came to Milan with us."

"That's right, Alf. Where did he go then?"

"Eh?"

"Where did he go then?"

"I don't rightly know," he said. "He didn't come back."

"Did he *say* where he was going?"

"Eh?"

I yelled again.

"No. He didn't say. Perhaps he told Billy. He was talking to Billy, see?"

I saw. I also saw that it was no use my ever asking Billy anything about anything. Yardman would have asked him, anyway, so if Simon had told Billy where he was going Yardman would have known. Unless, of course, Simon had asked Billy not to tell, and he hadn't. But Simon didn't like Billy and would never trust him with a secret.

"Where did Mr. Searle go, when you left the plane?"

I was getting hoarse before he answered.

"I don't know where he went. He was with Billy and the others. I went across on my own, like, to get a beer. Billy said they were just coming. But they never came."

"None of them came?"

There had been the two grooms from the stud besides Simon and Billy, on that trip.

Eventually Alf shook his head. "I finished my beer and went back to the plane. There was no one there as I ate my lunch."

I left it at that because my throat couldn't stand any more.

Coming back we were joined by some extra help in the shape of a large pallid man who didn't know what to do with his hands and kept rubbing them over the wings of his jodhpurs as if he expected to find pockets there. He was ostensibly accompanying a two-year-old, but I guessed tolerantly he was some relation of the owner or trainer traveling like that to avoid a translatlantic fare. I didn't get around to checking on it, because the double journey had been very tiring, and I slept soundly nearly all the way back. Alf had to shake me awake as we approached Gatwick. Yawning I set about the unloading — it was by then well into Sunday morning — and still feeling unusually tired, drove home afterward in a beeline to bed. A letter from Gabriella stopped me in the hall, and I went slowly upstairs reading it.

She had, she said, asked every single taxi driver and all the airport bus drivers if they had taken anywhere a big fat Englishman who couldn't speak Italian, had no luggage, and was wearing a green corduroy jacket. None of them could remember anyone like that. Also, she said, she had checked with the car hire firms which had agencies at the airport, but none of them had dealt with Simon. She had checked with all the airlines' passenger lists for the day he went to Milan, and the days after; he had not flown off to anywhere.

I lay in a hot bath and thought about whether I should go on trying to find him. Bringing in any professional help, even private detectives, would only set them searching in England for a reason for his disappearance, and they'd all too soon dig it up. A warrant out for his arrest was not what I wanted. It would effectively stop him coming back at all. Very likely he didn't want to be found in the first place, or he wouldn't have disappeared so thoroughly, or stayed away so long. But supposing something had happened to him . . . though what, I couldn't imagine. And I wouldn't have thought anything could have happened at all, were it not for Peters and Ballard.

There were Simon's partners in the fraud. His cousin, and the man in France. Perhaps I could ask them if they had heard from him. . . . I couldn't ask them, I thought confusedly; I didn't know their names. Simon had an elderly aunt somewhere, but I didn't know her name either . . . the whole thing was too much . . . and I was going to sleep in the bath.

I went to the wharf building the next morning at nine-thirty to collect my previous week's pay and see what was on the schedule for the future. True to his word, Yardman had arranged no air trips for the following three days of Cheltenham

165

Races. There was a big question mark beside a trip for six circus horses for Spain that same afternoon, but no question mark, I was glad to see, about a flight to Milan with brood mares on Friday.

Yardman, when I went down to see him, said the circus horses were postponed until the following Monday owing to their trainer having read in his stars that it was a bad week to travel. Yardman was disgusted. Astrology was bad for business.

"Milan on Friday, now," he said, sliding a pencil to and fro through his fingers. "I might come on that trip myself, if I can get away. It's most awkward, with Searle's work to be done. I've advertised for someone to fill his place . . . anyway, as I was saying, if I can get away I think I'd better go and see our opposite numbers out there. It always pays, you know, my dear boy. I go to all the countries we export to. About once a year. Keeps us in touch, you know."

I nodded. Good for business, no doubt.

"Will you ask them . . . our opposite numbers . . . if they saw Simon Searle any time after he landed?"

He looked surprised, the taut skin stretched over his jaw.

"I could, yes. But I shouldn't think he told them where he was going, if he didn't have the courtesy to tell me."

"It's only an outside chance," I agreed.

"I'll ask, though." He nodded. "I'll certainly ask."

I went upstairs again to Simon's room, shut his door, sat in his chair, and looked out of his window. His room, directly over Yardman's, had the same panoramic view of the river, from a higher angle. I would like to live there, I thought idly. I liked the shipping, the noise of the docks, the smell of the river, the coming and going. Quite simply, I supposed, I liked the business of transport.

The Finnish ship had gone from the berth opposite and another small freighter had taken her place. A limp flag swung fitfully at her masthead, red and white horizontal stripes with a navy blue triangle and a white star. I looked across at the nationality chart on Simon's wall. Puerto Rico. Well, well, one lived and learned. Three alphabetical flags lower down, when checked, proved to be E, Q and M. Mildly curious, I turned them up in the international code of signals. "I am delivering." Quite right and proper. I shut the book, twiddled my thumbs, watched a police launch swoop past doing twenty knots on the ebb, and reflected not for the first time that the London river was a fast, rough waterway for small boats.

After a while I picked up the telephone and rang up Fenland to book a plane for Sunday.

"Two o'clock?"

"That'll do me fine," I said. "Thanks."

"Wait a minute, Henry. Mr. Wells said if you

rang that he wanted a word with you."

"O.K."

There were some clicks, and then Tom's voice.

"Harry? Look, for God's sake, what is this job of yours?"

"I work for . . . a travel agency."

"Well, what's so special about it? Come here, and I'll pay you more." He sounded worried and agitated, not casually inviting as before.

"What's up?" I said.

"Everything's up except my planes. I've landed an excellent contract with a car firm in Coventry ferrying their executives, technicians, salesmen and so on all round the shop. They've a factory in Lancashire and tie-ups all over Europe, and they're fed-up with the airfield they've been using. They're sending me three planes. I'm to maintain them, provide pilots and have them ready when wanted."

"Sounds good," I said. "So what's wrong?"

"So I don't want to lose them again before I've started. And not only can I not find any out-of-work pilots worth considering, but one of my three regulars went on a skiing holiday last week and broke his leg, the silly bastard. So how about it?"

"It's not as easy as you make it sound," I said reluctantly.

"What's stopping you?"

"A lot of things . . . if you'll be around on Sunday, anyway, we could talk it over."

He sighed in exasperation. "The planes are due

168

here at the end of the month, in just over a fortnight."

"Get someone else, if you can," I said.

"Yeah . . . if I can." He was depressed. "And if I can't?"

"I don't know. I could do a day a week to help out, but even then . . ."

"Even then, what?"

"There are difficulties."

"Nothing to mine, Harry. Nothing to mine. I'll break you down on Sunday."

Everyone had troubles, even with success. The higher the tougher, it seemed. I wiggled the button, and asked for another number, the charter airline which Patrick worked for. The Gatwick office answered, and I asked them if they could tell me how to get hold of him.

"You're in luck. He's actually here, in the office. Who's speaking?"

"Henry Grey, from Yardman Transport."

I waited, and he came on the line.

"Hullo . . . how's things? How's Gabriella?"

"She," I said, "is fine. Other things are not. Could you do me a favor?"

"Shoot."

"Could you look up for me the name of the pilot who flew a load of horses to Milan for us a fortnight last Thursday? Also the names of the copilot and engineer, and could you also tell me how or when I could talk to one or all of them?"

"Trouble?"

"Oh, no trouble for your firm, none at all.

169

But one of our men went over on that trip and didn't come back, and hasn't got in touch with us since. I just wanted to find out if the crew had any idea what became of him. He might have told one of them where he was going . . . anyway, his work is piling up here and we want to find out if he intends to come back."

"I see. Hang on then. A fortnight last Thursday?"

"That's it."

He was away several minutes. The cranes got busy on the freighter from Puerto Rico. I yawned.

"Henry? I've got them. The pilot was John Kyle, copilot G. L. Rawlings, engineer V. N. Brede. They're not here, though; they've just gone to Arabia, ferrying mountains of luggage from London after some oil chieftain's visit. He brought about six wives, and they all went shopping."

"Wow," I said. "When do they get back?"

He consulted someone in the background.

"Sometime Wednesday. They have Thursday off, then another trip to Arabia on Friday."

"Some shopping," I said gloomily. "I can't get to see them on Wednesday or Thursday. I'm racing at Cheltenham. But I could ring them up on Wednesday night, if you can give me their numbers."

"Well . . . ," said Patrick slowly. "John Kyle likes his flutter on the horses."

"You don't think he'd come to Cheltenham, then?"

"He certainly might, if he isn't doing anything else."

"I'll get him a member's badge, and the others too, if they'd like."

"Fair enough. Let's see. I'm going to Holland twice tomorrow. I should think I could see them on Wednesday, if we all get back reasonably on schedule. I'll tell them what you want, and ring you. If they go to Cheltenham you'll see them, and if not you can ring them. How's that?"

"Marvelous. You'll find me at the Queen's Hotel at Cheltenham. I'll be staying there."

"Right . . . and oh, by the way, I see I'm down for a horse transport flight on Friday to Milan. Is that your mob, or not?"

"Our mob," I agreed. "What's left of it."

We rang off, and I leaned back in Simon's chair, pensively biting my thumbnail and surveying the things on his desk; telephone, tray of pens, black notepad, and a pot of paper clips and pins. Nothing of any help. Then slowly, methodically, I searched through the drawers. They were predictably packed with export forms of various sorts, but he had taken little of a personal nature to work. Some indigestion tablets, a screwdriver, a pair of green socks, and a plastic box labeled "spare keys." That was the lot. No letters, no bills, no private papers of any sort.

I opened the box of keys. There were about twenty or more, the silt of years. Suitcase keys, a heavy old iron key, car keys. I stirred them up with my finger. A Yale key. I picked it out and looked at it. It was a duplicate, cut for a few shillings from a blank, and had no number. The metal had been dulled by time, but not smoothed from use. I tapped it speculatively on the edge of the desk, thinking that anyway there would be no harm in trying.

9

Simon's home address, obtained off his insurance card via the dim typist, proved to be located in a dingy block of flats in the outer reaches of St. John's Wood. The grass on patchy lawns had remained uncut from about the previous August, which gave the graceless building a mournful look of having been thoughtlessly dumped in a hay-field. I walked through spotted glass entrance doors, up an uninspiring staircase, met no one, and came to a halt outside number fifteen in white twopenny plastic letters screwed on to cheap green-painted deal.

The Yale key slid raspingly into the lock as if it had never been there before, but it turned under my pressure and opened the door. There was a haphazard foot-high pile of newspapers and magazines just inside. When I pushed the door against them they slithered away, and I stepped in and round them, and shut the door behind me.

The flat consisted only of a tiny entrance hall, a small bedroom, poky kitchen and bathroom and a slightly larger sitting room. The prevailing color was maroon, which I found depressing, and the furniture looked as if it had been bought piece by piece from second-class second-hand shops. The total effect could have been harmonious, but it wasn't, not so much through lack of taste as lack of imagination. He had spent the minimum of trouble on his surroundings, and the result was gloomy. Cold dead air and a smell of mustiness seeped up my nose. There were unwashed, mold-growing dishes on the drainboard in the kitchen, and crumpled thrown-back bedclothes on the bed. He had left his shaving water in the washbasin and the scum had dried into a hard gray line round the edge. Poor Simon, I thought forlornly, what an existence. No wife, no warmth; no wonder he liked pubs.

One wall in the sitting room was lined with bookcases, and the newest, most obviously luxurious object in the flat was a big stereophonic radio standing behind the door. No television. No pictures on the dull coffee walls. Not a man of visual pleasures. Beside a large battered armchair, handy to perpetual reach, stood a wooden crate of bottled beer.

Wandering round his flat I realized what a fearful comment it was on myself that I had never been there before. This big tolerant dishonest man I would have counted my only real friend, yet I'd never seen where he lived. Never been asked; never thought of asking him to my own home. Even where I had wanted friendship, I hadn't known how to try. I felt as cold inside as Simon's flat; as uninhabited. Gabriella seemed very far away.

I picked up the heap of papers inside the front door and carried them into the sitting room. Sorted into piles, they consisted of sixteen dailies, three Sundays, three *Horse and Hounds*, three *Sporting Life* weeklies and one *Stud and Stable*. Several letters in brown unstuck envelopes looked unpromising, and with very little hesitation I opened all the rest. There were none from France, and none from the accomplice cousin. The only one of any help was written in a spiky black hand on dark-blue paper. It began "Dear Simon," thanked him for a birthday present, and was signed "your loving aunt Edna." The handwritten address at the top said 3 Gordon Cottages, East Road, Potter's Green, Berks., and there was no telephone number.

There was no desk as such in his flat. He kept his bills and papers clipped into labeled categories in the top drawer of a scratched chest in his bedroom, but if his cousin's name and address was among them, I couldn't recognize them. Alongside the papers lay a *Horse and Hound* rolled tightly into a tube and bound with wide brown sticky paper, ready to be posted. I picked it up and turned it round in my hands. It bore no address. The thick layers of brown sticky paper were tough, and even though I was careful with my penknife it looked as though a tiger had been chewing it when I finally hacked my way through. The magazine unrolled reluctantly, and I picked

175

it up and shook it. Nothing happened. It wasn't until one looked at it page by page that the money showed, five-pound notes stuck on with plastic tape. They were used notes, not new, and there were sixty of them. I rolled the *Horse and Hound* up again and laid it back in the drawer, seeing a vivid mental picture, as I picked up the brown pieces of gummed strips and put them in the wastebasket, of Simon listening to his radio and sticking his money into the journals, night after night, an endless job, working for his old age.

Potter's Green turned out to be a large village spreading out into tentacles of development around the edges. East Road was a new one, and Gordon Cottages proved to be one of several identical strips of council-built bungalows for old people. Number three like all the rest still looked clean and fresh, with nothing growing yet in the bathmat-sized flower bed under the front window. There was bright yellow paint clashing with pale pink curtains and a bottle of milk standing on the concrete doorstep.

I rang the bell. The pink curtains twitched, and I turned my head to see myself being inspected by a pair of mournful, faded eyes set in a large pale face. She flapped a hand at me in a dismissing movement, shooing me away, so I put my finger on the bell and rang again.

I heard her come round to the other side of the door.

"Go away," she said. "I don't want anything."

"I'm not selling," I said through the letter box. "I'm a friend of Simon's, your nephew Simon Searle."

"Who are you? I don't know you."

"Henry Grey. . . . I work with Simon at Yardman's. Could I please talk to you inside, it's very difficult like this, and your neighbors will wonder what's going on." There were in truth several heads at the front windows already, and it had its effect. She opened the door and beckoned me in.

The tiny house was crammed with the furniture she must have brought with her from a much larger place, and every available surface was covered with useless mass-produced ornaments. The nearest to me as I stood just inside the doorway was a black box decorated with "A present from Brighton" in shells. And next to that a china donkey bore panniers of dried everlasting flowers. Pictures of all sorts crowded the walls, interspersed by several proverbs done in poker-work on wood. "Waste not, want not" caught my eye, and farther round there was "Take care of the pence and the pounds will take care of you"; an improvement on the original.

Simon's stout aunt had creaking corsets and wheezing breath and smelled of mentholated cough pastilles. "Simon isn't here, you know. He lives in London, not here."

"I know, yes." Hesitatingly, I told her about Simon going away and not coming back. "I wondered," I finished, "if by any chance he has written to you. Sent you a picture postcard. That sort of thing."

"He will. He's sure to." She nodded several times. "He always does, and brings me a little souvenir when he's been away. Very considerate is Simon."

"But you haven't had a postcard yet."

"Not yet. Soon, I expect."

"If you do, would you write to me and let me know? You see, he hasn't said when he'll be back, and Mr. Yardman is advertising for someone to fill his job."

"Oh, dear." She was troubled. "I hope nothing has happened to him."

"I don't expect so; but if you hear from him, you will let us know?"

"Yes, yes, of course. Dear oh dear, I wonder what he is up to."

Her choice of phrase reminded me of what in fact he was up to, and I asked her if she knew Simon's cousin's name and address. Unhesitatingly she reeled it off. "He's my poor dead sister's son," she said. "But a surly man. I don't get on with him at all. Not easy, like Simon, now. Simon stayed with me a lot when he was little, when I kept the village shop. He never forgets my birthday, and always brings me nice little mementos like these." She looked proudly round her overflowing possessions. "Simon's very kind. I've only my old age pension, you know, and a little bit put by, and Simon's the only one who bothers with me much. Oh I've got my two daughters, of course, but one's married in Canada and the other's got enough troubles of her own. Simon's given me a hundred pounds for my birthday every year for the last three years; what do you think of that?"

"Absolutely splendid." A hundred pounds of taxpayers' money. Robin Hood stuff. Oh well.

"You'll let me know, then," I said, turning to go. She nodded, creaking as she moved round me to open the street door. Facing me in the little hall hung more timeworn poker-work. "See a pin and pick it up, all the day you'll have good luck. See a pin and let it lie, you will want before you die." So there, I thought, smiling to myself, was the origin of Simon's pin tidying habit, a proverb stretching back to childhood. He didn't intend to want before he died.

The accomplice cousin farmed in Essex, reasonably handy for Cambridge Airport, but a long haul for Gatwick. It was evident at once, however, that I could expect no easy help from him.

"You," he said forcefully, "you're the interfering bastard who's fouled up the works, aren't you? Well you can damn well clear off, that's what you can do. It's no business of yours where Simon's gone and in the future you keep your bloody nose out of things that don't concern you."

"If," I said mildly, "you prefer me to ask the police to find him, I will."

He looked ready to explode, a large red-faced man in khaki clothes and huge gum boots, standing four-square in a muddy yard. He struggled visibly between the pleasure of telling me to go to hell and fear of the consequences if he did so. Prudence just won.

"All right. All right. I don't know where he is and that's straight. He didn't tell me he was going, and I don't know when he's coming back."

Depressed, I drove home to Bedfordshire. The bulk and grandeur of the great house lay there waiting as I rolled slowly up the long drive. History in stone; the soul of the Creggans. Earl upon earl had lived there right back to the pirate who brought Spanish gold to Queen Bess, and since my father died I had only to enter to feel the chains fall heavily on me like a net. I stopped in the sweep of gravel in front instead of driving round to the garages as usual, and looked at what I had inherited. There was beauty, I admitted, in the great façade with its pillars and pediments and the two wide flights of steps sweeping up to meet at the door. The Georgian Palladian architect who had grafted a whole new mansion on to the Elizabethan and Stuart one already existing had produced a curiously satisfactory result, and as a Victorian incumbent had luckily confined his Gothic urges to a ruined folly in the garden, the only late addition had been a square red-bricked block of Edwardian plumbing. But for all its splendid outer show it had those beetles in the roof, miles of drafty passages, kitchens in the basement, and twenty bedrooms moldering into dust. Only a multimillionaire could maintain and fill such a place now with servants and guests, whereas after death duties I would be hard put to find a case of champagne once the useless pile had voraciously gulped what it cost just to keep standing.

Opening it to the public might have been a solution if I had been any sort of a showman. But to someone solitary by nature that way meant a lifetime of horrifying square-peggery. Slavery to a building. Another human sacrifice on the altar of tradition. I simply couldn't face it. The very idea made me wilt.

Since it was unlikely anyone would simply let me pull the whole thing down, the National Trust, I thought, was the only hope. They could organize the sight-seeing to their heart's content and they might let Mother live there for the rest of her life, which she needed.

Mother usually used the front entrance while Alice and I drove on and went in through one of the doors at the side, near the garages. That early evening, however, I left my little car on the gravel and walked slowly up the shallow steps. At the top I leaned against the balustrade and looked back over the calm wide fields and bare-branched trees just swelling into bud. I didn't really own all this, I thought. It was like the baton in a relay race, passed on from one, to be passed on to the next, belonging to none for more than a lap. Well, I wasn't going to pass it on. I was the last runner. I would escape from the track at a tangent and give the baton away. My son, if I ever had one, would have to lump it.

I pushed open the heavy door and stepped into the dusk-filled house. I, Henry Grey, descendant of the sea pirate, of warriors and explorers and empire builders and of a father who'd been decorated for valor on the Somme, I, the least of them, was going to bring their way of life to an end. I felt one deep protesting pang for their sakes, and that was all. If they had anything of themselves to pass on to me, it was already in my genes. I carried their inheritance in my body, and I didn't need their house.

Not only did John Kyle and his engineer come to Cheltenham, but Patrick as well.

"I've never been before," he said, his yellow eyes and auburn hair shining as he stood in the bright March sun. "These two are addicts. I just came along for the ride."

"I'm glad you did," I said, shaking hands with the other two. John Kyle was a bulky battered-looking young man going prematurely thin on top. His engineer, tall and older, had three racing papers and a form sheet tucked under his arm.

"I see," he said, glancing down at them, "th . . . that you won the United Hunts Ch . . . Challenge Cup yesterday." He managed his stutter unself-consciously. "W . . . w . . . well done."

"Thank you," I said. "I was a bit lucky. I wouldn't have won if Century hadn't fallen at the last."

"It d . . . d . . . d . . . does say that, in

the p . . . p . . . paper," he agreed disarmingly.

Patrick laughed and said, "What are you riding in today?"

"The Gold Cup and the Mildmay of Flete Challenge Cup."

"Clobber and Boathook," said John Kyle readily.

"I'll back you," Patrick said.

"M . . . m . . . money down the drain b . . . backing Clobber," said the engineer seriously.

"Thanks very much," I said with irony.

"F . . . form's all haywire. V . . . v . . . very inconsistent," he explained.

"Do you think you've got a chance?" Patrick asked.

"No, not much. I've never ridden him before. The owner's son usually rides him, but he's got jaundice."

"N . . . not a b . . . betting proposition," nodded the engineer.

"For God's sake, don't be so depressing, man," protested Kyle.

"How about Boathook?" I asked, smiling.

The engineer consulted the sky. The result wasn't written there, as far as I could see.

"B . . . B . . . Boathook," he remarked, coming back to earth, "m . . . m . . . might just do it. G . . . good for a p . . . place anyway."

"I shall back both, just the same," said Patrick firmly. I took them all to lunch and sat with them while they ate.

"Aren't you having any?" said Patrick.

"No. It makes you sick if you fall after eating."

"How often do you fall, then?" asked Kyle curiously, cutting into his cold red beef.

"On average, once in a dozen rides, I suppose. It varies. I've never really counted."

"When did you fall last?"

"Day before yesterday."

"Doesn't it bother you?" asked Patrick, shaking salt. "The prospect of falling?"

"Well, no. You never think you're going to, for a start. And a lot of falls are easy ones; you only get a bruise, if that. Sometimes when the horse goes right down you almost step off."

"And sometimes you break your bones," Kyle said dryly.

I shook my head. "Not often."

Patrick laughed. I passed him the butter for his roll, looked at my watch, and said, "I'll have to go and change soon. Do you think we could talk about the day you took Simon Searle to Milan?"

"Shoot," said Kyle. "What do you want to know?"

"Everything you can think of that happened on the way there and after you landed."

"I don't suppose I'll be much help," he said apologetically. "I was in the cockpit most of the time, and I hardly spoke to him at all. I went aft to the karzy once, and he was sitting in one of those three pairs of seats that were bolted on at the back."

I nodded. I'd bolted the seats on to the an-

184

chorages myself, after we had loaded all the horses. There was usually room for a few seats, and they made a change from hay bales.

"Was he alone?"

"No, there was a young fellow beside him. Your friend Searle was on the inside by the window, I remember, because this young chap had had his legs sprawled out in the gangway and I had to step over them. He didn't move."

"Billy." I nodded.

"After I came out I asked them if they were O.K. and said we'd be landing in half an hour. The young one said 'thanks, Dad' as if he was bored to death, and I had to step over his legs again to get past. I can't say I took to him enormously."

"You surprise me," I said sardonically. "Did Simon say anything?"

He hesitated. "It's three weeks ago. I honestly can't remember, but I don't think so. Nothing special, anyway."

I turned to the engineer. "How about you?"

He chewed, shook his head, swallowed, and took a sip of beer.

"D . . . d . . . don't think I'm much better. I w . . . w . . . was talking to him q . . . q . . . quite a lot at the beginning. In the g . . . g . . . galley. He said he'd come at the l . . . l . . . last minute instead of you. He t . . . t . . . talked about you quite a lot."

The engineer took a mouthful of salad and stuttered through it without embarrassment. A direct

185

man, secure in himself. "He s . . . said you were ice on a v . . . volcano. I said th . . . th . . . that didn't make sense, and he said it w . . . was the only w . . . way to describe you."

Without looking up from his plate Patrick murmured, "In a nutshell."

"That's no help at all," I said, disregarding him. "Didn't he say anything about where he was going, or what he might do, when you got to Milan?"

The engineer shook his head. "He m . . . m . . . meant to come straight back with us, in the afternoon, I'm sure of th . . . th . . . that."

"We didn't come straight back, of course," said Kyle matter-of-factly.

"You didn't?" I was surprised. "I didn't know that."

"We were supposed to. They got the return load of horses loaded up and then discovered there were no papers for one of the two they'd put in first. They had to get the whole lot out again, and they weren't very quick because there were only two of them, and by that time I said it was pointless loading again, as it would be too late to start, I'd be out of hours."

"They should have checked; they had all the papers before they loaded," I said.

"Well, they didn't."

"Only two of them," I said, frowning.

"That's right. The young one — Billy, did you say? — and one other. Not your friend Simon. A deaf old fellow."

"Alf," I said. "That's Alf. What about the two others who went over? They were two specials going with horses from the studs they worked in."

"From what I could make out from the old man, those two were going on with their horses right to the destination, somewhere farther south."

I thought it over. Simon obviously hadn't intended to come back at all, and it hadn't been the unexpected overnight stop which had given him the idea.

"You didn't see where Simon was headed, I suppose, when you got to Milan?" I spoke without much hope, and they both shook their heads.

"We got off the plane before him," Kyle said.

I nodded. The crew didn't have Customs and unloading to see to.

"Well . . . that's that. Thank you for coming today, anyway. And thank you," I said directly to the engineer, "for delivering that bottle of pills to the girl in the souvenir shop."

"P . . . pills? Oh yes, I remember." He was surprised. "How on earth d . . . d . . . did you know about that?"

"She told me a tall crew member brought them over for her."

"I f . . . f . . . found them on the plane, standing on the w . . . w . . . washbasin in the k . . . k . . . karzy. I th . . . th . . . thought I might as well give them to her, as I was g . . . going across anyway. I did . . . didn't

187

see how they got there, b . . . b . . . but they had her name on them."

"Simon was taking them to her from me," I explained.

"Oh, I s . . . see."

Patrick said, grinning, "Were they . . . ?"

"Yes, they were."

"He didn't go over to the airport building at all, then," said Patrick flatly. "He left the pills on board, hoping they would get to Gabriella somehow, and scooted from there."

"It looks like it," I agreed gloomily.

"You can get off that end of the airfield quite easily, of course. It's only scrubland and bushes, and if you walk down that road leading away from the unloading area, the one the horseboxes often use, you're off the place in no time. I should think that explains pretty well why no one saw him."

"Yes," I sighed, "that's what he must have done."

"But it doesn't explain why he went," said Patrick gently.

There was a pause.

"He had . . . troubles," I said at last.

"*In* trouble?" said Kyle.

"Looming. It might be because of something I discovered, that he went. I wanted to find him, and tell him it was . . . safe . . . to come back."

"On your conscience," said Patrick.

"You might say so."

They all nodded, acknowledging their final understanding of my concern for a lost colleague. The waiter brought their cheese and asked whether they would like coffee. I stood up.

"I'll see you again," I said. "How about after the fifth, outside the weighing room? After I've changed."

"Sure thing," said Patrick.

I ambled off to the weighing room and later got dressed in Mr. Thackery's red and blue colors. I'd never ridden in the Gold Cup before, and although I privately agreed with the engineer's assessment of the situation, there was still something remarkably stirring in going out in the best class race of the season. My human opponents were all handpicked professionals and all Clobber's bunch looked to have the beating of him, but nevertheless my mouth grew dry and my heart thumped.

I suspected Mr. Thackery had entered Clobber more for the prestige of having a Gold Cup runner than from any thought that he would win, and his manner in the parade ring confirmed it. He was enjoying himself enormously, untouched by the sort of anxious excitement characteristic of the hopeful.

"Julian's regards," he said, beaming and shaking hands vigorously. "He'll be watching on TV."

TV. There was always the fair chance that one of the people I knew at Fenland might be watching television, though none that I'd heard of was interested in racing. I turned my back on the cameras, as usual.

"Just don't disgrace me," said Mr. Thackery happily. "Don't disgrace me, that's all I ask."

"You could have got a professional," I pointed out.

"Oh, eh, I could. But frankly, it hasn't done me any harm, here and there, for folks to know you're riding my horses."

"A mutually satisfactory arrangement, then," I said dryly.

"Yes," said Mr. Thackery contentedly. "That's about it."

I swung up on his horse, walked out in the parade, and cantered down to the start. Clobber, an eight-year-old thoroughbred chestnut hunter, had only once won (thanks to being low in the handicap) in the company he was taking on now at level weights, but he shone with condition and his step was bursting with good feeling. Like so many horses, he responded well to spring air and sun on his back and my own spirits lifted with his. It was not, after all, going to be a fiasco.

We lined up and the tapes went up, and Clobber set off to the first fence pulling like a train. As he hadn't a snowball's hope in hell of winning, I thought Mr. Thackery might as well enjoy a few moments in the limelight, and I let Clobber surge his way to the front. Once he got there he settled down and stopped trying to run away with me and we stayed there, surprisingly leading the distinguished field for over two and a half of the three and a quarter miles.

Clobber had never been run in front before,

according to the form book, but from his willingness it was evidently to his liking. Holding him up against his inclination, I thought, probably accounted for his inconsistency; he must have lost interest on many occasions when thwarted, and simply packed up trying.

The others came up to him fast and hard going into the second last fence, and three went ahead before the last but Clobber jumped it cleanly and attacked the hill with his ears still pricked good-temperedly, and he finished fourth out of eight with some good ones still behind him. I was pleased with the result myself, having thoroughly enjoyed the whole race, and so it appeared was Mr. Thackery.

"By damn," he said, beaming, "that's the best he's ever run."

"He likes it in front."

"So it seems, yes. We've not tried that before, I must say."

A large bunch of congratulating females advanced on him and I rolled the girths round my saddle and escaped to the weighing room to change for the next race. The colors were those of Old Strawberry Leaves, who had commented sourly that it was disgraceful of me to ride in public only three weeks after my father's death, but had luckily agreed not to remove me from his horse. The truth was that he begrudged paying professionals when he could bully the sons of his friends and acquaintances for nothing. Boathook was his best horse, and for the pleasure of winning on him I could easily put up with the insults I got from losing on the others. On that day, however, there was one too good for him from Ireland, and for being beaten by half a length I got the customary bawling out. Not a good loser by any means, Old Strawberry Leaves.

All in all I'd had a good Cheltenham, I thought, as I changed into street clothes; a winner, a second, an also ran, one harmless fall, and a fourth in the Gold Cup. I wouldn't improve on it very easily.

Patrick and the other two were waiting for me outside, and after we'd watched the last race together, I drove them down to the station to catch the last train to London. They had all made a mint out of the engineer's tips and were in a fine collective state of euphoria.

"I can see why you like it," Patrick said on the way. "It's a magnificent sport. I'll come again."

"Good," I said, stopping at the station to let them out. "I'll see you tomorrow, then."

He grinned. "Milan first stop."

"Arabia again for us," said Kyle resignedly, shutting the door.

They waved their thanks and began to walk away into the station. An elderly man tottered slowly across in front of my car, and as I was waiting for him to pass the engineer's voice floated back to me, clear and unmistakable.

"It's f . . . funny," he said, "you qu . . . quite forget he's a L . . . Lord."

I turned my head round to them, startled. Patrick looked over his shoulder and saw that I had heard, and laughed. I grinned sardonically in return, and drove off reflecting that I was much in favor of people like him who could let me forget it too.

10

Fire can't burn without air. Deprived of an oxygen supply in a sealed space, it goes out. There existed a state of affairs like a smoldering room which had been shuttered and left to cool down in safety. Nothing much would have happened if I hadn't been trying to find Simon, but when I finally came on a trace of him, it was like throwing wide the door. Fresh air poured in and the whole thing banged into flames.

The fine Cheltenham weather was still in operation on the Friday, the day after the Gold Cup. The met reports in the charter company's office showed clear skies right across Europe, with an extended high-pressure area almost stationary over France. No breakup of the system was expected for at least twenty-four hours. Someone tapped me on the shoulder and I half turned to find Patrick reading over my shoulder.

"Trouble-free trip," he commented with satisfaction. "Piece of cake."

"We've got that old DC-4 again, I see," I said, looking out of the window across to where it stood on the tarmac.

"Nice reliable old bus."

"Bloody uncomfortable old bus."

Patrick grinned. "You'll be joining a union next."

"Workers unite," I agreed.

He looked me up and down. "Some worker. You remind me of Fanny Cradock."

"Of *who?*" I said.

"That woman on television who cooks in a ball gown without marking it."

"Oh." I looked down at my neat charcoal worsted, my black tie, and the fraction of white showing at the cuffs. Beside me, in the small overnight bag I now carried everywhere, was the high-necked black jersey I worked in, and a hanger for my jacket. Tidiness was addictive; one couldn't kick it, even when it was inappropriate.

"You're no slouch yourself," I pointed out defensively. He wore his navy gold-braided uniform with an air of authority, his handsome good-natured face radiating confidence. A wonderful bedside manner for nervous passengers, I thought. An inborn conviction that one only had to keep to the rules for everything to be all right. Fatal.

"Eight each way today?" he said.

"Eight out, four back. All brood mares."

"Ready to drop?"

"Let's hope not too ready."

"Let's indeed." He grinned and turned away to check over his flight plan with one of the office staff. "I suppose," he said over his shoulder, "you'd like me to organize an overnight delay at Milan?"

"You suppose correctly."

"You could do it yourself."

"How?"

"Load up all the horses and then 'lose' the papers for a front one. Like John Kyle said, by the time they'd unloaded and reloaded, it was too late to take off."

I laughed. "An absolutely brilliant idea. I shall act on it immediately."

"That'll be the day." He smiled over his papers, checking the lists.

The door opened briskly and Yardman came in, letting a blast of cold six-thirty air slip past him.

"All set?" he said, impressing on us his early hour alertness.

"The horses haven't arrived yet," I said mildly. "They're late again."

"Oh." He shut the door behind him and came in, putting down his brief case and rubbing his thin hands together for warmth. "They were due at six." He frowned and looked at Patrick. "Are you the pilot?"

"That's right."

"What sort of trip are we going to have?"

"Easy," said Patrick. "The weather's perfect."

Yardman nodded in satisfaction. "Good, good." He pulled out a chair and sat down, lifting and opening his brief case. He had brought all the brood mares' papers with him, and as he seemed content to check them with the airline people himself I leaned lazily against the office wall and thought about Gabriella. The office work went steadily on, regardless of the hour. No nine-to-five about an airline. As usual, some of the flying staff were lying there fast asleep, one on a canvas bed under the counter Patrick was leaning on, another underneath the big table where Yardman sat, and a third on my right, stretched along the top of a row of cupboards. They were all wrapped in blankets, heads and all, and were so motionless that one didn't notice them at first. They managed to sleep solidly through the comings and goings and telephoning and typing, and even when Yardman inadvertently kicked the one under the table he didn't stir.

The first of the horseboxes rolled past the window and drove across to the waiting plane. I peeled myself off the wall, temporarily banished Gabriella, and touched Yardman's arm.

"They're here," I said.

He looked round and glanced through the window. "Ah, yes. Well here you are, my dear boy, here's the list. You can load the first six, they are all checked. There's just one more to do . . . it seems there's some query of insurance on this one. . . ." He bent back to his work, riffling through his brief case for more papers.

I took the list and walked across to the plane. I had expected Timmie and Conker to arrive in a horsebox as they lived near the stud one lot of horses had come from, but when I got over there I found it was to be Billy and Alf again. They had come with Yardman, and were already sitting on the stacked box sides in the plane, eating sandwiches. With them sat a third man in jodhpurs and a grubby tweed jacket a size too small. He was wearing an old greenish cap and he didn't bother to look up.

"The horses are here," I said.

Billy turned his wide insolent glare full on and didn't answer. I bent down and touched Alf's knee, and pointed out of the oval window. He saw the horseboxes, nodded philosophically, and began to wrap up his remaining sandwiches. I left them and went down the ramp again, knowing very well that Billy would never obey an instruction of mine if I waited over him to see he did it.

The horsebox driver said they'd had to make a detour because of roadworks. A detour into a transport café, more like.

Two grooms who had traveled with the mares gave a hand with the loading, which made it easy. The man who had come with Billy and Alf, whose name was John, was more abstracted than skillful, but with six of us it was the quickest job I had done when Billy was along. I imagined that it was because he knew Yardman was within complaining distance that he left me alone.

Yardman came across with the all clear for the other two mares, and we stowed them on board. Then as always we trooped along to the Immigration Office in the main passenger building where a bored official collected our dogeared passports, flipped through them, and handed them back. Mine still had Mr. on it, because I'd originally applied for it that way, and I intended to put off changing it as long as possible.

"Four grooms and you," he said to Yardman. "That's the lot?"

"That's the lot." Yardman stifled a yawn. Early starts disagreed with him.

A party of bleary-eyed passengers from a cut-rate night flight shuffled past in an untidy crocodile.

"O.K. then." The passport man flicked the tourists a supercilious glance and retired into his office. Not everyone was at his best before breakfast.

Yardman walked back to the plane beside me.

"I've arranged to meet our opposite numbers for lunch," he said. "You know what business lunches are, my dear boy. I'm afraid it may drag on a little, and that you'll be kicking your heels about the airport for a few hours. Don't let any of them get . . . er . . . the worse for wear."

"No," I agreed insincerely. The longer his lunch, the better I'd be pleased. Billy drunk couldn't be worse than Billy sober, and I didn't intend to waste my hours at Malpensa supervising his intake.

Patrick and his crew were ready out by the plane, and had done their checks. The mobile battery truck stood by the nose cone with its power lead plugged into the aircraft. Patrick liked always to start his engines from the truck, so that he took off with the plane's own batteries fully charged.

Yardman and I followed Billy, Alf and John up the ramp at the rear, and Patrick with his copilot Bob, and the engineer Mike, climbed the forward stairs into the nose. The airport staff wheeled away the stairs and unfastened and removed the two long sections of ramp. The inner port propeller began to grind slowly round as I swung shut the double doors, then sparked into life with a roar, and the plane came alive with vibration. The moment of the first engine firing gave me its usual lift of the spirits and I went along the cabin checking the horses with a smile in my mind.

Patrick moved down the taxi truck and turned onto the apron set aside for power checks, the airframe quivering against the brakes as he pushed the throttles open. Holding two of the horses by their head collars I automatically followed him in imagination through the last series of checks before he closed the throttles, released the brakes and rolled round on to Gatwick's large single runway. The engine's note deepened and the plane began to move, horses and men leaning against the thrust as the speed built up to a hundred over the tarmac. We unstuck as per schedule and climbed away in a great wheeling turn, heading toward the Channel on course to the radio beacon at Dieppe. The heavy mares took the whole thing philosophically, and having checked round the lot of them I went forward into the galley, bending under the luggage racks and stepping over the guy chains as always in the cramped DC-4.

Mike, the engineer, was already writing the names on disposable cups with a red felt pen.

"All O.K.?" he asked, the eyebrow going up and down like a yo-yo.

"All fine," I said.

He wrote "Patrick" and "Bob" and "Henry" and asked the names of the others. "Mr. Y," "Billy," "Alf" and "John" joined the roll. He filled the crew's cups and mine, and I took Patrick's and Bob's forward while he went back to ask the others if they were thirsty. The rising sun blazed into the cockpit, dazzling after the comparative gloom of the cabin. Both pilots were wearing dark glasses, and Patrick already had his jacket off, and had started on the first of his attendant bunch of bananas. The chart lay handy, the usual unlikely mass of half-inch circles denoting radio stations, connected by broad pale-blue areas of authorized airlines, with the normal shape of the land beneath only faintly drawn in and difficult to distinguish. Bob pulled a tuft of cotton wool off a shaving cut, made it bleed again, and swore, his exact words inaudible against the racket of the engines. Both of them were wearing headsets, earphones combined with a microphone mounted on a metal band which curved round in front of the mouth. They spoke to each other by means of a transmitting switch set into the wheel on the control column, since normal speech in that noise was impossible. Giving me a grin and a thumbs-up sign for the coffee, they went on with their endless attention to the job in hand. I watched for a bit, then strolled back through the galley, picking up "Henry" en route, and relaxed on a hay bale to drink, looking down out of the oval window and seeing the coast of France tilt underneath as we passed the Dieppe beacon and set course for Paris.

A day like any other day, a flight like any other flight. And Gabriella waiting at the other end of it. Every half hour or so I checked round the mares, but they were a docile lot and traveled like veterans. Mostly horses didn't eat much in the air, but one or two were picking at their haynets, and a chestnut in the rearmost box was fairly guzzling. I began to untie her depleted net to fill it again for her from one of the bales when a voice said in my ear, "I'll do that."

I looked round sharply and found Billy's face two feet from my own.

"You?" The surprise and sarcasm got drowned by the engine noise.

He nodded, elbowed me out of the way, and finished untying the haynet. I watched with astonishment as he carried it away into the narrow starboard gangway and began to stuff it full again. He came back pulling the drawstring tight round the neck, slung it over to hang inside the box, and retied its rope onto the cleat. Wordlessly he treated me to a wide sneering glare from the searchlight eyes, pushed past, and flung himself with what suddenly looked like pent-up fury into one of the seats at the back.

In the pair of seats immediately behind him Yardman and John sat side by side. Yardman was frowning crossly at Billy, though to my mind he should have been giving him a pat on the head and medal for self-control.

Yardman turned his head from Billy to me and gave me his graveyard smile. "What time do we arrive?" he shouted.

"About half an hour."

He nodded and looked away through the window. I glanced at John and saw that he was dozing, with his grubby cap pushed back on his head and his hands lying limp on his lap. He opened his eyes while I was looking at him, and his relaxed facial muscles sharply contracted so that suddenly he seemed familiar to me, though I was certain I hadn't met him before. It puzzled me for only a second because Billy, getting up again, managed to kick my ankle just out of Yardman's sight. I turned away from him, lashed backward with my heel, and felt a satisfactory clunking jar as it landed full on his shin. One day, I thought, smiling to myself as I squeezed forward along the plane, one day he'll get tired of it.

We joined the circuit at Malpensa four hours from Gatwick; a smooth, easy trip. Holding the mares' heads I saw the familiar red and white checkered huts near the edge of the airfield grow bigger and bigger as we descended, then they were suddenly behind us at eye level as Patrick leveled out twenty feet from the ground at about a hundred and ten miles an hour. The bump from the tricycle under-carriage as we touched down with full flaps at a fraction above stalling speed wasn't enough to rock the mares on their feet. Top of the class, I thought.

The Customs man with his two helpers came on board, and Yardman produced the mares' papers from his brief case. The checking went on without a hitch, brisk but thorough. The Customs man handed the papers back to Yardman with a small bow and signed that the unloading could begin.

Yardman ducked out of any danger of giving a hand with that by saying that he'd better see if the opposite numbers were waiting for him inside the airport. As it was barely half-past eleven, it seemed doubtful, but all the same he marched purposefully down the ramp and away across the tarmac, a gaunt black figure with sunshine flashing on his glasses.

The crew got off at the sharp end and followed him, a navy-blue trio in peaked caps. A large yellow Shell tanker pulled up in front of the aircraft, and three men in white overalls began the job of refueling.

We unloaded into the waiting horseboxes in record time, Billy seemingly being as anxious as me to get it done quickly, and within half an hour of landing I had changed my jersey for my jacket and was pushing open the glass doors of the airport. I stood just inside, watching Gabriella.

She was selling a native doll, fluffing up the rich dark skirt to show the petticoats underneath, her face solemn and absorbed. The heavy dark club-cut hair swung forward as she leaned across the counter, and her eyes were cool and quiet as she shook her head gently at her customer, the engineer Mike. My chest constricted at the sight of her, and I wondered how I was possibly going to bear leaving again in three hours' time. She looked up suddenly as if she felt my gaze, and she saw me and smiled, her soft mouth curving sweet and wide.

Mike looked quite startled at the transformation and turned to see the reason.

"Henry," said Gabriella, with welcome and gaiety shimmering in her voice. "Hullo, darling."

"Darling?" exclaimed Mike, the eyebrow doing its stuff.

Gabriella said in French, "I've doubled my English vocabulary, as you see. I know two words now."

"Essential ones, I'm glad to say."

"Hey," said Mike. "If you can talk to her, Henry, ask her about this doll. It's my elder girl's birthday tomorrow, and she's started collecting these things, but I'm damned if I know whether she'll like this one."

"How old is she?"

"Twelve."

I explained the situation to Gabriella, who promptly produced a different doll, much prettier and more colorful, which she wrapped up for

205

him while he sorted out some lire. Like Patrick's his wallet was stuffed with several different currencies, and he scattered a day's pay in deutschmarks over the merchandise before finding what he wanted. Collecting his cash in an untidy handful he thanked her cheerfully in basic French, picked up his parcel and walked off upstairs into the restaurant. There were always lunches provided for us on the planes, tourist-class lunches packed in boxes, but both Mike and Bob preferred eating on the ground, copiously and in comfort.

I turned back to Gabriella and tried to satisfy my own sort of hunger by looking at her and touching her hand. And I could see in her face that to her too this was like a bowl of rice to the famine of India.

"When do you go?" she said.

"The horses arrive at two-thirty. I have to go then to load them. I might get back for a few minutes afterward, if my boss dallies over his coffee."

She sighed, looking at the clock. It was ten past noon. "I have an hour off in twenty minutes. I'll make it two hours. . . ." She turned away into swift chatter with the girl along on the duty-free shop, and came back smiling. "I'm doing her last hour today, and she'll do the gift shop in her lunch hour."

I bowed my thanks to the girl and she laughed back with a flash of teeth, very white against the gloom of her bottle shop.

"Do you want to have lunch up there?" I suggested to Gabriella, pointing where Mike and Bob had gone.

She shook her head. "Too public. Everyone knows me so well. We've time to go in to Milan, if you can do that?"

"If the horses get here early, they can wait."

"Serve them right." She nodded approvingly, her lips twitching.

A crowd of outgoing passengers erupted into the hall and swarmed round the gift counter. I retired to the snack bar at the far end to wait out the twenty minutes, and found Yardman sitting alone at one of the small tables. He waved me to join him, which I would just as soon not have done, and told me to order myself a double gin and tonic, like his.

"I'd really rather have coffee."

He waved a limp hand permissively. "Have whatever you like, my dear boy."

I looked casually around the big airy place, at the glass, the polished wood, the terrazza. Along one side, next to a stall of sweets and chocolates, stretched the serving counter with coffee and beer rubbing shoulders with milk and gin. And down at the far end, close-grouped round another little table and clutching pint glasses, sat Alf and Billy, and with his back to us, John. Two and a half hours of that, I thought wryly, and we'd have a riotous trip home.

"Haven't your people turned up?" I asked Yardman.

"Delayed," he said resignedly. "They'll be here

about one, though."

"Good," I said, but not for his sake. "You won't forget to ask them about Simon?"

"Simon?"

"Searle."

"Searle . . . oh yes. Yes, all right, I'll remember."

Patrick walked through the hall from the office department, exchanged a greeting with Gabriella over the heads of her customers and came on to join us.

"Drink?" suggested Yardman, indicating his glass. He only meant to be hospitable, but Patrick was shocked.

"Of course not."

"Eh?"

"Well . . . I thought you'd know. One isn't allowed to fly within eight hours of drinking alcohol."

"Eight hours," repeated Yardman in astonishment.

"That's right. Twenty-four hours after a heavy party, and better not for forty-eight if you get paralytic."

"I didn't know," said Yardman weakly.

"Air Ministry regulations," Patrick explained. "I'd like some coffee, though."

A waitress brought him some, and he unwrapped four sugars and stirred them in. "I enjoyed yesterday," he said, smiling at me with his yellow eyes. "I'll go again. When do you race next?"

"Tomorrow."

"That's out for a start. When else?"

I glanced at Yardman. "It depends on the schedules." Patrick turned to him in his usual friendly way. "I went to Cheltenham yesterday and saw our Henry here come fourth in the Gold Cup. Very interesting."

"You know each other well, then?" Yardman asked. His deep-set eyes were invisible behind the glasses, and the slanting sunlight showed up every blemish in his sallow skin. I still had no feeling for him either way, not liking, not disliking. He was easy to work for. He was friendly enough. He was still an enigma.

"We know each other," Patrick agreed. "We've been on trips together before."

"I see."

Gabriella came down toward us, wearing a supple brown suede coat over her black working dress. She had flat black round-toed patent-leather shoes and swung a handbag with the same shine. A neat, composed, self-reliant, nearly beautiful girl who took work for granted and a lover for fun.

I stood up as she came near, trying to stifle a ridiculous feeling of pride, and introduced her to Yardman. He smiled politely and spoke to her in slow Italian, which surprised me a little, and Patrick translated for me into one ear.

"He's telling her he was in Italy during the war. Rather tactless of him, considering her grandfather was killed fighting off the invasion of Sicily."

"Before she was born," I protested.

"True." He grinned. "She's pro-British enough now, anyway."

"Miss Barzini tells me you are taking her to lunch in Milan," Yardman said.

"Yes," I agreed. "If that's all right with you? I'll be back by two-thirty when the return mares come."

"I can't see any objection," he said mildly. "Where do you have in mind?"

"Trattoria Romana," I said promptly. It was where Gabriella, Patrick and I had eaten on our first evening together.

Gabriella put her hand in mine. "Good. I'm very hungry." She shook hands with Yardman and waggled her fingers at Patrick. "Arrivederci."

We walked away up the hall, the voltage tingling gently through our joined palms. I looked back once, briefly, and saw Yardman and Patrick watching us go. They were both smiling.

11

Neither of us had much appetite, when it came to the point. We ate half our lasagna and drank coffee, and needed nothing else but proximity. We didn't talk a great deal, but at one point, clairvoyantly reading my disreputable thoughts, she said out of the blue that we couldn't go to her sister's flat as her sister would be in, complete with two or three kids.

"I was afraid of that," I said wryly.

"It will have to be next time."

"Yes." We both sighed deeply in unison, and laughed.

A little later, sipping her hot coffee, she said, "How many pills were there in the bottle you sent with Simon Searle?"

"I don't know. Dozens. I didn't count them. The bottle was over three-quarters full."

"I thought so." She sighed. "The baker's wife rang up last night to ask me whether I could let her have some more. She said the bottom of the bottle was all filled up with paper, but if you ask me she's given half of them away to a friend, or something, and now regrets it."

"There wasn't any paper in the bottle. Only cotton wool on top."

"I thought so." She frowned, wrinkling her nose in sorrow. "I wish she'd told me the truth."

I stood up abruptly. "Come on," I said. "Leave the coffee."

"Why?" She began to put on her coat.

"I want to see that bottle."

She was puzzled. "She'll have thrown it away."

"I hope to God she hasn't," I said urgently, paying the bill. "If there's paper in the bottle, Simon put it there."

"You mean . . . it could matter?"

"He thought I was giving the pills to you. He didn't know they'd go to someone else. And I forgot to tell him you didn't speak English. Perhaps he thought when you'd finished the pills you'd read the paper and tell me what it said. Heaven knows. Anyway, we must find it. It's the first and only trace of him we've had."

We hurried out of the restaurant, caught a taxi, and sped to the bakery. The baker's wife was fat and motherly and looked fifty, though she was probably only thirty-five. Her warm smile for Gabriella slowly turned anxious as she listened, and she shook her head and spread her hands wide.

"It's in the dustbin," Gabriella said. "She threw it away this morning."

"We'll have to look. Ask her if I can look for it."

The two women consulted.

212

"She says you'll dirty your fine suit."

"Gabriella. . . ."

"She says the English are mad, but you can look."

There were three dustbins in the backyard, two luckily empty and one full. We turned this one out and I raked through the stinking contents with a broom handle. The little brown bottle was there, camouflaged by wet coffee grounds and half a dozen noodles. Gabriella took it and wiped it clean on a piece of newspaper while I shoveled the muck back into the dustbin and swept the yard.

"The paper won't come out," she said. She had the cap off and was poking down the neck of the bottle with her finger. "It's quite right. There is some in there." She held it out to me.

I looked and nodded, wrapped the bottle in newspaper, put it on the ground, and smashed it with the shovel. She squatted beside me as I unfolded the paper and watched me pick out from the winking fragments of brown glass the things which had been inside.

I stood up slowly, holding them. A strip torn off the top of a piece of Yardman's stationery. A banknote of a currency I did not recognize, and some pieces of hay. The scrap of writing paper and the money were pinned together, and the hay had been folded up inside them.

"They are nonsense," said Gabriella slowly.

"Do you have any idea where this comes from?" I touched the note. She flicked it over to see both sides.

"Yugoslavia. One hundred dinars."

"Is that a lot?"

"About five thousand one hundred lire."

Three pounds. Wisps of hay. A strip of paper. In a bottle.

Gabriella took the money and paper out of my hands and removed the pin which joined them.

"What do they mean?" she asked.

"I don't know."

A message in a bottle.

"There are some holes in the paper."

"Where he put the pin."

"No. More holes than that. Look." She held it up to the sky. "You can see the light through."

The printed heading said in thick red letters "Yardman Transport Ltd., Carriers." The strip of paper was about six inches across and two inches deep from the top smooth edge to the jagged one where it had been torn off the page. I held it up to the light.

Simon had pinpricked four letters. S.M.E.N. I felt the first distant tremor of cold apprehension.

"What is it?" she asked. "What does it say?"

"Yardman Transport." I showed her. "See where he has added to it. If you read it with the pin hole letters tacked on, it says: 'Yardman Transports MEN.' "

She looked frightened by the bleakness in my voice, as if she could feel the inner coldness growing. "What does it mean?"

"It means he didn't have a pencil," I said grimly, evading the final implication. "Only pins in his coat."

A message in a bottle, washed ashore.

"I've got to think it out," I said. "I've got to remember."

We perched on a pile of empty boxes stacked in one corner of the baker's yard, and I stared sightlessly at the whitewashed wall opposite and at the single bush in a tub standing in one corner.

"Tell me," Gabriella said. "Tell me. You look so . . . so terrible."

"Billy," I said. "Billy put up a smoke screen, after all."

"Who is Billy?"

"A groom. At least, he works as one. Men. . . . Every time Billy has been on a trip, there has been a man who didn't come back."

"Simon?" she said incredulously.

"No, I don't mean Simon, though he went with Billy. . . . No. Someone who went as a groom, but wasn't a groom at all. And didn't come back. I can't remember any of their faces, not to be sure, because I never talked to any of them much. Billy saw to that."

"How?"

"Oh, by insults and . . ." I stopped, concentrating back. "The first time I went with Billy, there was a very fat man called John. At least, that was what I was told he was called. He was absolutely useless. Didn't know how to handle horses at all. We did two trips to France that day, and I think he wanted to vanish after the first. I saw him arguing furiously with Billy just before we came back the first time. But Billy made him do the double journey . . . and when he told me John had gone to Paris instead of coming back with us, he poured beer over my foot, so that I'd think about that, and not about John. And he made sure of it by picking a fight on the plane coming back. . . ."

"But who was this John?"

I shook my head. "I've no idea."

"And were there others?"

"Yes . . . we went to New York next, he and I. There was a groom traveling with a half-bred Norwegian horse. He hardly talked at all, said he didn't speak English much. I understood he was staying in the States for a fortnight: but who knows if he came back? And on that trip Billy smashed a bar across my fingers so that they hurt all the way across, and I thought about them, not the Norwegian groom."

"Are you sure?" She was frowning.

"Oh yes, I'm sure. I thought once before that Billy had done it for a purpose. I just got the purpose wrong." I pondered. "There was a day we took a man with a large bushy mustache to France, and a fortnight later we brought a man with a large bushy mustache back again. I never looked beyond the mustache. . . . I think it could have been two different men."

"What did Billy do, those times?"

"On the way over he poured sirupy coffee on my head, and I spent nearly all the time in the washroom getting it out. And on the way back he hit me with a chain, and I went up into the

216

galley all the way with the engineer to avoid any more."

She looked at me very gravely. "Is that . . . is that the lot?"

I shook my head. "We went to New York last week. I told Yardman if Billy didn't leave me alone I'd quit. The journey out went quite all right, but coming back . . . there was a man who was plainly not a horseman. He wasn't even comfortable in the riding clothes he had on. I thought at the time he was the owner's nephew or something, cadging a free ride, but again I didn't talk to him much. I slept all the way back. All ten hours . . . I don't usually get tired like that, but I thought it was only because it was my fourth Atlantic crossing in six days. . . ."

"A sleeping pill?" she said slowly.

"It might have been. Alf brought some coffee back for me soon after we left. There was a restive colt in the aft box and I was trying to soothe him. . . . It could have been in that. "

"Alf?"

"An old deaf man, who always goes with Billy."

"Do you think it *was* a sleeping pill?"

"It could have been. . . . I was still tired long after I got home. I even went to sleep in the bath."

"It's serious," she said.

"Today," I said. "There's a stranger with us today. His name is John too. I've never met him before, but there's something about him. . . . I was looking at him on the plane and wondering what it was, and Billy kicked me on the ankle. I kicked him back, but I went away, and stopped thinking about that man."

"Can you think now?"

"Well . . . his hands are wrong for one thing. Stablemen's hands are rough and chafed from being wet so often in cold weather, with washing tack and so on, but his are smooth, with well-shaped nails."

She picked up one of my hands and looked at it, running the tips of her fingers over the roughness which had developed since I left my desk job.

"They are not like yours, then."

"Not like mine. But it's his expression really. I watched him wake up. It was what came into his face with consciousness. . . ." I could remember that moment vividly, in spite of Billy's kick. I knew that expression very well . . . so what was it? "Oh," I exclaimed in enlightenment, half laughing at my own stupidity. "I know what it is . . . he went to the same school as I did."

"You do know him then, I mean, you've seen him before, if you were at school together."

"Not together. He's older. He must have left about five years before I went. No, I've never seen him before, but the look he has is typical of some of the boys there. Not the nicest ones . . . only the ones who think they are God's gift to mankind and everyone else is a bit inferior. He's one of those. Definitely *not* a groom. He looked as if wearing the grubby riding clothes he's got on was a kick in the dignity."

"But you don't wear riding clothes," she pointed out. "It isn't necessary for him if he doesn't like them."

"It is though. Alf wears jodhpurs, Billy wears jeans. The two grooms who travel turn about with these two, Timmie and Conker, they both wear breeches to work in. It's a sort of office. . . . No one would think twice about a man arriving on a horse transport dressed in breeches or jodhpurs."

"No, I see that."

"No one bothers much about our passports," I said. "Look how simply I came out into Milan today, through the airport staff door. Hardly any airports, especially the very small ones, take much notice of you, if you work on airplanes. It's dead easy just to walk off most airfields round at the loading bays without ever being challenged. The Americans are strictest, but even they are used to our comings and goings."

"But people do look at your passports sometimes, surely," she protested.

I produced mine, battered and dog-eared in the last three months after several years of dark-blue stiffness. "Look at it. It gets like that from always being in my pocket, but it doesn't get stamped much." I turned through the pages. "American visa, certainly. But look, the only stamp from Milan is the time I came on a scheduled flight and went through immigration with the other passengers. Hardly a mark for France, and I've been over there several times. . . . Of course it gets looked at, but never very thoroughly. It must be easy to fake one in this condition, and even traveling without one wouldn't be impossible. A pilot told me he'd done it for three weeks once, all over the world."

"People who work on aircraft would go mad if everyone started checking their passports thoroughly every time they walked in or out."

"Well . . . normally there's no need for it. It isn't all that easy to get on a single one-way flight as a worker. Impossible, if you haven't a strong pull somewhere or other. Just any odd person who fancies a quiet trip to foreign parts wouldn't have a hope of getting himself into a horse transport. But if the transport agency itself, or someone working for it, is ready to export people illegally along with the horses, then it's easy."

"But . . . what people?"

"What indeed! Billy can hardly advertise his service in the daily press. But he has no shortage of customers."

"Crooks, do you think?" Gabriella asked, frowning.

I fingered the banknote and twisted the small pieces of hay.

"Hay," I said. "Why hay?"

Gabriella shrugged. "Perhaps he found the money in some hay."

"Of course!" I exclaimed. "You're dead right. Haynets. Carried openly on and off the planes and never searched by Customs officers. Perhaps they're transporting currency as well as men." I told her about Billy refilling the net for me on the trip over, and how astonished I had been.

"But, Henry darling, what I really do not understand is why you were not astonished all along at the unpleasant things Billy has been doing to you. I would have thought it utterly extraordinary, and I would have made a very big fuss about it." She looked solemn and doubtful.

"Oh, I thought it was simply because I . . ." I stopped.

"Because you what?"

I smiled slightly. "Because I belong to a sort of people he thinks should be exterminated."

"Henry!" Her mouth lost its severity. "What sort of people?"

"Well . . . you have counts and countesses still in Italy. . . ."

"But you're not . . . you're not, are you . . . a count?"

"Sort of. Yes."

She looked at me doubtfully, halfway to laughing, not sure that I was not teasing her.

"I don't believe you."

"The reason I wasn't astonished at Billy knocking me about was that I knew he hated my guts for having a title."

"That makes sense, I suppose." She managed to frown and smile at the same time, which looked adorable. "But if you have a title, Henry, why are you working in a horse transport?"

"You tell me why," I said.

She looked at me searchingly for a moment, then she put her arms round my neck and her cheek on mine, with her mouth against my ear.

"It isn't enough for you to have a title," she said. "It isn't enough for anyone. It is necessary to show also that you are . . ." She fished around in her French vocabulary, and came up with a word: ". . . véritable. Real."

I took a deep breath of relief and overspilling love, and kissed her neck where the dark hair swung below her ear.

"My wife will be a countess," I said. "Would you mind that?"

"I could perhaps bear it."

"And me? Could you bear me? For always?"

"I love you," she said in my ear. "Yes. For always. Only, Henry . . ."

"Only what?"

"You won't stop being real?"

"No," I said sadly.

She pulled away from me, shaking her head.

"I'm stupid. I'm sorry. But if even I can doubt you . . . and so quickly . . . you must always be having to prove . . ."

"Always," I agreed.

"Still, you don't have to go quite so far."

My heart sank.

"It's not everyone," she said, "who gets proposed to in a baker's backyard surrounded by dustbins." Her mouth trembled and melted into a heart-wrenching smile.

"You wretch, my love."

"Henry," she said. "I'm so happy I could burst."

I kissed her and felt the same, and lived another half minute of oblivion before I thought again of Simon.

"What is it?" she said, feeling me straighten.

"The time. . . ."

"Oh."

"And Simon. . . ."

"I fear for him," she said, half under her breath.

"I too."

She took the piece of paper out of my hand and looked at it again.

"We've been trying to avoid realizing what this means."

"Yes," I said softly.

"Say it, then."

"This was the only message he had a chance of sending. The only way he could send it." I paused, looking into her serious dark eyes. After ten silent seconds I finished it. "He is dead."

She said in distress, "Perhaps he is a prisoner."

I shook my head. "He's the third man who's disappeared. There was a man called Ballard who used to arrange trips from this end, and the man who used to have my own job, a man called Peters. They both vanished, Ballard over a year ago, and no one's heard of them since."

"This Billy . . ." she said slowly, her eyes anxious.

"This Billy," I said, "is young and heartless,

223

and carries a loaded revolver under his left arm."

"Please . . . don't go back with him."

"It will be quite safe as long as I keep quiet about this." I took the hurried, desperate, pin-pricked message back, folded it up with the banknote and the hay, and put them all in my wallet. "When I get back to England, I'll find out who I have to tell."

"The police," she said, nodding.

"I'm not sure. . . ." I thought about the Yu-goslav currency and remembered Gabriella saying on our first evening, "Communists begin at Tri-este." I felt like someone who had trodden through a surface into a mole run underneath, and had suddenly realized that it was part of a whole dark invisible network. I thought it very unlikely that the men I'd flown with were or-dinary crooks. They were couriers, agents . . . heaven knew what. It seemed fantastic to me to have brushed so closely with people I had known must exist but never expected to see; but I sup-posed the suburban people who had lived next door to Peter and Helen Kroger in Cranley Drive, Ruislip, had been pretty astonished too.

"Billy must have unloaded whatever he brought over in the haynets today," I said. "But going back . . ."

"No," Gabriella said vehemently. "Don't look. That's what Simon must have done. Found the money. And Billy saw him."

It might have been like that. And there had been two extra grooms on that trip, men I'd never seen before. Somehow, on the way, Simon had come across something I'd been blind to, perhaps because there was one more man than he'd arranged for, perhaps because Billy couldn't distract his attention by the methods he'd used on me, perhaps because of other happenings in the past which I didn't know about. In any case, Simon had found Billy out, and had let Billy know it. I thought drearily of Simon suddenly realizing toward the end of that flight that Ballard and Peters had never come back, and that he wouldn't get a chance to put Billy in jail. Billy, the young thug, with his ready gun. A few minutes in the lavatory, that was all the time he'd had. No pencil. Only his pins, and the little bottle I'd given him in the privacy of the airlines office; the bottle Billy didn't know existed, with Gabriella's name on it. Pills into loo. Banknote and paper with its inadequate message into bottle. Simon into eternity.

"Please don't search the haynets," Gabriella said again.

"No," I agreed. "Someone official had better do it, next time Billy goes on a trip."

She relaxed with relief. "I'd hate you to disappear."

I smiled. "I won't do that. I'll go back most of the way up front with the crew, with Patrick and the man who bought the doll. And when I get to England I'll telephone you to let you know I arrived safely. How's that?"

"It would be wonderful. I could stop worrying."

"Don't start," I said confidently. "Nothing will go wrong."

How the local gods must have laughed their Roman heads off.

12

We went through the baker's shop and out into the street. I looked somewhat anxiously at my watch and calculated a dead heat with the brood mares.

"We need a taxi," I said.

Gabriella shook her head. "Very unlikely to find one in this quarter. We'd better catch a tram back to the center, and take one on from there."

"All right," I agreed. "Tram or taxi, whichever comes first."

The trams ran along the busy street at the end of the quiet empty road where the baker lived, and we began to walk toward them with some dispatch.

"I didn't realize how late it is," Gabriella said, catching sight of a clock with the hands together pointing northeast.

"And that one's slow. It's a quarter past."

"Oh dear."

One of the long green and cream single-decker trams rolled across the end of the road, not far ahead.

"Run," Gabriella said. "The stop's just around

the corner. We must catch it."

We ran, holding hands. It couldn't have been more than ten strides to the corner. Not more.

Gabriella cried out suddenly and stumbled, whirling against me as I pulled her hand. There was a sharp searing stab in my side and we fell down on the pavement, Gabriella's weight pulling me over as I tried to save her from hurting herself.

Two or three passers-by stopped to help her up, but she didn't move. She was lying face down, crumpled. Without belief, I stared at the small round hole near the center of the back of her coat. Numbly, kneeling beside her, I put my left hand inside my jacket against my scorching right side, and when I brought it out it was covered in blood.

"Oh no," I said in English. "Oh dear God, no."

I bent over her and rolled her up and on to her back in my arms. Her eyes were open. They focused on my face. She was alive. It wasn't much.

"Henry," her voice was a whisper. "I can't . . . breathe."

The three passers-by had grown to a small crowd. I looked up desperately into their inquiring faces.

"Doctor," I said. "Medico." That was Spanish. "Doctor."

"Si si," said a small boy at my elbow. "Un dottore, si."

There was a stir in the crowd and a great deal of speculation of which I understood only one word. "Inglese," they said, and I nodded. "Inglese."

I opened gently the front of Gabriella's brown suede coat. There was a jagged tear in the right side, nearest me, and the edges of it were dark. Underneath, the black dress was soaking. I waved my arm wildly round at the people to get them to stand back a bit, and they did take one pace away. A motherly-looking woman produced a pair of scissors from her handbag and knelt down on Gabriella's other side. She pointed at me to open the coat again, and when I'd tucked it back between Gabriella's body and my own she began to cut away the dress. Gentle as she was, Gabriella moved in my arms and gave a small gasping cry.

"Hush," I said, "my love, it's all right."

"Henry. . . ." She shut her eyes.

I held her in anguish while the woman with the scissors carefully cut and peeled away a large piece of dress. When she saw what lay underneath her big face filled with overwhelming compassion, and she began to shake her head. "Signor," she said to me, "mi dispiace molto. Molto."

I took the clean white handkerchief out of my top pocket, folded it inside out, and put it over the terrible wound. The bullet had smashed a rib on its way out. There were splinters of it showing in the bleeding area just below the breast. The bottom edge of her white bra had a new scarlet border. I gently untucked the coat and put it over her again to keep her warm and I thought in utter agony that she would die before the doctor came.

A carabiniere in glossy boots and greenish khaki breeches appeared beside us, but I doubt if I could have spoken to him even if he'd known the same language. The crowd chattered to him in subdued voices and he left me alone.

Gabriella opened her eyes. Her face was gray and wet with the sweat of appalling pain.

"Henry. . . ."

"I'm here."

"I can't . . . breathe."

I raised her a little more so that she was half sitting, supported by my arm and my bent knee. The movement was almost too much for her. Her pallor became pronounced. The short difficult breaths passed audibly through her slackly open mouth.

"Don't . . . leave me."

"No," I said. "Hush, my dearest love."

"What . . . happened?"

"You were shot," I said.

"Shot. . . ." She showed no surprise. "Was it . . . Billy?"

"I don't know. I didn't see. Don't talk, my sweet love, don't talk. The doctor will be here soon."

"Henry. . . ." She was exhausted, her skin the color of death. "Henry . . . I love you."

Her eyes flickered shut again, but she was still conscious, her left hand moving spasmodically and restlessly on the ground beside her and the lines of suffering deepening in her face.

I would have given anything, anything on earth, to have had her whole again, to have taken that pain away.

The doctor, when at last he came, was young enough to have been newly qualified. He had thick black curly hair and thin clever hands; this was what I most saw of him as he bent over Gabriella, and all I remember. He looked briefly under my white handkerchief and turned to speak to the policeman.

I heard the words "auto ambulanza" and "pallota," and eager information from the crowd.

The young doctor went down on one knee and felt Gabriella's pulse. She opened her eyes, but only a fraction.

"Henry. . . ."

"I'm here. Don't talk."

The young doctor said something soothing to her in Italian, and she said faintly "Si." He opened his case beside him on the ground and with quick skillful fingers prepared an injection, made a hole in her stocking, swabbed her skin with surgical spirit, and pushed the needle firmly into her thigh. Again he spoke to her gently, and again felt her pulse. I could read nothing but reassurance in his manner, and the reassurance was for her, not me.

After a while she opened her eyes wider and looked at me, and a smile struggled on to her damp face.

"That's better," she said. Her voice was so

weak as to be scarcely audible, and she was growing visibly more breathless. Nothing was better, except the pain.

I smiled back. "Good. You'll be all right soon, when they get you to hospital."

She nodded a fraction. The doctor continued to hold her pulse, checking it on his watch.

Two vehicles drove up and stopped with a screech of tires. A Citroën police car and an ambulance like a large estate car. Two carabinieri of obvious seniority emerged from one, and stretcher bearers from the other. These last, and the doctor, lifted Gabriella gently out of my arms and on to the stretcher. They piled blankets behind her to support her, and I saw the doctor take a look at what he could see of the small hole in her back. He didn't try to take off her coat.

One of the policemen said, "I understand you speak French."

"Yes," I said, standing up. I hadn't felt the hardness of the pavement until that moment. The leg I'd been kneeling on was numb.

"What are the young lady's name and address?"

I told him. He wrote them down.

"And your own?"

I told him.

"What happened?" he said, indicating the whole scene with a flickering wave of the hand.

"We were running to catch the tram. Someone shot at us, from back there." I pointed down the empty street toward the baker's.

"Who?"

"I didn't see." They were lifting Gabriella into the ambulance. "I must go with her," I said.

The policeman shook his head. "You can see her later. You must come with us, and tell us exactly what happened."

"I said I wouldn't leave her. . . ." I couldn't bear to leave her. I took a quick stride and caught the doctor by the arm. "Look," I said, pulling open my jacket.

He looked. He tugged my bloodstained shirt out of my trousers to inspect the damage more closely. A ridged furrow five inches long along my lowest rib. Not very deep. It felt like a burn. The doctor told the policeman who also looked.

"All right," said the one who spoke French, "I suppose you'd better go and have it dressed." He wrote an address on a page of his notebook, tore it off and gave it to me. "Come here, afterwards."

"Yes."

"Have you your passport with you?"

I took it out of my pocket and gave it to him, and put the address he'd given me in my wallet. The doctor jerked his head toward the ambulance to get in, and I did.

"Wait," said the policeman as they were shutting the door. "Did the bullet go through the girl into you?"

"No," I said. "Two bullets. She was hit first, me after."

"We will look for them," he said.

Gabriella was still alive when we reached the hospital. Still alive when they lifted her, stretcher and all, onto a trolley. Still alive while one of the ambulance men explained rapidly to a doctor what had happened, and while that doctor and another took in her general condition, left my handkerchief undisturbed, and whisked her away at high speed.

One doctor went with her. The other, a thickset man with the shoulders of a boxer, stayed behind and asked me a question.

"Inglese." I shook my head. "Non parlo italiano."

"Sit down," he said in English. His accent was thick, his vocabulary tiny, but it was a relief to be able to talk to him at all. He led me into a small white cubicle containing a hard, high narrow bed and a chair. He pointed to the chair and I sat on it. He went away and returned with a nurse carrying some papers.

"The name of the miss?"

I told him. The nurse wrote it all down, name, address and age, gave me a comforting smile, took the papers away and came back with a trolley of equipment and a message.

She told it to the doctor, and he translated, as it was for me.

"Telephone from carabinieri. Please go to see them before four."

I looked at my watch, blank to the time. It

234

was still less than an hour since Gabriella and I had run for the tram. I had lived several ages.

"I understand," I said.

"Please now, remove the coat," the doctor said.

I stood up, took off my jacket and slid my right arm out of my shirt. He put two dressings over the bullet mark, an impregnated gauze one and a slightly padded one with adhesive tape. He pressed the tapes firmly into my skin and stood back. I put my arm back into my shirt sleeve.

"Don't you feel it?" he said. He seemed surprised.

"No."

His rugged face softened. "E sua moglie?"

I didn't understand.

"I am sorry . . . is she your wife?"

"I love her," I said. The prospect of losing her was past bearing. There were tears suddenly in my eyes and on my cheeks. "I love her."

"Yes." He nodded, sympathetic and unembarrassed, one of a nation who saw no value in stiff upper lips. "Wait here. We will tell you. . . ." He left the sentence unfinished and went away, and I didn't know whether it was because he didn't want to tell me she was dying or because he simply didn't know enough English to say what he meant.

I waited an hour I couldn't endure again. At the end of it another doctor came, a tall gray-haired man with a fine-boned face.

"You wish to know about Signora Barzini?"

His English was perfect, his voice quiet and very precise.

I nodded, unable to ask.

"We have cleaned and dressed her wound. The bullet passed straight through her lung, breaking a rib on the way out. The lung was collapsed. The air from it, and also a good deal of blood, had passed into the chest cavity. It was necessary to remove the air and blood at once so that the lung would have room to inflate again, and we have done that." He was coolly clinical.

"May I . . . may I see her?"

"Later," he said, without considering it. "She is unconscious from the anesthetic and she is in the post-operative unit. You may see her later."

"And . . . the future?"

He half smiled. "There is always danger in such a case, but with good care she could quickly recover. The bullet itself hit nothing immediately fatal; none of the big blood vessels. If it had, she would have died soon, in the street. The longer she lived, the better were her chances."

"She seemed to get worse," I said, not daring to believe him.

"In some ways that was so," he explained patiently. "Her injury was very painful, she was bleeding internally, and she was suffering from the onset of shock, which as you may know is a physical condition often as dangerous as the original damage."

I nodded, swallowing.

"We are dealing with all those things. She is

young and healthy, which is good, but there will be more pain and there may be difficulties. I can give you no assurances. It is too soon for that. But hope, yes definitely, there is considerable hope."

"Thank you," I said dully, "for being so honest."

He gave his small smile again. "Your name is Henry?"

I nodded.

"You have a brave girl," he said.

If I couldn't see her yet, I thought, I would have to go and talk to the police. They had said to be with them by four and it was already twenty past; not that that mattered a jot.

I was so unused to thinking in the terms of the strange half-world into which I had stumbled that I failed to take the most elementary precautions. Distraught about Gabriella, it didn't even cross my mind that if I had been found and shot at in a distant back street I was equally vulnerable outside the hospital.

There was a taxi standing in the forecourt, the driver reading a newspaper. I waved an arm at him, and he folded the paper, started the engine and drove over. I gave him the paper with the address the policeman had written out for me, and he looked at it in a bored sort of way and nodded. I opened the cab door and got in. He waited politely till I was settled, his head half turned, and then drove smoothly out of the hospital gates. Fifty yards away he turned right down a tree-lined secondary road beside the hospital, and fifty yards down there he stopped. From a tree one yard from the curb a little figure peeled itself, wrenched open the nearest door, and stepped inside.

He was grinning fiercely, unable to contain his triumph. The gun with the silencer grew in his hand as if born there. I had walked right into his ambush.

Billy the Kid.

"You took your bloody time, you stinking bastard," he said.

I looked at him blankly, trying to keep the shattering dismay from showing. He sat down beside me and shoved his gun into my ribs, just above the line it had already drawn there.

"Get cracking, Vittorio," he said. "His effing Lordship is late."

The taxi rolled smoothly away and gathered speed.

"Four o'clock we said," said Billy, grinning widely. "Didn't you get the message?"

"The police. . . ." I said weakly.

"Hear that, Vittorio?" Billy laughed. "The hospital thought you were the police. Fancy that. How extraordinary."

I looked away from him, out of the window on my left.

"You just try it," Billy said. "You'll have a bullet through you before you get the door open."

I looked back at him.

"Yeah," he grinned. "Takes a bit of swallowing, don't it, for you to have to do what I say. Sweet, I call it. And believe me, matey, you've hardly bloody started." I didn't answer. It didn't worry him. He sat sideways, the gloating grin fixed like a rictus.

"How's the bird . . . Miss what's her name?" He flicked his fingers. "The girl friend."

I did some belated thinking.

I said stonily, "She's dead."

"Well, well," said Billy gleefully. "How terribly sad. Do you hear that, Vittorio? His Lordship's bit of skirt has passed on."

Vittorio's head nodded. He concentrated on his driving, mostly down side streets, avoiding heavy traffic. I stared numbly at the greasy back of his neck and wondered what chance I had of grabbing Billy's gun before he pulled the trigger. The answer to that, I decided, feeling its steady pressure against my side, was none.

"Come on now, come on," said Billy. "Don't you think I'm clever?"

I didn't answer. Out of the corner of my eye I sensed the grin change from triumph to vindictiveness.

"I'll wipe that bloody superior look off your face," he said. "You sodding blue-arsed —"

I said nothing. He jerked the gun hard into my ribs.

"You just wait, your high and mighty Lordship, you just bloody well wait."

There didn't in fact seem to be much else I

could do. The taxi bowled steadily on, leaving the city center behind.

"Hurry it up, Vittorio," said Billy. "We're late."

Vittorio put his foot down and we drove on away from the town and out into an area of scrubland. The road twisted twice and then ran straight, and I stared in astonishment and disbelief at what lay ahead at the end of it. It was the broad open sweep of Malpensa Airport. We had approached it from the side road leading away from the loading bay, the road the horseboxes sometimes took.

The DC-4 stood there on the tarmac less than a hundred yards away, still waiting to take four mares back to England. Vittorio stopped the taxi fifty yards from the loading area. "Now," said Billy to me, enjoying himself again, "you listen and do as you are told, otherwise I'll put a hole in you. And it'll be in the breadbasket, not the heart. That's a promise." I didn't doubt him. "Walk down the road, straight across to the plane, up the ramp and into the toilet. Get it? I'll be two steps behind you, all the way."

I was puzzled, but greatly relieved. I had hardly expected such a mild end to the ride. Without a word I opened the door and climbed out. Billy wriggled agilely across and stood up beside me, the triumphant sneer reasserting itself on his babyish mouth.

"Go on," he said.

There was no one about at that side of the airfield. Four hundred yards ahead there were people moving round the main building, but four hundred yards across open tarmac looked a very long way. Behind lay scrubland and the taxi. Mentally shrugging, I followed Billy's instructions, walked down the short stretch of road, across to the plane, and up the ramp. Billy stalked a steady two paces behind me, too far to touch, too near to miss.

At the top of the ramp stood Yardman. He was frowning heavily, though his eyes were as usual inscrutable behind the glasses, and he was tapping his watch.

"You've cut it very fine," he said in annoyance. "Another quarter of an hour and we'd have been in trouble."

My chief feeling was still of astonishment and unreality. Billy broke the bubble, speaking over my shoulder.

"Yeah, he was dead late coming out of the hospital. Another five minutes, and we'd have had to go in for him."

My skin rose in goose pimples. The ride had after all led straight to the heart of things. The pit yawned before me.

"Get in then," Yardman said. "I'll go and tell the pilot our wandering boy has at last returned from lunch and we can start back for England." He went past us and down the ramp, hurrying.

Billy sniggered. "Move, your effing Lordship," he said. "Open the toilet door and go in. The one on the left." The pistol jabbed against the bottom of my spine. "Do as you're told."

I walked the three necessary steps, opened the left-hand door, and went in.

"Put your hands on the wall," said Billy. "Right there in front of you, so that I can see them."

I did as he said. He swung the door shut behind him and leaned against it. We waited in silence. He sniggered complacently from time to time, and I considered my blind stupidity.

Yardman. Yardman transports men. Simon had fought through to a conclusion, where I had only gone halfway. Billy's smoke screen had filled my eyes. I hadn't seen beyond it to Yardman. And instead of grasping from Simon's message and my own memory that it had to be Yardman too, I had kissed Gabriella and lost the thread of it. And five minutes later she had been bleeding on the pavement. . . .

I shut my eyes and rested my forehead momentarily against the wall. Whatever the future held it meant nothing to me if Gabriella didn't live.

After a while Yardman returned. He rapped on the door and Billy moved over to give him room to come in.

"They're all coming across, now," he said. "We'll be away shortly. But before we go . . . how about the girl?"

"Croaked," said Billy laconically.

"Good," Yardman said. "One less job for Vittorio."

My head jerked.

"My dear boy," said Yardman. "Such a pity.

242

Such a nice girl too." In quite a different voice he said to Billy, "Your shooting was feeble. You are expected to do better than that."

"Hey," there was a suspicion of a whine in Billy's reply. "They started running."

"You should have been closer."

"I *was* close. Close enough. Ten yards at the most. I was waiting in a doorway, ready to pump it into them just after they'd passed me. And then they just suddenly started running. I got the girl all right, though, didn't I? I mean I got her, even if she lingered a bit, like. As for him, well, granted I did miss him, but she sort of swung round and knocked him over just as I pulled the trigger."

"If Vittorio hadn't been with you. . . ." Yardman began coldly.

"Well, he was with me, then, wasn't he?" Billy defended himself. "After all, it was me that told him to worm into that crowd round the girl and keep his ears flapping. Granted it was Vittorio who heard the police telling this creep to go and see them straight from the hospital, but it was me that thought of ringing up the hospital and winkling him out. And anyway, when I rang you up the second time, didn't you say it was just as well, you could do with him back here alive as you'd got a use for him?"

"All right," said Yardman. "It's worked out all right, but it was still very poor shooting."

He opened the door, letting in a brief murmur of people moving the ramp away, and closed it

243

behind him. Billy sullenly delivered a long string of obscenity, exclusively concerned with the lower part of the body. Not one to take criticism sweetly.

The aircraft trembled as the engines started one after the other. I glanced at my watch, on a level with my eyes. If it had been much later, Patrick would have refused to take off that day. As it was, there was little enough margin for him to get back to Gatwick within fifteen hours of going on duty that morning. It was the total time which mattered, not just flying hours, with inquiries and fines to face for the merest minutes over.

"Kneel down," Billy said, jabbing me in the spine. "Keep your hands on the wall. And don't try lurching into me accidental like when we take off. It wouldn't do you an effing bit of good."

I didn't move.

"You'll do as you're ruddy well told, matey," said Billy, viciously kicking the back of one of my knees. "Get down."

I knelt on the floor. Billy said, "There's a good little earl," with a pleased sneer in his voice, and rubbed the snout of his pistol up and down the back of my neck.

The plane began to taxi, stopped at the perimeter for power checks, rolled forward on to the runway, and gathered speed. Inside the windowless lavatory compartment it was impossible to tell the exact moment of unstick, but the subsequent climb held me close anyway against the wall, as I faced the tail, and Billy stopped himself from overbalancing onto me by putting his gun between my shoulder blades and leaning on it. I hoped remotely that Patrick wouldn't strike an air pocket.

Up in the cockpit, as far away in the plane as one could get and no doubt furious with me for coming back so late, he would be drinking his first coffee, and peeling his first banana. A mile from imagining I could need his help. He completed a long climbing turn and after a while leveled off and reduced power. We were well on the first leg south to the Mediterranean.

The Mediterranean. A tremor as nasty as the one I'd had on finding Yardman at the heart of things fluttered through my chest. The DC-4 was unpressurized. The cabin doors could be opened in flight. Perhaps Billy had simply opened the door and pushed Simon out.

The traceless exit. Ten thousand feet down to the jewel-blue sea.

13

Yardman came back, edging round the door.

"It's time," he said.

Billy sniggered. "Can't be too soon."

"Stand by, stand up, my dear boy," Yardman said. "You look most undignified down there. Face the wall all the time."

As I stood up he reached out, grasping my jacket by the collar, and pulled it backward and downward. Two more jerks and it was off.

"I regret this, I do indeed," he said. "But I'm afraid we must ask you to put your hands together behind your back."

I thought that if I did I was as good as dead. I didn't move. Billy squeezed round into the small space between me and the washbasin and put the silencer against my neck.

Yardman's unhurried voice floated into my ear. "I really must warn you, my dear boy, that your life hangs by the merest thread. If Billy hadn't clumsily missed you in the street, you would be in the Milan morgue by now. If you do not do as we ask, he will be pleased to rectify his mistake immediately."

I put my hands behind my back.

"That's right," Yardman said approvingly. He tied them together with a rough piece of rope.

"Now, my dear boy," he went on. "You are going to help us. We have a little job for you."

Billy's searchlight eyes were wide and bright, and I didn't like his smile.

"You don't ask what it is," Yardman said. "So I will tell you. You are going to persuade your friend the pilot to alter course."

Alter course. Simple words. Premonition shook me to the roots. Patrick wasn't strong enough.

I said nothing. After a moment Yardman continued conversationally, "We were going to use the engineer originally, but as I find you and the pilot are good friends I am sure he will do as you ask."

I still said nothing.

"He doesn't understand," Billy sneered.

I understood all right. Patrick would do what they told him. Yardman opened the washroom door. "Turn round," he said.

I turned. Yardman's eyes fell immediately to the dried bloodstains on my shirt. He reached out a long arm, pulled the once white poplin out of my trousers and saw the bandage underneath.

"You grazed him," he said to Billy, still critical.

"Considering he was running and falling at the same time that isn't bad, not with a silencer."

"Inefficient." Yardman wasn't letting him off the hook.

"I'll make up for it," Billy said viciously.

"Yes, you do that."

Yardman turned his head back to me. "Outside, dear boy."

I followed him out of the washroom into the cabin, and stopped. It looked utterly normal. The four mares stood peacefully in the two middle boxes, installed, I presumed, by Yardman and Alf. The foremost and aft boxes were strapped down flat. There were the normal bales of hay dotted about. The noise was the normal noise, the air neither hotter nor colder than usual. All familiar. Normal. As normal as a coffin.

Yardman walked on.

"This way," he said. He crossed the small area at the back of the plane, stepped up onto the shallow platform formed by the flattened rear box, walked across it, and finished down again on the plane's floor, against the nearest box containing mares. Billy prodded his gun into my back. I joined Yardman.

"So wise, my dear boy," nodded my employer. "Stand with your back to the box."

I turned round to face the tail of the aircraft. Yardman took some time fastening my tied hands to the center banding bar round the mares' box. Billy stood up on the flattened box and amused himself by pointing his gun at various parts of my anatomy. He wasn't going to fire it. I took no notice of his antics but looked beyond him, to the pair of seats at the back. There was a man sitting there, relaxed and interested. The

248

man who had flown out with us, whose name was John. Milan hadn't been the end of his journey, I thought. Yardman wanted to land him somewhere else.

He stood up slowly, his pompous manner a complete contradiction to his grubby ill-fitting clothes.

"Is this sort of thing really necessary?" he asked, but with curiosity, not distress. His voice was loud against the beat of the engine.

"Yes," said Yardman shortly. I turned my head to look at him. He was staring gravely at my face, the bones of his skull sharp under the stretched skin. "We know our business."

Billy got tired of waving his gun about to an unappreciative audience. He stepped off the low platform and began dragging a bale of hay into the narrow alleyway between the standing box and the flattened one, settling it firmly longwise between the two. On top of that bale he put another, and on top of that another and another. Four bales high. Jammed against these, on top of the flattened box, he raised three more, using all the bales on the plane. Together, they formed a solid wall three feet away on my left. Yardman, John and I watched him in silence.

"Right," Yardman said when he'd finished it. He checked the time and looked out of the window. "Ready?"

Billy and John said they were. I refrained from saying that I wasn't, and never would be.

All three of them went away up the plane,

crouching under the luggage racks and stumbling over the guy chains. I at once discovered by tugging that Yardman knew his stuff with a rope. I couldn't budge my hands. Jerking them in vain, I suddenly discovered Alf watching me. He had come back from somewhere up front, and was standing on my right with his customary look of missing intelligence.

"Alf," I shouted. "Untie me."

He didn't hear. He simply stood and looked at me without surprise. Without feeling. Then he slowly turned and went away. Genuinely deaf; but it paid him to be blind too, I thought bitterly. Whatever he saw he didn't tell. He had told me nothing about Simon.

I thought achingly of Gabriella hanging on to life in Milan. She must still be alive, I thought. She must. Difficulties, the doctor had said. There might be difficulties. Like infection. Like pneumonia. Nothing would matter if she died . . . but she wouldn't . . . she couldn't. Anxiety for her went so deep that it pretty well blotted out the hovering knowledge that I should spare some for myself. The odds of her survival were about even; I wouldn't have taken a hundred to one on my own.

After ten eternal minutes Yardman and Billy came back, with Patrick between them. Patrick stared at me, his face tight and stiff with disbelief. I knew exactly how he felt. Billy pushed him to the back with his gun, and Yardman pointed to the pair of seats at the back. He and Patrick sat down on them, side by side, fifteen feet away. A captive audience, I reflected sourly. Front row of the stalls.

Billy put his mouth close to my ear. "He doesn't fancy a detour, your pilot friend. Ask him to change his mind."

I didn't look at Billy, but at Patrick. Yardman was talking to him unhurriedly, but against the engine noise I couldn't hear what he said. Patrick's amber eyes looked dark in the gauntness of his face, and he shook his head slightly, staring at me beseechingly. Beseech all you like, I thought, but don't give in. I knew it was no good. He wasn't tough enough.

"Ask him," Billy said.

"Patrick," I shouted.

He could hear me. His head tilted to listen. It was difficult to get urgency and conviction across when one had to shout to be heard at all, but I did my best. "Please . . . fly back to Milan."

Nothing happened for three seconds. Then Patrick tried to stand up and Yardman pulled him back, saying something which killed the beginning of resolution in his shattered face. Patrick, for God's sake, I thought, have some sense. Get up and go.

Billy unscrewed the silencer from his gun and put it in his pocket. He carefully unbuttoned my shirt, pulled the collar back over my shoulders, and tucked the fronts round into the back of my trousers. I felt very naked and rather silly.

Patrick's face grew, if anything, whiter.

Billy firmly clutched the dressing over the bullet mark and with one wrench pulled the whole thing off.

"Hey," he shouted to Yardman. "I don't call that a miss."

Yardman's reply got lost on the way back.

"Want to know something?" Billy said, thrusting his sneering face close to mine. "I'm enjoying this."

I saved my breath.

He put the barrel of his revolver very carefully against my skin, laying it flat along a rib just above the existing cut. Then he pushed me round until I was half facing the wall he had made of the hay bales. "Keep still," he said. He drew the revolver four inches backward with the barrel still touching me and pulled the trigger. At such close quarters, without the silencer, the shot was a crashing explosion. The bullet sliced through the skin over my ribs and embedded itself in the wall of hay. The spit of flame from the barrel scorched in its wake. In the box behind me, the startled mares began making a fuss. It would create a handy diversion, I thought, if they were frightened into dropping their foals.

Patrick was on his feet, aghast and swaying. I heard him shouting something unintelligible to Billy, and Billy shouting back, "Only you can stop it, mate."

"Patrick," I yelled. "Go to Milan."

"That's bloody enough," Billy said. He put his

gun back on my side, as before. "Keep still."

Yardman couldn't afford me dead until Patrick had flown where they wanted. I was all for staying alive as long as possible, and jerking around under the circumstances could cut me off short. I did as Billy said, and kept still. He pulled the trigger.

The flash, the crash, the burn, as before.

I looked down at myself, but I couldn't see clearly because of the angle. There were three long furrows now, parallel and fiery. The top two were beginning to bleed.

Patrick sat down heavily as if his knees had given way and put his hands over his eyes. Yardman was talking to him, clearly urging him to save me. Billy wasn't for waiting. He put his gun in position, told me to keep still, and shot.

Whether he intended it or not, that one went deeper, closer to the bone. The force of it spun me round hard against the mares' box and wrenched my arms, and my feet stumbled as I tried to keep my balance. The mares whinnied and skittered around, but on the whole they were getting less agitated, not more. A pity.

I had shut my eyes, that time. I opened them slowly to see Patrick and Yardman much nearer, only eight feet away on the far side of the flattened box. Patrick was staring with unreassuring horror at Billy's straight lines. Too soft-hearted, I thought despairingly. The only chance we had was for him to leave Billy to get on with it and go and turn back to Milan. We weren't much more than half an hour out. In half an hour we could be back. Half an hour of this. . . .

I swallowed and ran my tongue round my dry lips.

"If you go where they say," I said urgently to Patrick, "they will kill us all."

He didn't believe it. It wasn't in his nature to believe it. He listened to Yardman instead.

"Don't be silly, my dear boy. Of course we won't kill you. You will land, we will disembark, and you can all fly off again, perfectly free."

"Patrick," I said desperately. "Go to Milan."

Billy put his gun along my ribs.

"How long do you think he can keep still?" he asked, as if with genuine interest. "What'll you bet?"

I tried to say, "They shot Gabriella," but Billy was waiting for that. I got the first two words out but he pulled the trigger as I started her name, and the rest of it got lost in the explosion and my own gasping breath.

When I opened my eyes that time, Patrick and Yardman had gone.

For a little while I clung to a distant hope that Patrick would turn back, but Billy merely blew across the top of his hot revolver and laughed at me, and when the plane banked it was to the left, and not a one-eighty-degree turn. After he had straightened out I looked at the acute angle of the late afternoon sun as it sliced forward in narrow slivers of brilliance through the row of oval windows on my right.

No surprise, I thought drearily.

We were going east.

Billy had a pocket full of bullets. He sat on the flattened box, feeding his gun. The revolving cylinder broke out sideways with its axis still in line with the barrel, and an ejector rod, pushed back toward the butt, had lifted the spent cartridges out into his hand. The empty cases now lay beside him in a cluster, rolling slightly on their rims. When all the chambers were full again he snapped the gun shut and fondled it. His eyes suddenly switched up to me, the wide stare full of malice.

"Stinking earl," he said.

A la lanterne, I thought tiredly. And all that jazz.

He stood up suddenly and spoke fiercely, with some sort of inner rage.

"I'll make you," he said.

"What?"

"Ask."

"Ask what?"

"Something . . . anything. I'll make you bloody well ask me for something."

I said nothing.

"Ask," he said savagely.

I stared past him as if he wasn't there. Fights, I thought with some chill, weren't always physical.

"All right," he said abruptly. "All right. You'll ask in the end. You bloody sodding well will."

I didn't feel sure enough to say I bloody sodding well wouldn't. The taunting sneer reappeared on his face, without the same infallible confidence perhaps, but none the less dangerous for that. He nodded sharply, and went off along the alleyway toward the nose, where I hoped he'd stay.

I watched the chips of sunshine grow smaller and tried to concentrate on working out our course, more for distraction than from any hope of needing the information for a return journey. The bullets had hurt enough when Billy fired them, but the burns, as burns do, had hotted up afterwards. The force generated inside the barrel of a pistol was, if I remembered correctly, somewhere in the region of five tons. A bullet left a revolver at a rate of approximately seven hundred feet per second and if not stopped carried about five hundred hards. The explosion which drove the bullet spinning on its way also shot out flames, smoke, hot propulsive gases and burning particles of gunpowder, and at close quarters they made a very dirty mess. Knowing these charming facts was of no comfort at all. The whole ruddy area simply burned and went on burning, as if someone had stood an electric iron on it and had forgotten to switch it off.

After Billy went away it was about an hour before I saw anyone again, and then it was Alf. He shuffled into my sight round the corner of the box I was tied to, and stood looking at me with one of the disposable mugs in his hand. His lined old face was, as usual, without expression.

"Alf," I shouted. "Untie me."

There wasn't anywhere to run to. I just wanted

to sit down. But Alf either couldn't hear, or wouldn't. He looked unhurriedly at my ribs, a sight which as far as I could see produced no reaction in him at all. But something must have stirred somewhere, because he took a slow step forward, and being careful not to touch me, lifted his mug. It had "Alf" in red where Mike had written it that morning, in that distant sane and safe lost world of normality.

"Want some?" he said.

I nodded, half afraid he'd pour it out on the floor, as Billy would have done; but he held it up to my mouth, and let me finish it all. Lukewarm, oversweet neo-coffee. The best drink I ever had.

"Thank you," I said.

He nodded, produced the nearest he could do to a smile, and shuffled away again. Not an ally. A non-combatant, rather.

More time passed. I couldn't see my watch or trust my judgment, but I would have guessed it was getting on for two hours since we had turned. I had lost all sense of direction. The sun had gone, and we were traveling into dusk. Inside the cabin the air grew colder. I would have liked to have had my shirt on properly, not to mention my jersey, but the mares behind my back provided enough warmth to keep me from shivering. On a full load in that cramped plane eight horses generated a summer's day even with icing conditions outside, and we seldom needed the cabin heaters. It was far too much to hope in the circumstances that Patrick would think of switching them on.

Two hours' flying. We must, I thought, have been down near Albenga when we turned, which meant that since then, if we were still going east and the winds were the same as in the morning, we could have been crossing Italy somewhere north of Florence. Ahead lay the Adriatic, beyond that, Yugoslavia, and beyond that, Roumania.

It didn't matter a damn where we went, the end would be the same.

I shifted wearily, trying to find some ease, and worried for the thousandth time whether Gabriella was winning, back in Milan. The police there, I supposed, wrenching my mind away from her, would be furious I hadn't turned up. They still had my passport. There might at least be a decent investigation if I never went back for it, and Gabriella knew enough to explain what I'd inadvertently got caught up in. If she lived. If she lived. . . .

The plane banked sharply in a steep turn to the left. I leaned against the roll and tried to gauge its extent. Ninety-degree turn, I thought. No; more. It didn't seem to make much sense. But if — if — we had reached the Adriatic I supposed it was possible we were now going up it, northwest, back toward Venice . . . and Trieste. I admitted gloomily to myself that it was utter guesswork; that I was lost, and in more than one sense.

Ten minutes later the engine note changed and

the volume of noise decreased. We had started going down. My heart sank with the plane. Not much time left. Oncoming night and a slow descent, the stuff of death.

There were two rows of what looked like car headlights marking each end of a runway. We circled one so steeply that I caught a glimpse of them through the tipped window, and then we leveled out for the approach and lost speed, and the plane bumped down on to a rough surface. Grass, not tarmac. The plane taxied round a bit, and then stopped. One by one the four engines died. The place was quiet and dark, and for three long deceptive minutes at my end of it there was peace.

The cabin lights flashed on, bright overhead. The mares behind me kicked the box. Farther along, the other pair whinnied restlessly. There was a clatter in the galley, and the noise of people coming back through the plane, stumbling over the chains.

Patrick came first, with Billy after. Billy had screwed the silencer back on his gun.

Patrick went past the flattened box into the small area in front of the two washroom doors. He moved stiffly, as if he couldn't feel his feet on the floor, as if he were sleepwalking.

Billy had stopped near me, on my right.

"Turn round, pilot," he said.

Patrick turned, his body first and his legs untwisting after. He staggered slightly, and stood swaying. If his face had been white before, it was leaden gray now. His eyes were stretched and glazed with shock, and his good-natured mouth trembled.

He stared at me with terrible intensity.

"He . . . shot . . . them," he said. "Bob . . . and Mike. Bob and Mike." His voice broke on the horror of it.

Billy sniggered quietly.

"You said . . . they would kill us all." A tremor shook him. "I didn't . . . believe it."

His eyes went down to my side. "I couldn't. . . ." he said. "They said they'd go on and on. . . ."

"Where are we?" I said sharply.

His eyes came back in a snap, as if I'd kicked his brain.

"Italy," he began automatically. "Southwest of. . . ."

Billy raised his gun, aiming high for the skull.

"No." I yelled at him in rage and horror at the top of my voice. "No."

He jumped slightly, but he didn't even pause. The gun coughed through the silencer and the bullet hit its target. Patrick got both his hands halfway to his head before the blackness took him. He spun on his collapsing legs and crashed headlong, face down, his long body still and silent, the auburn hair brushing against the washroom door. The soles of his feet were turned mutely up, and one of his shoes needed mending.

14

Yardman and John edged round Billy and the flattened box and stood in the rear area, looking down at Patrick's body.

"Why did you do it back here?" John said.

Billy didn't answer. His gaze was fixed on me.

Yardman said mildly, "Billy, Mr. Rous-Wheeler wants to know why you brought the pilot here to shoot him?"

Billy smiled and spoke to me. "I wanted you to watch," he said.

John — Rous-Wheeler — said faintly "My God," and I turned my head and found him staring at my ribs.

"Pretty good shooting," said Billy complacently, following the direction of his eyes and taking his tone as a compliment. "There's no fat on him and the skin over his ribs is thin. See where I've got every shot straight along a bone? Neat, that's what it is. A bit of craftsmanship I'd say. These lines are what I'm talking about," he was anxious to make his point, "not all that black and red around them. That's only dried blood and powder burn."

Rous-Wheeler, to do him justice, looked faintly sick.

"All right, Billy," Yardman said calmly. "Finish him off."

Billy lifted his gun. I had long accepted the inevitability of that moment, and I felt no emotion but regret.

"He's not afraid," Billy said. He sounded disappointed.

"What of it?" Yardman asked.

"I want him to be afraid."

Yardman shrugged. "I can't see what difference it makes."

To Billy it made all the difference in the world. "Let me take a little time over him, huh? We've got hours to wait."

Yardman sighed. "All right, Billy, if that's what you want. Do all the other little jobs first, eh? Shut all the curtains in the plane first, we don't want to advertise ourselves. And then go down and tell Giuseppe to turn those landing lights off; the stupid fool's left them on. He'll have ladders and paint waiting for us. He and you and Alf can start straight away on painting out the airline's name and the plane's registration letters."

"Yeah," said Billy. "O.K. and while I'm doing it I'll think of something." He put his face close to mine, mocking. "Something special for your effing Lordship."

He put the gun in its holster and the silencer in his pocket, and drew all the curtains in the back part of the plane, before starting forward to do the rest.

Rous-Wheeler stepped over Patrick's body, sat down in one of the seats, and lit a cigarette. His hands were shaking.

"Why do you let him?" he said to Yardman. "Why do you let him do what he likes?"

"He is invaluable," Yardman sighed. "A natural killer. They're not at all common, you know. That combination of callousness and enjoyment, it's unbeatable. I let him have his way if I can as a sort of reward, because he'll kill anyone I tell him to. I couldn't do what he does. He kills like stepping on a beetle."

"He's so young," Rous-Wheeler protested.

"They're only any good when they're young," Yardman said. "Billy is nineteen. In another seven or eight years, I wouldn't trust him as I do now. And there's a risk a killer will turn maudlin any time after thirty."

"It sounds," Rous-Wheeler cleared his throat trying to speak as unconcernedly as Yardman, "it sounds rather like keeping a pet tiger on a leash."

He began to cross his legs and his shoes knocked against Patrick's body. With an expression of distaste he said, "Can't we cover him up?"

Yardman nodded casually and went away up the plane. He came back with a gray blanket from the pile in the luggage bay, opened it out, and spread it over, covering head and all. I spent the short time that he was away watching Rous-

263

Wheeler refuse to meet my eyes and wondering just who he was, and why he was so important that taking him beyond Milan was worth the lives of three totally uninvolved and innocent airmen.

An unremarkable-looking man of about thirty-five, with incipient bags under his eyes, and a prim mouth. Unused to the violence surrounding him, and trying to wash his hands of it. A man with his fare paid in death and grief.

When Yardman had covered Patrick he perched himself down on the edge of the flattened box. The overhead lights shone on the bald patch on his skull and the black spectacle frames made heavy bars of shadow on his eyes and cheeks.

"I regret this, my dear boy, believe me, I regret it sincerely," he said, eyeing the result of Billy's target practice. Like Rous-Wheeler he took out a cigarette and lit it. "He really has made a very nasty mess."

But only skin-deep, if one thought about it. I thought about it. Not much good.

"Do you understand what Billy wants?" Yardman said, shaking out his match.

I nodded.

He sighed. "Then couldn't you . . . er . . . satisfy him, my dear boy? You will make it so hard for yourself, if you don't."

I remembered the stupid boast I'd made to Billy the first day I'd met him, that I could be as tough as necessary. Now that I looked like having to prove it, I had the gravest doubts.

When I didn't answer Yardman shook his head

sorrowfully. "Foolish boy, whatever difference would it make, after you are dead?"

"Defeat. . . ." I cleared my throat and tried again. "Defeat on all levels."

He frowned. "What do you mean?"

"Communists are greedy," I said.

"Greedy," he echoed. "You're wandering, my dear boy."

"They like to . . . crumble . . . people, before they kill them. And that's . . . gluttony."

"Nonsense," said Rous-Wheeler in a vintage Establishment voice.

"You must have read newspaper accounts of trials in Russia," I said, raising an eyebrow. "All those 'confessions.' "

"The Russians," he said stiffly, "are a great, warm, simple people."

"Oh, sure," I agreed. "And some are like Billy."

"Billy is English."

"So are you," I said, "and where are you going?"

He compressed his lips and didn't answer.

"I hope," I said, looking at the blanket which covered Patrick, "that your travel agents have confirmed your belief in the greatness, warm-heartedness and simplicity of the hemisphere you propose to join."

"My dear boy," interrupted Yardman smoothly, "what eloquence!"

"Talking," I explained, "takes the mind off . . . this and that."

A sort of recklessness seemed to be running in my blood, and my mind felt clear and sharp. To have even those two to talk to was suddenly a great deal more attractive than waiting for Billy on my own.

"The end justifies the means," said Rous-Wheeler pompously, as if he'd heard it somewhere before.

"Crap," I said inelegantly. "You set yourself too high."

"I am . . ." he began angrily, and stopped.

"Go on," I said. "You are what? Feel free to tell me. Moriturus, and all that."

It upset him, which was pleasant. He said stiffly, "I am a civil servant."

"Were," I pointed out.

"Er, yes."

"Which ministry?"

"The Treasury," he said, with the smugness of those accepted in the inner of inner sanctums.

The Treasury. It was a stopper, that one.

"What rank?" I asked.

"Principal." There was a grudge in his voice. He hadn't risen.

"And why are you defecting?"

The forthcomingness vanished. "It's none of your business."

"Well it is rather," I said in mock apology, "since your change of allegiance looks like its having a fairly decisive effect on my future."

He looked mulish and kept silent.

"I suppose," I said with mild irony, "you are

266

going where you think your talents will be appreciated."

For a second he looked almost as spiteful as Billy. A petty-minded man I thought, full of imagined slights, ducking the admission that he wasn't as brilliant as he thought he was. None of that lessened one jot the value of the information he carried in his head.

"And you," I said to Yardman. "Why do you do it? All this."

He looked back gravely, the tight skin pulling over his shut mouth.

"Ideology?" I suggested.

He tapped ash off his cigarette, made a nibbling movement with his lip, and said briefly, "Money."

"The brand of goods doesn't trouble you, as long as the carriage is paid?"

"Correct," he said.

"A mercenary soldier. Slaughter arranged. Allegiance always to the highest bidder?"

"That," he said, inclining his head, "is so."

It wasn't so strange, I thought inconsequentially, that I'd never been able to understand him.

"But believe me, my dear boy," he said earnestly, "I never really intended you any harm. Not you."

"Thanks," I said dryly.

"When you asked me for a job I nearly refused you . . . but I didn't think you'd stay long, and your name gave my agency some useful respectability, so I agreed." He sighed. "I must admit, you surprise me. You were very good at that job, if it's of any comfort to you. Very good. Too good. I should have stopped it when your father died, when I had the chance, before you stumbled on anything . . . it was selfish of me. Selfish."

"Simon Searle stumbled," I reminded him. "Not me."

"I fear so," he agreed without concern. "A pity. He too was invaluable. An excellent, accurate man. Very hard to replace."

"Would you be so good as to untuck my shirt?" I said. "I'm getting cold."

Without a word he stood up, came round, tugged the bunched cloth out of the back of my trousers and pulled the collar and shoulders back to their right place. The shirt fronts fell together edge to edge, the light touch of the cloth on the burns being more than compensated by the amount of cool air shut out.

Yardman sat down again where he had been before and lit another cigarette from the stub of the first, without offering one to Rous-Wheeler.

"I didn't mean to bring you on this part of the trip," he said. "Believe me, my dear boy, when we set off from Gatwick I intended to organize some little delaying diversion for you in Milan, so that you wouldn't embark on the trip back."

I said bleakly, "Do you call sh . . . shooting my girl a little diversion?"

He looked distressed. "Of course not. Of course

not. I didn't know you had a girl until you introduced her. But then I thought it would be an excellent idea to tell you to stay with her for a day or two, we could easily manage without you on the way back. He," he nodded at Patrick's shrouded body, "told me you were . . . er . . . crazy about her. Unfortunately for you, he also told me how assiduous you had been in searching for Searle. He told me all about the bottle of pills. Now, my dear boy, that was a risk we couldn't take."

"Risk," I said bitterly.

"Oh yes, my dear boy, of course. Risk is something we can't afford in this business. I always act on risk. Waiting for certain knowledge may be fatal. And I was quite right in this instance, isn't that so? You had told me yourself where you were going to lunch, so I instructed Billy to go and find you and follow you from there, and make sure it was all love's young dream and no excitement. But you went bursting out of the restaurant and off at high speed to an obscure little bakery. Billy followed you in Vittorio's cab and rang me up from near there." He spread his hands. "I told him to kill you both and search you under cover of helping, as soon as you came out."

"Without waiting to find out if there was anything in the bottle except pills?"

"Risk," he nodded. "I told you. We can't afford it. And that reminds me; where is Searle's message?"

"No message," I said wearily.

"Of course there was, my dear boy," he chided. "You've shown so little surprise, asked so few questions. It was clear to me at once that you knew far too much when Billy brought you back to the plane. I have experience in these things, you see."

I shrugged a shoulder. "In my wallet," I said.

He drew on his cigarette, gave me an approving look, stepped over Patrick, and fetched my jacket from the washroom. He took everything out of the wallet and spread the contents beside him in the flattened box. When he picked out the hundred-dollar note and unfolded it, the pieces of writing paper and hay fell out.

He fingered the note. "It was plain carelessness on Billy's part," he said. "He didn't hide the canisters properly."

"There was a lot of money, then, on the plane?"

"Wheels have to be oiled," Yardman said reasonably, "and it's no good paying Yugoslavs in sterling. All agents insist on being paid in the currency they can spend without arousing comment. I do, myself."

I watched him turn the scrap of his stationery over and over, frowning. He saw the pin holes in the end, and held them up to the light. After a few seconds he put it down and looked from me to Rous-Wheeler.

"Men," he said without inflection. "And when you read that, my dear boy, you understood a great deal." A statement, not a question.

270

Gabriella, I thought dumbly, for God's sake live. Live and tell. I shut my eyes and thought of her as she had been at lunch. Gay and sweet and vital. Gabriella my dearest love. . . .

"Dear boy," said Yardman in his dry unconcerned voice, "are you feeling all right?"

I opened my eyes and shut Gabriella away out of reach of his frightening intuition.

"No," I said with truth.

Yardman actually laughed. "I like you, my dear boy, I really do. I shall miss you very much in the agency."

"Miss. . . ." I stared at him. "You are going back?"

"Of course." He seemed surprised, then smiled his bony smile. "How could you know; I was forgetting. Oh yes, of course we're going back. My transport system . . . is . . . er . . . much needed, and much appreciated. Yes. Only the plane and Mr. Rous-Wheeler are going on."

"And the horses?" I asked.

"Those too," he nodded. "They carry good blood lines, those mares. We expected to have to slaughter them, but we have heard they will be acceptable alive on account of their foals. No, my dear boy, Billy and I go back by road, halfway with Giuseppe, the second half with Vittorio."

"Back to Milan?"

"Quite so. And tomorrow morning we learn the tragic news that the plane we missed by minutes this afternoon has disappeared and must be presumed lost with all souls, including yours, my dear boy, in the Mediterranean."

"There would be a radar trace. . . ." I began.

"My dear boy, we are professionals."

"Oiled wheels?" I said ironically.

"So quick," he said nodding. "A pity I can't tempt you to join us."

"Why can't you?" said Rous-Wheeler truculently.

Yardman answered with slightly exaggerated patience. "What do I offer him?"

"His life," Rous-Wheeler said with an air of triumph.

Yardman didn't even bother to explain why that wouldn't work. The Treasury, I thought dryly, really hadn't lost much.

Billy's voice suddenly spoke from the far end of the plane.

"Hey, Mr. Yardman," he called. "Can't you and Mr. Rous-flipping-Wheeler come and give us a hand? This ruddy airplane's bloody covered with names and letters. We're practically having to paint the whole sodding crate."

Yardman stood up. "Yes, all right," he said.

Rous-Wheeler didn't want to paint. "I don't feel . . ." he began importantly.

"And you don't want to be late," Yardman said flatly.

He stood aside to let the deflated Rous-Wheeler pass, and they both made their way up past the two boxes, through the galley, and down the telescopic ladder from the forward door.

Desperation can move mountains. I'd never

hoped to have another minute alone to put it to the test, but I'd thought of a way of detaching myself from the mare's box, if I had enough strength. Yardman had had difficulty squeezing the rope down between the banding bar and the wooden box side when he'd tied me there; he'd had to push it through with the blade of his pen-knife. It wouldn't have gone through at all, I thought, if either the box side wasn't a fraction warped or the bar a shade bent. Most of the bars lay flat and tight along the boxes, with no space at all between them.

I was standing less than two feet from the corner of the box, and along at the corner the bar was fastened by a lynch pin.

I got splinters in my wrists, and after I'd moved along six inches I thought I'd never manage it. The bar and the box seemed to come closer together the farther I went, and jerking the rope along between them grew harder and harder, until at last it was impossible. I shook my head in bitter frustration. Then I thought of getting my feet to help, and bending my knee put my foot flat on the box as high behind me as I could get leverage. Thrusting back with my foot, pulling forward on the bar with my arms, and jerking my wrists sideways at the same time, I moved along a good inch. It worked. I kept at it grimly and finally arrived at the last three inches. From there, twisting, I could reach the lynch pin with my fingers. Slowly, agonizingly slowly, I pushed it up from the bottom, transferred my weak grip to the rounded top, slid it fraction by fraction up in my palm, and with an enormous sense of triumph felt it come free. The iron bands parted at the corner, and it required the smallest of jerks to tug the rope out through the gap.

Call that nothing, I said to myself with the beginnings of a grin. All that remained was to free my hands from each other.

Yardman had left my jacket lying on the flattened box, and in my jacket pocket was a small sharp penknife. I sat down on the side of the shallow platform, trying to pretend to myself that it wasn't because my legs were buckling at the knees but only the quickest way to reach the jacket. The knife was there, slim and familiar. I clicked open the blade, gripped it firmly, and sawed away blindly at some unseen point between my wrists. The friction of dragging the rope along had frayed it helpfully, and before I'd begun to hope for it I felt the strands stretch and give, and in two more seconds my hands were free. With stiff shoulders I brought them round in front of me. Yardman had no personal brutality and hadn't tied tight enough to stop the blood. I flexed my fingers and they were fine.

Scooping up wallet and jacket I began the bent walk forward under the luggage rack and over the guy chains, stepping with care so as not to make a noise and fetch the five outdoor decorators in at the double. I reached the galley safely and went through it. In the space behind the cockpit I stopped dead for a moment. The body of Mike the engineer lay tumbled in a heap against the left-hand wall.

Tearing both mind and eyes away from him I edged toward the way out. On my immediate right I came first to the luggage bay, and beyond that lay the door. The sight of my overnight bag in the bay made me remember the black jersey inside it. Better than my jacket, I thought. It had a high neck, was easier to move in, and wouldn't be so heavy on my raw skin. In a few seconds I had it on, and had transferred my wallet to my trousers.

Five of them round the plane, I thought. The exit door was ajar, but when I opened it the light would spill out, and for the time it took to get onto the ladder they would be able to see me clearly. Unless by some miracle they were all over on the port side, painting the tail. Well, I thought coldly, I would just be unlucky if the nearest to me happened to be Billy with his gun.

It wasn't Billy, it was the man I didn't know, Giuseppe. He was standing at the foot of the starboard wing painting out the airline's name on the fuselage, and he saw me as soon as I opened the door not far below him. I pulled the door shut behind me and started down the ladder, hearing Giuseppe shouting and warning all the others. They had ladders to get down too, I thought. I could still make it.

Giuseppe was of the hard core, a practicing militant Communist. He was also young and extremely agile. Without attempting to reach a ladder he ran along the wing to its tip, put his hands down, swung over the edge, and dropped ten feet to the ground. Seeing his running form outlined on the wing against the stars I veered away to the left as soon as I had slid down the ladder, and struck out forward, more or less on the same axis as the plane.

My eyes weren't accustomed to the light as theirs were. I couldn't see where I was going. I heard Giuseppe shouting in Italian, and Yardman answering. Billy tried a shot which missed by a mile. I scrambled on, holding my arms up defensively and hoping I wouldn't run into anything too hard. All I had to do, I told myself, was to keep going. I was difficult to see in black and moved silently over the grass of the field. If I got far enough from the plane they wouldn't be able to find me, not five of them with Alf no better than a snail. Keep going and get lost. After that I'd have all night to search out a bit of civilization and someone who could speak English.

The field seemed endless. Endless. And running hurt. What the hell did that matter, I thought dispassionately, with Billy behind me. I had also to refrain from making a noise about it in case they should hear me, and with every rib-stretching breath that got more difficult. In the end I stopped, went down on my knees, and tried to get air in shallow silent gulps. I could hear nothing behind but a faint breeze, see nothing above but the stars, nothing ahead but the dark. After a few moments I stood up again and went on, but more slowly. Only in nightmares did fields go on forever. Even airfields.

At the exact second that I first thought I'd got away with it, bright white lights blazed out and held me squarely in their beams. A distant row of four in front, a near row of four behind, and a black figure in the flarepath. Sick, devastating understanding flooded through me. I had been trying to escape down the runway.

Sharply, almost without missing a step, I wheeled left and sprinted; but Giuseppe wasn't very far behind after all. I didn't see or hear him until the last moment when he closed in from almost in front. I swerved to avoid him, and he threw out his leg at a low angle and tripped me up.

Even though I didn't fall very heavily, it was enough. Giuseppe very slickly put one of his feet on each side of my head and closed them tight on my ears. Grass pressed into my eyes, nose and mouth, and I couldn't move in the vise.

Billy came up shouting as if with intoxication, the relief showing with the triumph.

"What you got there then, my friend? A bleeding aristocrat, then? Biting the dust, too, ain't that a gas?"

I guessed with a split second to spare what he would do, and caught his swinging shoe on my elbow instead of my ribs.

Yardman arrived at a smart military double.

"Stop it," he said. "Let him get up."

Giuseppe stepped away from my head and when

I put my hands up by my shoulders and began to push myself up, Billy delivered the kick I had avoided before. I rolled half over, trying not to care. The beams from the runway lights shone through my shut eyelids, and the world seemed a molten river of fire, scarlet and gold.

Without, I hoped, taking too long about it I again started to get up. No one spoke. I completed the incredibly long journey to my feet and stood there, quiet and calm. We were still on the runway between the distant lights. Yardman close in front of me, Giuseppe and Billy behind, with Rous-Wheeler struggling breathlessly up from the plane. Yardman's eyes, level with mine, were lit into an incandescent greenness by the glow. I had never clearly seen his eyes before. It was like drawing back curtains and looking into a soul.

A soldier without patriotism. Strategy, striking power and transport were skills he hired out, like any other craftsman. His pride was to exercise his skill to the most perfect possible degree. His pride overrode all else.

I think he probably meant it when he said he liked me. In a curious way, though I couldn't forgive him Gabriella, I felt respect for him, not hatred. Battle against him wasn't personal or emotional, as with Billy. But I understood that in spite of any unexpected warmth he might feel, he would be too prudent to extend foolish mercy to the enemy.

We eyed each other in a long moment of cool appraisal. Then his gaze slid past me, over my

278

shoulder, and he paid me what was from his point of view a compliment.

"You won't crack him, Billy. Kill him now. One shot, nice and clean."

15

I owed my life to Billy's greed. He was still hungry, still unsatisfied, and he shook his head to Yardman's request. Seeing the way Yardman delicately deferred to Billy's wishes it struck me that Rous-Wheeler's simile of a tiger on a leash might not be too far off the mark. In any case for the first time I was definitely glad of Billy's lust to spill my blue blood ounce by ounce, as I really was most averse to being shot down on the spot; and I acknowledged that I already had him to thank that I was still breathing at all. If I'd been anyone but who I was I would have died with the crew.

We walked back up the runway, I in front, the other four behind. I could hear Rous-Wheeler puffing, the only one not physically fit. Fit. . . . It was only yesterday, I thought incredulously, that I rode in the Gold Cup.

The plane was a faintly lit shape to the left of the end of the runway. A hundred yards short of it Yardman said, "Turn left, dear boy. That's it. Walk straight on. You will see a building. Go in."

There was, in fact, a building. A large one. It resembled an outsize prefabricated garage, made of asbestos sheets on a metal frame. The door was ajar and rimmed by light. I pushed it open, and with Billy's gun touching my back, walked in.

The right-hand two-thirds of the concrete floor space was occupied by a small four-seater single-engined airplane, a new-looking high-winged Cessna with an Italian registration. On its left stood a dusty black Citroën, its bonnet toward me. Behind the car and the plane the whole far wall consisted of sliding doors. No windows anywhere. Three metal girders rose from floor to ceiling on the left of the car, supporting the flat roof and dividing the left-hand part of the hangar into a kind of bay. In that section stood Alf.

"Right," said Yardman briskly. "Well done, Alf, turn them off now." His voice echoed hollowly in space.

Alf stared at him without hearing.

Yardman went up to him and shouted in his ear. "Turn the runway lights off."

Alf nodded, walked up to the wall on the left of the door I had come in by, and pushed up a heavy switch beside a black fuse box. A second similar box worked, I suppose, the fluorescent strips across the ceiling and the low-powered radiant heaters mounted high on both side walls. Beside the switches stood a mechanic's bench with various tools and a vise, and farther along two sturdy brackets held up a rack of gardening implements: spades, fork, rake, hoe and shears. Filling all the back of the bay was a giant motor mower with a seat for the driver, and dotted about there were some five-gallon petrol cans, funnels, tins of paint, an assortment of overalls and several greasy-looking metal chairs.

That Cessna, I thought briefly; I could fly it like riding a bicycle. And the car . . . if only I had known they were there.

Yardman searched among the clutter on the bench and produced a length of chain and two padlocks, one large, one small. Billy had shut the door and was standing with his back to it, the gun pointing steadily in my direction. Alf, Rous-Wheeler and Giuseppe had prudently removed themselves from his line of fire.

Yardman said, "Go over to that first girder, my dear boy, and sit down on the floor."

To say I was reluctant to be tied again is to put it mildly. It wasn't only that it was the end of any hope of escape, but I had a strong physical repugnance to being attached to things, the result of having been roped to a fir in a Scottish forest one late afternoon in a childhood game by some cousins I was staying with; they had run away to frighten me and got lost themselves, and it had been morning before the subsequent search had found me.

When I didn't obey at once, Yardman, Giuseppe and Billy all took a step forward as if moved by the same mind. There was no percentage in having them jump on me; I was sore enough already. I walked over to the girder and sat down facing them, leaning back idly against the flat metal surface.

"That's better," Yardman said. He came round and knelt down on the ground at my back. "Hands behind, my dear boy."

He twined the chain round my wrists and clicked on both padlocks. Tossing the keys on his palm he stood up and came round in front of me. All five of them stared down with varying degrees of ill-feeling and I stared glassily back.

"Right," said Yardman after a pause. "We'd better get out and finish the painting. But this time we must leave someone with him, just in case." He reviewed his available troops, and alighted on Rous-Wheeler. "You sit here," he said to him, picking up a chair and taking it over beside the switches, "and if he does anything you aren't sure about, switch on the runway lights and we'll come at once. Clear?"

Rous-Wheeler was delighted to avoid any more painting and accepted his new task with enthusiasm.

"Good." Yardman looked at his watch. "Go on then, Billy." Billy, Alf and Giuseppe filed out and Yardman stopped as he followed them to say to Rous-Wheeler, "The cargo will be arriving soon. Don't be alarmed."

"Cargo?" said Rous-Wheeler in surprise.

"That's right," Yardman said. "Cargo. The reason for this . . . um . . . operation."

"But I thought I . . ." began Rous-Wheeler.

"My dear Rous-Wheeler, no," said Yardman. "Had it been just you, I could have sent you down the usual discreet pipeline from Milan. Your journey would have been just as secret as it is now. No, we needed the plane for a rather special cargo, and as you know, my dear boy," he swung round to speak directly to me with a small ironic smile, "I do hate wasting space on flights. I always try to make up a full load, so as not to neglect an opportunity."

"What is this cargo, then?" asked Rous-Wheeler with a damaged sense of self-importance.

"Mm?" said Yardman, putting the padlock keys down on the bench. "Well now, it's the brain child of a brilliant little research establishment near Brescia. A sort of machine. An interesting little development, one might say. Broadly speaking, it's a device for emitting ultrasonic rays on the natural frequency of any chosen mineral substance."

"Ultrasonics have been extensively researched," Rous-Wheeler said testily.

Yardman smiled tightly. "Take it from me, dear fellow, this particular development has great possibilities. Our friends have been trying to arrange photographs of the drawings and specifications, but these have been too well guarded. It proved easier in the end to . . . er . . . remove some vital parts of the device itself. But that of course presented a transport problem, a difficult transport problem, requiring my own personal supervision." He was talking for my benefit as much as Rous-Wheeler's, letting me know how expert he was at his job. "Once we were committed to the plane, of course it was the easiest way to take you too."

No opportunity wasted. But he hadn't originally intended to take me as well, to give him his due.

Yardman went out of the hangar. Rous-Wheeler sat on his hard chair and I on the hard concrete and again my presence and/or predicament embarrassed him. "Played any good wall games lately?" I said at length.

A hit, a palpable hit. He hadn't expected any needling school chums on his little trip. He looked offended.

"Have you been to . . . er . . . wherever you're going . . . before?" I asked.

"No," he said shortly. He wouldn't look at me.

"And do you speak the language?"

He said stiffly, "I am learning."

"What are they offering you?"

Some heavy smugness crept into his manner. "I am to have a flat and a car, and a better salary. I will of course be in an important advisory position."

"Of course," I said dryly.

He flicked me his first glance. Disapproving.

"I am to be a consultant interpreter of the British way of life. . . . I pride myself that in my own small way I shall be promoting better understanding between two great peoples and making a positive contribution to the establishment of fruitful relations."

He spoke as if he really meant it; and if he were as self-satisfied as that, he wouldn't consider turning round and going back. I tried again without success to do a Houdini on Yardman's chain job, and Rous-Wheeler watched me.

"What branch of the Treasury were you in?" I asked, giving it up.

"Initial Finance," he replied stiffly.

"What does that mean?"

"Grants."

"You mean, your department settles who gets grants of public money, and how much?"

"That is so."

"Development, research, defense, and so on?"

"Precisely."

"So that you personally would know what projects are in hand . . . or contemplated?"

"Yes."

They wouldn't have bothered with him, I supposed, for any less.

After a pause, I said, "What about this ultrasonic transmitter?"

"What about it? It isn't a British project, if that's what you mean."

"Did I get it right . . . that it will emit waves on the natural frequency of any mineral substance?"

"I believe that's what Yardman said," he agreed stiffly.

"It would break things . . . like sound breaks glass?"

"I am not a scientist. I've no idea." And from the tone of his voice he didn't care.

I stared gloomily at the floor and wondered what made a man change his allegiance. Rous-Wheeler might have been self-important and disappointed and have refused to face his own limitations, but thousands of men were like that, and thousands of men didn't give away a slice of their nation's future in return for a flat, a car, and a pat on the back. There had to be more to it. Deep obsessive murky convoluted motives I couldn't guess at, pushing him irresistibly over. But he would be the same man wherever he went; in five years or less, again dismantled and passed over. A useless, dispensable piece of flotsam.

He, it appeared, took as pessimistic a view of my future as I of his.

"Do you think," he cleared his throat. "Do you think Billy will really kill you?"

"Be your age," I said. "You saw what he did to the crew."

"He keeps putting it off," he said.

"Saving the icing till last."

"How can you be so frivolous?" he exclaimed. "Your position is very serious."

"So is yours," I said. "And I wouldn't swap."

He gave me a small pitying smile of contemptuous disbelief, but it was true enough. Everyone dies sometime, as Simon had once said, and one was probably as little eager at eighty as at twenty-six. And there really were, I reflected with a smile for Victorian melodramas, fates worse than death.

A heavy van or lorry of some sort pulled up with a squeak of brakes somewhere near the door and after a few moments its driver came into the hangar. He was like Giuseppe, young, hard, cold-eyed and quick. He looked at me without apparent surprise and spoke to Rous-Wheeler in rapid Italian, of which the only intelligible word as far as I was concerned was Brescia.

Rous-Wheeler held up a hand, palm toward the driver. "I don't understand you, my good fellow. Wait until I fetch Yardman."

This proved unnecessary as my ex-employer had already seen the lorry's arrival. Followed by his entourage carrying ladders, paint pots, brushes and overalls, Yardman came forward into the hangar and exchanged some careful salutations with the driver.

"Right," Yardman said in English to Billy. "There should be several small light cases and one large heavy one. It will be easiest to load the light cases up through the forward door and stow them in the luggage bay. Then we will open the back doors, haul the heavy case in on the block and tackle, and stand it in the peat tray of the last box, the one that's now flattened. Clear?"

Billy nodded.

I opened my mouth to speak, and shut it again.

Yardman noticed. "What is it?" he said sharply.

"Nothing." I spoke listlessly.

He came over to me and looked down. Then he squatted on his haunches to peer on a level with my face.

"Oh yes, my dear boy, there is something. Now what, what?"

He stared at me as if he could read my thoughts while the calculations ticked over in his own. "You were going to tell me something, and decided not to. And I feel I really should know what it is. I feel it must be to my disadvantage, something definitely to my disadvantage, as things stand between us."

"I'll shoot it out of him," Billy offered.

"It'll be quicker if I guess it. . . . Now, what is wrong with stowing the cases the way I suggested? Ah yes, my dear boy, you know all about loading airplanes, don't you? You know what I said was wrong. . . ." He snapped his fingers and stood up. "The heavy case at the back is wrong. Billy, move the mares forward so that they occupy the two front boxes, and put the heavy case in the second to back box, and leave the rear one as it is."

"Move the mares?" Billy complained.

"Yes, certainly. The center of gravity is all-important, isn't that right, my dear boy?" He was pleased with himself, smiling. Quick as lightning. If I gave him even a thousandth of a second of suspicion that Gabriella was still alive . . .

Billy came over and stood looking down at me with a revoltingly self-satisfied smile.

"Not long now," he promised.

"Load the plane first," Yardman said. "The van has to go back as soon as possible. You can . . . er . . . have your fun when I go to fetch the pilot. And be sure he's dead by the time I get back."

"O.K.," Billy agreed. He went away with Alf, Giuseppe and the driver, and the van ground away on the short stretch to the DC-4.

"What pilot?" Rous-Wheeler asked.

"My dear Rous-Wheeler," Yardman explained with a touch of weary contempt. "How do you think the plane is going on?"

"Oh . . . Well, why did you kill the other one? He would have flown to wherever you said."

Yardman sighed. "He would have done no such thing without Billy at hand to shoot pieces off our young friend here. And frankly, my dear fellow, quite apart from the problem of Billy's and my return journey, it would have been embarrassing for us to kill the crew in your new country. Much better here. Much more discreet, don't you think?"

"Where exactly . . . where are we?" asked Rous-Wheeler. A good question if ever there was one.

"A private landing field," Yardman said. "An elderly and respected nobleman lets us use it from time to time."

Elderly and respected; Yardman's voice held some heavy irony.

"The usual sort of blackmail?" I asked. "Filmed in a bed he had no right in?"

Yardman said "No," unconvincingly.

"What's he talking about?" Rous-Wheeler asked testily.

"I'm talking about the methods employed by your new friends," I said. "If they can't get help and information by bamboozling and subverting people like you, they do it by any form of blackmail or intimidation that comes to hand."

Rous-Wheeler was offended. "I haven't been bamboozled."

"Nuts," I said. "You're a proper sucker."

Yardman took three threatening steps toward me with the anger he had shown. "That's enough."

"Nothing's enough," I said mildly. "What the hell do you think I have to lose?"

Yardman's glasses flashed in the light, and he looked from me to Rous-Wheeler with a taut mouth. "I have to go over to the plane, Mr. Rous-Wheeler, and I think it would be best if you came with me." He came behind me and bent down to check that his chains were still effective, which unfortunately they were. "You look so gentle, dear boy," he said into my ear. "So misleading, isn't it?"

They went away and left me alone. I had another go at the chains, tantalized by the Cessna standing so close behind me; but this time Yardman had been more careful. The girder was rooted in concrete, the chain wouldn't fray like rope, and try as I might I couldn't slide my hands out.

Little time to go, I thought. And no question left. There wasn't much profit in knowing the answers, since in a very short while I would know nothing at all. I thought about that too. I didn't believe in any form of afterlife. To die was to finish. I'd been knocked out several times in racing falls, and death was just a knockout from which one didn't awake. I couldn't honestly say that I much feared it. I never had. Undoubtedly on my part a defect of the imagination, a lack of sensitivity. All I felt was a strong reluctance to leave the party so soon when there was so much I would have liked to do. But there was the messy business of Billy to be got through first . . . and I admitted gloomily to myself that I would have avoided that if I could have dredged up the smallest excuse.

Alf shuffled into the hangar, went across to the rack of gardening tools and took down a spade. I shouted to him, but he showed no sign of having heard, and disappeared as purposefully as he'd come.

More minutes passed. I spent them thinking about Gabriella. Gabriella alive and loving, her solemnity a crust over depths of warmth and strength. A girl for always. For what was left of always.

The lorry came back, halted briefly outside, and rumbled away into the distance. Yardman and all his crew except Alf trooped into the hangar. Giuseppe walked past me across to the sliding doors at the back and opened a space behind the Citroën. A cool draft blew in and sent the dust round in little swirls on the concrete floor, and outside the sky was an intense velvety black.

Yardman said, "Right, Billy. If the crew are on time, we'll be back with them in a little over an hour. I want you ready to go then, immediately the plane has taken off. All jobs done. Understood?"

"O.K." Billy nodded. "Relax."

Yardman walked over and paused in front of me, looking down with a mixture of regret and satisfaction.

"Good-by, my dear boy."

"Good-by," I answered politely.

His taut mouth twisted. He looked across at Billy. "Take no chances, Billy, do you understand? You underestimate this man. He's not one of your fancy nitwits, however much you may want him to be. You ought to know that by now. And Billy, I'm warning you, I'm warning you, my dear Billy, that if you should let him escape at this stage, knowing everything that he does, you may as well put one of your little bullets through your own brain, because otherwise, rest assured, my dear Billy, I will do it for you."

Even Billy was slightly impressed by the cold menace in Yardman's usually uninflected voice. "Yeah," he said uneasily. "Well, he won't bloody escape, not a chance."

"Make sure of it." Yardman nodded, turned, and went and sat in the front passenger seat of the Citroën. Giuseppe beside him started the engine, reversed the car out of the hangar, and drove smoothly away, Yardman facing forward and not looking back. Billy slid the door shut again behind them and came slowly across the concrete, putting his feet down carefully and silently like a stalker. He stopped four paces away, and the silence slowly thickened.

Rous-Wheeler cleared his throat nervously, and it sounded loud.

Billy flicked him a glance. "Go for a walk," he said.

"A . . . walk?"

"Yeah, a walk. One foot in front of the other." He was offensive. "Down the runway and back should just about do it."

Rous-Wheeler understood. He wouldn't meet my eyes and he hadn't even enough humanity to plead for me. He turned his back on the situation and made for the exit. So much for the old school tie.

"Now," said Billy. "Just the two of us."

16

He walked cat-footed round the hangar in his quiet shoes, looking for things. Eventually he came back toward me carrying an old supple broken bicycle chain and a full flat five-gallon tin of petrol. I looked at these objects with what I hoped was fair impassiveness and refrained from asking what he intended to do with them. I supposed I would find out soon enough.

He squatted on his haunches and grinned at me, his face level with mine, the bicycle chain in one hand and the petrol can on the floor in the other. His gun was far away, on the bench.

"Ask me nicely," he said. "And I'll make it easy."

I didn't believe him anyway. He waited through my silence and sniggered.

"You will," he said. "You'll ask all right, your sodding Lordship."

He brought forward the bicycle chain, but instead of hitting me with it as I'd expected he slid it round my ankle and tied it there into two half-hitches. He had difficulty doing this but once the knots were tied the links looked like holding forever. The free end he led through the handle of the petrol can and again bent it back on itself into knots. When he had finished there was a stalk of about six inches between the knots on my ankle and those on the can. Billy picked up the can and jerked it. My leg duly followed, firmly attached. Billy smiled, well satisfied. He unscrewed the cap of the can and let some of the petrol run out over my feet and make a small pool on the floor. He screwed the cap back on, but looser.

Then he went round behind the girder and unlocked both the padlocks on my wrists. The chain fell off, but owing to a mixture of surprise and stiffened shoulders I could do nothing toward getting my hands down to undo the bicycle chain before Billy was across the bay for his gun and turning with it at the ready.

"Stand up," he said. "Nice and easy. If you don't, I'll throw this in the petrol." This, in his left hand, was a cigarette lighter, a gas lighter with a top which stayed open until one snapped it shut. The flame burned bright as he flicked his thumb.

I stood up stiffly, using the girder for support, the sick and certain knowledge of what Billy intended growing like a lump of ice in my abdomen. So much for not being afraid of death. I had changed my mind about it. Some forms were worse than others.

Billy's mouth curled. "Ask then," he said.

I didn't. He waved his pistol slowly toward

the floor. "Outside, matey. I've a little job for you to do. Careful now, we don't want a bleeding explosion in here if we can help it." His face was alight with greedy enjoyment. He'd never had such fun in his life. I found it definitely irritating.

The can was heavy as I dragged it along with slow steps to the door and through onto the grass outside. Petrol slopped continuously in small amounts through the loosened cap, leaving a highly flammable trail in my wake. The night air was sweet and the stars were very bright. There was no moon. A gentle wind. A beautiful night for flying.

"Turn right," Billy said behind me. "That's Alf along there where the light is. Go there, and don't take too bloody long about it, we haven't got all night." He sniggered at his feeble joke.

Alf wasn't more than a tennis court away, but I was fed up with the petrol can before I got there. He had been digging, I found. A six- or seven-foot square of grass had been cut out, the turf lying along one edge in a tidy heap, and about a foot of earth had been excavated into a crumbling mound. A large torch standing on the pile of turf shone on Alf's old face as he stood in the shallow hole. He held the spade loosely and looked at Billy inquiringly.

"Go for a walk," Billy said loudly. Alf interpreted the meaning if not the words, nodded briefly, leaned the spade against the turf, stepped up on to the grass and shuffled away into the engulfing dark.

"O.K., then," said Billy. "Get in there and start digging. Any time you want to stop, you've only got to ask. Just ask."

"And if I do?"

The light shone aslant on Billy's wide bright eyes and his jeering delighted mouth. He lifted the pistol a fraction. "In the head," he said. "And I'll have bloody well beaten you, your effing bloody Lordship. And it's a pity I haven't got the whole lot like you here as well."

"We don't do any harm," I said, and wryly knew that history gave me the lie. There'd been trampling enough done in the past, and resentment could persist for centuries.

"Keep both hands on the spade," he said. "You try and untie the bicycle chain, and you've had it."

He watched me dig, standing safely out of reach of any slash I might make with the spade and snapping his lighter on and off. The smell of petrol rose sharply into my nostrils as it oozed drop by drop through the leaking cap and soaked into the ground I stood on. The earth was soft and loamy, not too heavy to move, but Billy hadn't chosen this task without careful malice aforethought. Try as I might, I found I could scarcely shift a single spadeful without in some way knocking or rubbing my arm against my side. Jersey and shirt were inadequate buffers, and every scoop took its toll. The soreness increased like a geometrical progression.

Billy watched and waited. The hole grew slowly deeper. I told myself severely that a lot of other people had had to face far worse than this, that others before me had dug what they knew to be their own graves, that others had gone up in flames for a principle . . . that it was possible, even if not jolly.

Billy began to get impatient. "Ask," he said. I threw a spadeful of earth at him in reply and very nearly ended things there and then. The gun barrel jerked up fiercely at my head, and then slowly subsided. "You'll be lucky," he said angrily. "You'll have to go down on your bloody knees."

When I was sure my feet must be below his line of sight I tugged my foot as far away from the petrol can as the chain would allow, and jammed the spade down hard on the six inches of links between the knots. It made less noise than I'd feared on the soft earth. I did it again and again with every spadeful, which apart from being slightly rough on my ankle produced no noticeable results.

"Hurry up," Billy said crossly. He flicked the lighter. "Hurry it up."

Excellent advice. Time was fast running out and Yardman would be back. I jammed the spade fiercely down and with a surge of long dead hope felt the battered links begin to split. It wasn't enough. Even if I got free of the petrol can I was still waist deep in a hole, and Billy still had the revolver; but even a little hope was better than none at all. The next slice of the spade split the chain further. The one after that severed it, but I had hit it with such force that when it broke I fell over, sprawling on hands and knees.

"Stand up," Billy said sharply. "Or I'll . . ."

I wasn't listening to him. I was acknowledging with speechless horror that the grave which was big enough for Patrick and Mike and Bob as well as myself was already occupied. My right hand had closed on a piece of cloth which flapped up through the soil. I ran my fingers along it, burrowing, and stabbed them into something sharp. I felt, and knew. A row of pins.

I stood up slowly and stared at Billy. He advanced nearly to the edge of the hole, looked briefly down, and back at me.

"Simon," I said lifelessly. "It's . . . Simon."

Billy smiled. A cold, terrible, satisfied smile.

There was no more time. Time was only the distance from his gun to my head, from his gas lighter to my petrol-soaked shoes and the leaking can at my feet. He'd only been waiting for me to find Simon. His hunger was almost assuaged.

"Well," he said, his eyes wide. "Ask. It's your last chance."

I said nothing.

"Ask," he repeated furiously. "You must."

I shook my head. A fool, I thought, I'm a bloody fool. I must be mad.

"All right," he said, raging. "If I had more time you'd ask. But if you won't . . ." His voice died, and he seemed suddenly almost as afraid as I was at what he was going to do. He hesitated, half lifting the gun instead; but the moment passed and his nerve came back, renewed and pitiless.

He flicked the lighter. The flame shot up, sharp and blazing against the night sky. He poised it just for a second so as to be sure to toss it where I couldn't catch it on the way; and in that second I bent down, picked up the petrol can, and flung it at him. The loose cap unexpectedly came right off on the way up, and the petrol splayed out in a great glittering volatile stream, curving round to meet the flame.

A split second for evasion before the world caught fire.

The flying petrol burned in the air with a great rushing noise and fell like a fountain over both the spots where Billy and I had just been standing. The can exploded with a gust of heat. The grave was a square blazing pit and flames licked over the mound of dug-out soil like brandy on an out-size plum pudding. Five gallons made dandy pyrotechnics.

I rolled out on my back over the lip of the grave with nothing to spare before it became a crematorium, and by some blessed miracle my feet escaped becoming part of the general holocaust. More than I had hoped.

Billy was running away screaming with his coat on fire along the left shoulder and down his arm. He was making frantic efforts to get it off but he was still clinging to his gun and this made it impossible. I had to have the gun and would have fought for it, but as I went after him I saw him drop it and stagger on, tearing at his jacket buttons in panic and agony, and my spine and scalp shuddered at the terror I had escaped.

With weak knees I half stumbled, half ran for the place where the revolver had fallen. The light of the flames glinted on it in the grass, and I bent and took it into my hand, the bulbous silencer heavy on the barrel and the butt a good fit in my palm.

Billy had finally wrenched his jacket off and it lay on the ground ahead in a deserted smoldering heap. Billy himself was still on his feet and making for the hangar, running and staggering and yelling for Alf.

I went after him.

Alf wasn't in the hangar. When I reached it Billy was standing with his back to me in the place where the car had been, rocking on his feet and still yelling. I stepped through the door and shut it behind me.

Billy swung round. The left sleeve of his shirt had burned into ribbons and his skin was red and glistening underneath. He stared unbelievingly at me and then at his gun in my hand. His mouth shut with a snap; and even then he could still raise a sneer.

"You won't do it," he said, panting.

"Earl's sons," I said, "learn to shoot."

"Only birds." He was contemptuous. "You haven't the guts."

302

"You're wrong, Billy. You've been wrong about me from the start."

I watched the doubt creep in and grow. I watched his eyes and then his head move from side to side as he looked for escape. I watched his muscles bunch to run for it. And when I saw that he finally realized in a moment of stark astonishment that I was going to, I shot him.

17

The Cessna had full tanks. Hurriedly I pressed the master switch in the cockpit and watched the needles swing round the fuel gauges. All the instruments looked all right, the radio worked, and the latest date on the maintenance card was only three days old. As far as I could tell from a cursory check, the little aircraft was ready to fly. All the same . . .

Alf and Rous-Wheeler came bursting in together through the door, both of them startled and wild looking and out of breath. Back from their little walks and alarmed by the bonfire. Alf gave an inarticulate cry and hurried over to Billy's quiet body. Rous-Wheeler followed more slowly, not liking it.

"It's Billy," he said, as if stupefied. "Billy."

Alf gave no sign of hearing. They stood looking down at Billy as he lay on his back. There was a small scarlet star just left of his breastbone, and he had died with his eyes wide open, staring sightlessly up to the roof. Alf and Rous-Wheeler looked lost and bewildered.

I climbed quickly and quietly out of the Cessna

and walked round its tail. They turned after a moment or two and saw me standing there not six paces away, holding the gun. I wore black. I imagine my face was grim. I frightened them.

Alf backed away two steps, and Rous-Wheeler three. He pointed a shaking arm at Billy.

"You . . . you killed him."

"Yes." My tone gave him no comfort. "And you too, if you don't do exactly as I say."

He had less difficulty in believing it than Billy. He made little protesting movements with his hands, and when I said, "Go outside; take Alf," he complied without hesitation.

Just outside the door I touched Alf's arm, pointed back at Billy and then down to where the grave was. The flames had burned out.

"Bury Billy," I shouted in his ear.

He heard me, and looked searching into my face. He too found no reassurance, and he was used to doing what I said. Accepting the situation with only a shade more dumb resignation than usual he went slowly back across the concrete. I watched him shut the glazing eyes with rough humane fingers, and remembered the cup of coffee he'd given me when I badly needed it. He had nothing to fear from me as long as he stayed down by the grave. He picked Billy up, swung him over his shoulder in a fireman's lift, and carried him out and away across the grass, a sturdy old horseman who should never have got caught up in this sort of thing. Any more than I should.

I stretched an arm back into the hangar and

pulled down the lever which controlled the runway lights. At each end of the long strip the four powerful beams sprang out, and in that glow Alf could see where he was going and what he was going to do.

That Cessna, I thought, glancing at it, probably had a range of about six or seven hundred miles. . . .

"You," I said abruptly to Rous-Wheeler. "Go and get into the plane we came in. Go up the forward steps, back through the galley, right back through the cabin, and sit down on those seats. Understand?"

"What . . . ?" he began nervously.

"Hurry up."

He gave me another frightened glance and set off to the plane, a lumbering gray shape behind the runway lights. I walked three steps behind him and unsympathetically watched him stumble in his fear.

"Hurry," I said again, and he stumbled faster. The thought of the Citroën returning was like a devil on my tail. I was just not going to be taken again. There were five bullets left in the gun. The first for Rous-Wheeler, the next for Yardman, and after that . . . he would have Giuseppe with him, and at least two others. Not nice.

"Faster," I said.

Rous-Wheeler reached the ladder and stumbled up it, tripping over half the steps. He went awkwardly back through the plane just as I had said and flopped down panting on one of the seats. I followed him. Someone, Alf I supposed, had given the mares some hay, and one of the bales from Billy's now dismantled wall had been clipped open and split. The binding wire from it lay handy on the flattened aft box. I picked it up to use on Rous-Wheeler, but there was nothing on the comfortable upholstered double seat I could tie him to.

He made no fuss when I bound his wrists together. His obvious fear made him flabby and malleable, and his eyes looked as if he could feel shock waves from the violence and urgency which were flowing through me.

"Kneel down," I said, pointing to the floor in front of the seats. He didn't like that. Too undignified.

"Kneel," I said. "I haven't got time to bother about your comfort."

With a pained expression that at any other time would have been funny he lowered himself onto his knees. I slid the end of the wire through one of the holes in the seat anchorages on the floor, and fastened him there securely by the wrists.

"I s . . . say," he protested.

"You're bloody lucky to be alive at all, so shut up."

He shut up. His hands were tied only a couple of feet away from the blanket which covered Patrick. He stared at the quiet mound and he didn't like that either. Serve him right, I thought callously.

"What . . . what are you going to do?" he
said.

I didn't answer. I went back up the cabin, looking at the way they'd re-stored the cargo. Aft
box still flat. The walls of the next one, dismantled, had been stacked in the starboard alley.
On the peat tray now stood a giant packing case
six feet long, four feet wide, and nearly five feet
tall. Chains ran over it in both directions, fastening
it down to the anchorages. It had rope handles
all the way round, and Yardman had said something about using a block and tackle, but all the
same maneuvering it into its present position must
have been a tricky sweaty business. However,
for the sake of forwarding the passage of this
uninformative crate Yardman had also been prepared to steal a plane and kill three airmen. Those
who had no right to it wanted it very badly.

I went up farther. The four mares were unconcernedly munching at full haynets and paid
me scant attention. Through the galley and into
the space behind the cockpit, where Mike's body
still lay. Burial had been the last of the jobs.
Uncompleted.

The luggage compartment held four more
crates, the size of tea chests. They all had rope
handles and no markings.

Beyond them was the open door. It represented
to me a last chance of not going through with
what I had in mind. Yardman hadn't yet come
back, and the Cessna was ready. If I took it,
with its radio and full tanks, I would undoubtedly

be safe, and Yardman's transport business would be busted. But he'd still have the DC-4 and the packing cases. . . .

Abruptly I pulled up the telescopic ladder and shut the door with a clang. Too much trouble, I told myself, to change my mind now. I'd have to take Rous-Wheeler all the way back to the Cessna or shoot him, and neither course appealed. But the situation I found in the cockpit nearly defeated me before I began.

Billy had shot Bob as he sat, through the back of the head. The upper part of him had fallen forward over the wheel, the rest held firmly to the seat by the still fastened safety strap across his thighs. In the ordinary way even stepping into the copilot's seat in the cramped space was awkward enough, and lifting a dead man out of it bodily was beyond me. Blacking my mind to the sapping thought that this was a man I had known, and considering him solely as an object which spelled disaster to me if I didn't move it I undid the seat belt, heaved the pathetic jack-knifed figure round far enough to clear his feet and head from the controls, and fastened the belt tight across him again in his new position, his back half toward me.

With the same icy concentration I sat in Patrick's place and set about starting the plane. Switches. Dozens of switches everywhere. On the control panel, on the roof, in the left side wall and in the bank of throttles on my right. Each labeled in small metal letters, and too many having to be set correctly before the plane would fly.

Patrick had shown me how. Quite different from doing it. I pared the pre-starting checks down to the barest minimum; fuel supply on, mixture rich, propeller revs maximum, throttle just open, brakes on, trimmer central, direction indicator synchronized with the compass.

My boats were burned with the first ignition switch, because it worked. The three-bladed propeller swung and ground and the inner port engine roared into action with an earsplitting clatter. Throttle too far open. Gently I pulled the long lever with its black knob down until the engine fell back to warming-up speed, and after that in quick succession and with increasing urgency I started the other three. Last, I switched on the headlights. Alf might not have heard the engines, but he would certainly see the lights. It couldn't be helped. I had to be able to see where I was going. With luck he wouldn't know what to do, and do nothing.

I throttled back a bit and took the brakes off and the plane began to roll. Too fast. Too fast. I was heading straight for the runway lights and could smash them, and I needed them alight. I pulled the two starboard throttles back for a second and the plane slued round in a sort of skid and missed the lights and rolled forward on to the runway.

The wind was behind me, which meant taxiing to the far end and turning back to take off. No one ever taxied a DC-4 faster. And at the far end I skipped all the power checks and everything else I'd been taught and swung the plane round facing the way I'd come and without a pause pushed forward all the four throttles wide open.

The great heavy plane roared and vibrated and began to gather speed with what seemed to me agonizing slowness. The runway looked too short. Grass was slower than tarmac, the strip was designed for light aircraft, and heaven alone knew the weight of that packing case. . . . For short runways, lower flaps. The answer came automatically from the subconscious, not as a clear coherent thought. I put my hand on the lever and lowered the trailing edges of the wings. Twenty degrees. Just under halfway. Full flaps were brakes. . . .

Yardman came back.

Unlike Alf, he knew exactly what to do, and wasted no time doing it. Toward the far end the Citroën was driven straight out onto the center line of the runway, and my headlights shone on distant black figures scrambling out and running toward the hangar. Swerve wide enough to miss the car, I thought, and I'll get unbalanced on rough ground and pile up. Go straight up the runway and not be able to lift off in time, and I'll hit it either with the wheels or the propellers. . . .

Yardman did what Alf didn't. He switched off the runway lights. Darkness clamped down like a sack over the head. Then I saw that the plane's bright headlights raised a gleam on the car now frighteningly close ahead and at least gave me the direction to head for. I was going far too fast to stop, even if I'd felt like it. Past the point of no return, and still on the ground. I eased gently back on the control column, but she wouldn't come. The throttles were wide; no power anywhere in reserve. I ground my teeth and with the car coming back to me now at a hundred miles an hour hung on for precious moments I couldn't spare, until it was then or never. No point in never. I hauled back on the control column and at the same time slammed up the lever which retracted the undercarriage. Belly flop or car crash; I wasn't going to be around to have second thoughts. But the DC-4 flew. Unbelievably there was no explosive finale, just a smooth roaring upward glide. The plane's headlights slanted skyward, the car vanished beneath, the friction of the grass fell away. Airborne was the sweetest word in the dictionary.

Sweat was running down my face; part exertion, part fear. The DC-4 was heavy, like driving a fully loaded pantechnicon after passing a test on empty minis, and the sheer muscle power needed to hold it straight on the ground and get it into the air was under the circumstances exhausting. But it was up, and climbing steadily at a reasonable angle, and the hands were circling reassuringly round the clock face of the altimeter. Two thousand, three thousand, four thousand feet. I leveled out at that and closed the throttles a little as the airspeed increased to two-twenty knots. A slow old plane, built in 1945. Two-twenty was the most it could manage.

The little modern Cessna I'd left behind was just about as fast. Yardman had brought a pilot. If he too took off without checks, he could be only scant minutes behind.

Get lost, I thought. I'd the whole sky to get lost in. The headlights were out, but from habit I'd switched on the navigation lights on the wing tips and tail and also the revolving beacon over the cockpit. The circling red beam from it washed the wings alternately with pale pink light. I switched it out, and the navigation lights too. Just one more broken law in a trail of others.

The runway had been laid out from due east to west. I had taken off to the west and flown straight on, urgent to get out, regardless of where. Too easy for them. I banked tentatively to the left and felt the plane respond cumbrously, heavy on my arms. Southwest, into the wind. I straightened up and flew on, an invisible shell in the darkness, and after five minutes knew they wouldn't find me. Not with the Cessna, anyway.

The tight-strung tension of my nerves relaxed a little, with most uncomfortable results. I was suddenly far too aware of the wicked square of burn over my ribs, and realized that I hadn't really felt it since the moment I found Simon. Under the pressure of events its insistent message hadn't got through. Now it proceeded to rectify that with enthusiasm.

Weakness seeped down my limbs. I shivered,

although I was still sweating from exertion. My hands started trembling on the wheel, and I began to realize the extent to which I was unfit to fly anything, let alone take a first try at an airliner way out of my normal class. But far worse than the physical stress was the mental let down which accompanied it. It was pride which had got me into that plane and up into the air. Nothing but pride. I was still trying to prove something to Billy, even though he was dead. I hadn't chosen the DC-4 because of any passionate conviction that the ultlrasonic gadget needed saving at all costs, but simply to show them, Yardman and Billy's ghost, that there wasn't much I couldn't do. Childish, vainglorious, stupid, ridiculous: I was the lot.

And now I was stuck with it. Up in the air in thundering tons of metal, going I didn't know where.

I wiped the sleeve of my jersey over my face and tried to think. Direction and height were vital if I were ever to get down again. Four thousand feet, I thought, looking at the altimeter; at that height I could fly straight into a mountain . . . if there were any. Southwest steady, but southwest from where? I hunted round the cockpit for a map of any sort, but there wasn't one to be found.

Patrick had said we were in Italy, and Giuseppe was Italian, and so was the registration on the Cessna, and the ultrasonic device had been driven straight from Brescia. Conclusive, I thought.

Northern Italy, probably somewhere near the east coast. Impossible to get closer than that. If I continued southwest, in the end I'd be over the Mediterranean. And before that . . . new sweat broke out on my forehead. Between the northern plain and the Mediterranean lay the Apennines, and I couldn't remember at all how high they were. But four thousand was much too low . . . and for all I knew they were only a mile ahead. . . .

I put the nose up and opened the throttles and slowly gained height. Five thousand, six thousand, seven thousand, eight. That ought to be enough . . . The Alps only reached above twelve thousand at the peaks, and the Apennines were a good deal lower. I was guessing. They might be higher than I thought. I went up again to ten thousand.

At that height I was flying where I had no business to be, and at some point I'd be crossing the airways to Rome. Crossing a main road in the dark, without lights. I switched the navigation lights on again, and the revolving beacon too. They wouldn't give much warning to a jetliner on a collision course, but possibly better than none.

The thunderous noise of the engines was tiring in itself. I stretched out a hand for Patrick's head-set and put it on, the padded earphones reducing the din to a more manageable level. I had taken it for granted from the beginning that Yardman would have put the radio out of order before ever asking Patrick to change course, and some short tuning with the knobs confirmed it. Not a peep or crackle from the air. There had been just a chance that he wouldn't have disconnected the V.O.R. — Very high frequency Omni-Range — by which one navigated from one radio beacon to the next; it worked independently of two-way ground-to-air communication, and he might have needed to use it to find the airfield we had landed on. But that too was dead.

Time, I thought. If I didn't keep track of the time I'd be more lost than ever. I looked at my watch. Half-past eleven. I stared at the hands blankly. If they'd said half nine or half one it would have felt the same. The sort of time one measured in minutes and hours had ceased to exist in a quiet street in Milan. I shook myself. Half-past eleven. From now on it was important. Essential. Without maps or radio, time and the compass were going to decide my fate. Like all modern pilots I had been taught to stick meticulously to using all the aids and keeping all the regulations. The "seat of the pants" stuff of the pioneers was held to be unscientific and no longer necessary. This was a fine time to have to learn it from scratch.

If I'd been up for a quarter of an hour, I thought, and if I'd started from the northern plain, and if I could only remember within a hundred miles how broad Italy was, then I might have some idea of when I'd be over the sea. Not yet, anyway. There were pinpricks of light below me, and several small clusters of towns. No conveniently lit airports with welcoming runways.

If I'd taken the Cessna, I thought wretchedly, it would have been easy. Somewhere, by twiddling the knobs, I'd have raised radio contact with the ground. The international air language was English. A piece of cake. They'd have told me my position, what course to set, how to get down, everything. But if I'd taken the Cessna, I would have had to leave the DC-4 intact, because of the mares. I'd thought at first of piling a couple more five-gallon cans under the big plane and putting a match to it, and then remembered the living half of the cargo. Yardman might be cold-bloodedly prepared to kill three airmen, but I balked at roasting alive four horses. And I couldn't get them out, because the plane carried no ramp. With time I could have put the engines out of action . . . and with time they could have mended them again. But I hadn't had time. If I'd done that, I couldn't have got the Cessna out and away before Yardman's return.

The useless thoughts squirreled round and round, achieving nothing. I wiped my face again on the sleeve of my jersey and understood why Patrick had nearly always flown in shirt sleeves, even though it was winter.

Italy couldn't be much wider than England, if as wide. A hundred and twenty, a hundred and forty nautical miles. Perhaps more. I hadn't looked at the time when I took off. I should have. It was routine. I hadn't a hope if I couldn't concentrate better than that. A hundred and forty

317

miles at two-twenty knots . . . say a hundred-and sixty miles to be sure . . . it would take somewhere between forty and forty-five minutes. If I'd had the sense to look at my watch earlier I would have known how far I'd gone.

The lights below grew scarcer and went out. It was probably too soon to be the sea . . . it had to be mountains. I flew on for some time, and then checked my watch. Midnight. And still no lights underneath. The Apennines couldn't be so broad . . . but if I went down too soon, I'd hit them. I gave it another five minutes and spent them wishing Billy's burns would let up again. They were a five-star nuisance.

Still no lights. I couldn't understand it. I couldn't possibly still be over the narrow Apennines. It was no good. I'd have to go down for a closer look. I throttled back, let the nose go down, and watched the altimeter hands go anti-clockwise through seven, six, five, four. At four thousand feet I leveled out again, and the night was as black as ever. I'd certainly hit no mountains, but for all I could see I was a lost soul in Limbo. It wasn't a safe feeling, not at all.

When at last I saw lights ahead I was much more uneasy than reassured. It was twelve-fifteen by my watch, which meant I had come nearly two hundred miles already, and Italy couldn't be as wide as that. Or at least I wouldn't have thought so.

The lights ahead resolved themselves into little

clusters strung out in a horizontal line. I knew the formation too well to mistake it. I was approaching a coastline. Incredulity swamped me. I was approaching *from the sea.*

Nightmares weren't in it. I felt a great sense of unreality, as if the world had spun and rearranged its face, and nothing was ever going to be familiar again. I must be somewhere, I thought, taking a fierce grip on my escaping imagination. But where on earth, where literally on earth, was I?

I couldn't go on flying blindly southwest forever. The coastline must have a shape. About three miles short of it I banked to the right, wheeling northward, guided by nothing more rational than instinct, and flew along parallel with the few and scattered lights on the shore. The sea beneath was black but the land was blacker. The line where they met was like ebony against coal, a shadowy change of texture, a barely perceptible rub of one mass against another.

I couldn't, I thought, bullying my mind into some sort of order, I couldn't possibly have flown straight across the Gulf of Genoa and now be following the Italian coast northward from Alassio. There weren't enough lights, even for that time of night. And I knew that coastline well. This one, I didn't. Moreover, it ran due north for far too long. I had already been following it for fifteen minutes; fifty-five miles.

It had to be faced that I'd been wrong about where I started from. Or else the directional gyro was jammed. It couldn't be. . . . I'd checked it twice against the remote reading compass, which worked independently. I checked again: they matched. They couldn't both be wrong. But I *must* have started in Italy. I went right back in my mind to the flight out, when Patrick had first turned east. It had been east. I was still sure of that, and that was all.

There was a flashing light up ahead, on the edge of the sea. A lighthouse. Very useful if I'd had a nautical chart, which I hadn't. I swept on past the lighthouse and stopped dead in my mental tracks. There was no land beyond.

I banked the plane round to the left and went back. The lighthouse stood at the end of a long narrow finger of land pointing due north. I flew southward along the western side of it for about twenty miles until the sporadic lights spread wider and my direction swung again to the southwest. A fist pointing north.

Supposing I'd been right about starting from Italy, but wrong about being so far east. Then I would have been over the sea when I thought I was over the mountains. Supposing I'd been going for longer than a quarter of an hour when I first looked at my watch; then I would have gone farther than I guessed. All the same, there simply wasn't any land this shape in the northern Mediterranean, not even an island.

An island of this size. . . .

Corsica.

It couldn't be, I thought. It couldn't be so far

south. I wheeled the plane round again and went back to the lighthouse. If it was Corsica and I flew northwest I'd reach the south of France and be back on the map: If it was Corsica I'd started from right down on the southern edge of the northern plain, not near Trieste or Venice as I'd imagined. It wasn't impossible. It made sense. The world began to fall back into place. I flew northwest over the black invisible sea. Twenty-seven minutes. About a hundred miles.

The strings and patterns of lights along the French coast looked like lace sewn with diamonds, and were just as precious. I turned and followed them westward, looking for Nice Airport. It was easy to spot by day; the runways seemed to be almost on the beach, as the airfield had been built on an outward curve of the shoreline. But either I was farther west than I thought, or the airport had closed for the night, because I missed it. The first place I was sure of was Cannes with its bay of embracing arms, and that was so close to Nice that if the runway had been lit I must have seen it.

A wave of tiredness washed through me, along with a numb feeling of futility. Even if I could find one, which was doubtful, I couldn't fly into a major airport without radio, and all the minor ones had gone to bed. I couldn't land anywhere in the dark. All I looked like being able to do was fly around in circles until it got light again and land at Nice . . . and the fuel would very likely give out before then.

It was at that depressing point that I first thought about trying to go all the way to England. The homing instinct in time of trouble. Primitive. I couldn't think of a thing against it except that I was likely to go to sleep from tiredness on the way, and I could do that even more easily going round in circles outside Cannes.

Committed from the moment I'd thought of it, I followed the coast until it turned slightly north again and the widespread lights of Marseilles lay beneath. The well-known way home from there lay up the Rhone Valley over the beacons at Montélimar and Lyons, with a left wheel at Dijon to Paris. But though the radio landmarks were unmistakable the geographical ones weren't, and I couldn't blindly stumble into the busy Paris complex without endangering every other plane in the area. North of Paris was just as bad, with the airlines to Germany and the east. South, then. A straight line across France south of Paris. It would be unutterably handy to have known where Paris lay; what precise bearing. I had to guess again . . . and my first guesses hadn't exactly been a riotous triumph.

Three-twenty degrees, I thought. I'd try that. Allow ten degrees for wind drift from the south-west. Three ten. And climb a bit . . . the center of France was occupied by the Massif Central and it would be fairly inefficient to crash into it. I increased the power and went back up to ten thousand feet. That left fuel the worst problem of all.

I'd taken off on the main tanks and the gauges now stood at half full. I switched over to the auxiliaries and they also were half full. And half empty, too. The plane had been refueled at Milan that morning, ten centuries ago. It carried . . . I thought searchingly back to Patrick's casually thrown out snippets of information the first day I flew with him . . . it carried twelve hundred United States gallons, giving a range of approximately eighteen hundred miles in normal conditions with a normal load. The load, though unconventional, was normal enough in weight. The condition of the weather was perfect, even if the condition of the pilot wasn't. Nine hundred miles from Marseilles would see me well over England, but it wouldn't take much more than four hours at the present speed until the tanks ran dry and it would still be too dark. . . .

There was just one thing to be done about that. I put my hand on the throttle levers and closed them considerably. The airspeed fell back from two-twenty, back through two hundred, one-eighty, steadied on one-fifty. I didn't dare go any slower than that because one thing Patrick hadn't told me was the stalling speed, and a stall I could do without. The nose wanted to go down heavily with the decreased airspeed and I was holding it up by brute strength, the wheel of the control column lodged against my whole left forearm. I stretched my right hand up to the trimmer handle in the roof and gave it four complete turns, and cursed as a piece of shirt which was sticking to the furrows and burns unhelpfully unstuck itself. The nose of the plane steadied; ten thousand feet at one-fifty knots; and blood oozed warmly through my jersey.

A hundred and fifty knots should reduce the petrol consumption enough for me to stay in the air until long enough after dawn to find an airfield. I hoped. It also meant not four hours ahead, but more than five, and I'd had enough already. Still, now that I knew roughly where I was going, the plane could fly itself. I made small adjustments to the trimmer until the needle on the instrument which showed whether she was climbing or descending pointed unwaveringly to level, and then switched in the automatic pilot. I took my hands off the wheel and leaned back. The DC-4 flew straight on. Very restful.

Nothing happened for several minutes except that I developed a thirst and remembered Rous-Wheeler for the first time since takeoff. Still on his knees, I supposed, and extremely uncomfortable. His bad luck.

There was water in the galley only five or six steps behind me, cold and too tempting. Gingerly I edged out of my seat. The plane took no notice. I took two steps backward. The instruments didn't quiver. I went into the galley and drew a quick cup of water, and went back toward the cockpit drinking it. Clearly the plane was doing splendidly without me. I returned to the galley for a refill of the cold delicious liquid, and when I'd got it, nearly dropped it.

Even above the noise of the engines I could hear Rous-Wheeler's scream. Something about the raw terror in it raised the hair on my neck. That wasn't pain, I thought, not the sort he'd get from cramp anyway. It was fear.

He screamed again, twice.

One of the horses, I thought immediately. If Billy hadn't boxed them properly . . . My newly irrigated mouth went dry again. A loose horse was just too much.

I went back to the cockpit, hurrying. Nothing had moved on the instrument panel. I'd have to risk it.

The plane had never seemed longer, the chains and racks more obstructing. And none of the mares was loose. They weren't even fretting, but simply eating hay. Half relieved, half furious, I went on past the packing case. Rous-Wheeler was still there, still kneeling. His eyes protruded whitely and his face was wet. The last of his screams hung like an echo in the air.

"What the hell's the matter?" I shouted to him angrily.

"He . . ." His voice shrieked uncontrollably. "He . . . moved."

"Who moved?"

"Him." His eyes were staring fixedly at the blanket covering Patrick.

He couldn't have moved. Poor, poor Patrick. I went across and pulled the rug off and stood looking down at him, the tall silent body, the tumbled hair, the big pool of blood under his down-turned face.

Pool of blood.

It was impossible. He hadn't had time to bleed as much as that. I knelt down beside him and rolled him over, and he opened his yellow eyes.

18

He'd been out cold for six hours and he was still unconscious. Nothing moved in his eyes, and after a few seconds they fell slowly shut again.

My fingers were clumsy on his wrist and for anxious moments I could feel nothing; but his pulse was there. Slow and faint, but regular. He was on his way up from the depths. I was so glad that he wasn't dead that had Rous-Wheeler not been there I would undoubtedly have wept. As it was, I fought against the flooding back of the grief I'd suppressed when Billy shot him. Odd that I should be tumbled into such intense emotion only because the reason for it was gone.

Rous-Wheeler stuttered. "What . . . what is it?" with a face the color and texture of putty, and I glanced at him with dislike.

"He's alive," I said tersely.

"He can't be."

"Shut up."

Billy's bullet had hit Patrick high, above the hairline and at a rising angle, and instead of penetrating his skull had slid along outside it. The long, swollen and clotted wound looked dreadful, but was altogether beautiful in comparison with a neat, round hole. I stood up and spread the blanket over him again, to keep him warm. Then, disregarding Rous-Wheeler's protest, I went away up the plane.

In the cockpit nothing had changed. The plane roared steadily on its three-ten heading and all the instruments were like rocks. I touched the back of the copilot, aware again to his presence. The silence in him was eternal; he wouldn't feel my sympathy, but he had it.

Turning back a pace or two, I knelt down beside Mike. He too had been shot in the head, and about him too there was no question. The agile eyebrow was finished. I straightened him out from his crumpled position and laid him flat on his back. It wouldn't help any, but it seemed to give him more dignity. That was all you could give the dead, it seemed; and all you could take away.

The four packing cases in the luggage bay were heavy and had been thrust in with more force than finesse, pushing aside and crushing most of the things already there. Shifting the first case a few inches I stretched a long arm past it and tugged out a blanket, which I laid over Mike. Armed with a second one I went back into the galley. Sometime in the past I'd seen the first-aid box in one of the cupboards under the counter, and to my relief it was still in the same place.

Lying on top of it was a gay parcel wrapped in the striped paper of Malpensa Airport. The doll for Mike's daughter. I felt the jolt physically.

Nothing could soften the facts. I was taking her a dead father for her birthday.

And Gabriella . . . anxiety for her still hovered in my mind like a low cloud ceiling, thick, threatening and unchanged. I picked up the parcel she had wrapped and put it on the counter beside the plastic cups and the bag of sugar. People often did recover from bullets in the lungs; I knew they did. But the precise Italian doctor had only offered hope, and hope had tearing claws. I was flying home to nothing if she didn't live.

Taking the blanket and the first-aid kit I went back to Patrick. In the lavatory compartment I washed my filthy hands and afterward soaked a chunk of cotton wool with clean water to wipe his blood-streaked face. Dabbing dry with more cotton wool I found a large hard lump on his forehead where it had hit the floor; two heavy concussing shocks within seconds, his brain had received. His eyelids hadn't flickered while I cleaned him and with a new burst of worry I reached for his pulse; but it was still there, faint but persevering.

Sighing with relief I broke open the wrappings of a large sterile wound dressing, laid it gently over the deep gash in his scalp, and tied it on with the tape. Under his head I slid the second blanket, folded flat, to shield him a little from the vibration in the aircraft's metal skin. I loosened his tie and undid the top button of his shirt and also the waistband of his trousers, and beyond that there was no help I could give him. I stood up slowly with the first-aid kit and turned to go.

With anxiety bordering on hysteria Rous-Wheeler shouted, "You aren't going to leave me like this again, are you?"

I looked back at him. He was half sitting, half kneeling, with his hands still fastened to the floor in front of him. He'd been there for nearly three hours, and his flabby muscles must have been cracking. It was probably too cruel to leave him like that for the rest of the trip. I put the first-aid kit down on the flattened box, pulled a bale of hay along on the starboard side and lodged it against the ultrasonic packing case. Then with Alf's cutter I clipped through the wire round his wrists and pointed to the bale.

"Sit there."

He got up slowly and stiffly, crying out. Shuffling, half falling, he sat where I said. I picked up another piece of wire and in spite of his protests bound his wrists together again and fastened them to one of the chains anchoring the crate. I didn't want him bumbling all over the plane and breathing down my neck.

"Where are we going?" he said, the pomposity reawakening now that he'd got something from me.

I didn't answer.

"And who is flying the plane?"

"George," I said, finishing his wrists with a twirl he'd never undo. "Naturally."

"George who?"

"A good question," I said, nodding casually.

He was beautifully disconcerted. I left him to stew in it, picked up the first-aid kit, checked again that Patrick's pulse was plodding quietly along, and made my way back to the galley.

There were a number of dressings in the first-aid box, including several especially for burns, and I wasn't keen on my shirt sticking and tearing away again. Gingerly I pulled my jersey up under my arms and tucked the side of the shirt away under it. No one except Billy would have found the view entertaining, and the air at once started everything going again at full blast. I opened one of the largest of the burn dressings and laid it in place with that exquisite kind of gentleness you only give to yourself. Even so, it was quite enough. After a moment I fastened it on and pulled my shirt and jersey down on top. It felt so bad for a bit that I really wished I hadn't bothered.

I drank another cup of water, which failed to put out the fire. The first-aid kit, on further inspection, offered a three-way choice in pain killers: a bottle each of aspirin and codeine tablets, and six ampoules of morphine. I shook out two of the codeines, and swallowed these. Then I packed everything back into the box, shut the lid, and left it on the counter.

Slowly I went up to the cockpit and stood looking at the instruments. All working fine. I fetched a third blanket from the luggage bay and tucked it over and round the body of Bob. He became immediately less of a harsh reality, and I wondered if that was why people always covered the faces of the dead.

I checked the time. An hour from Marseilles. Only a hundred and fifty miles, and a daunting way still to go. I leaned against the metal wall and shut my eyes. It was no good feeling the way I did with so much still to do. Parts of Air Ministry regulations drifted ironically into my mind. . . . "Many flying accidents have occurred as a result of pilots flying while medically unfit . . . and the more exacting the flying task the more likely are minor indispositions to be serious . . . so don't go up at all if you are ill enough to need drugs . . . and if coffee isn't enough to keep you awake you are not fit to fly."

Good old Air Ministry, I thought; they'd hit the nail on the head. Where they would have me be was down on the solid earth, and I wholeheartedly agreed.

The radio, I thought inconsequentially. Out of order. I opened my eyes, pushed myself off the wall, and set about finding out why. I hadn't far to look. Yardman had removed all the circuit breakers, and the result was like an electric light system with no fuses in the fuse box. Every plane carried spares, however. I located the place where the spares should have been, and there weren't any. The whole lot in Yardman's pockets, no doubt.

Fetching a fresh cup of water, I climbed again into Patrick's seat and put on the headset to reduce the noise. I leaned back in the comfortable leather upholstery and rested my elbows on the stubby arms, and after a while the codeine and the bandage turned in a reasonable job.

Outside the sky was still black and dotted with brilliant stars, and the revolving anti-collision beacon still skimmed pinkly over the great wide span of the wings, but there was also a new misty grayish quality in the light. Not dawn. The moon coming up. Very helpful of it, I thought appreciatively. Although it was well on the wane I would probably be able to see what I was doing the next time I flew out over the coastline. I began to work out what time I would get there. More guesses. Northwest across France coast to coast had to be all of five hundred miles. It had been one-forty when I left Marseilles; was three-ten now. E.T.A. English Channel, somewhere about five.

Patrick's being alive made a lot of difference to everything. I was now thankful without reservation that I had taken the DC-4 however stupid my motive at the time, for if I'd left it, and Yardman had found him alive, they would simply have pumped another bullet into him, or even buried him as he was. The tiring mental merry-go-round of whether I should have taken the Cessna troubled me no more.

I yawned. Not good. Of all things I couldn't afford to go to sleep. I shouldn't have taken those pills, I thought; there was nothing like the odd spot of agony for keeping you awake. I rubbed my hand over my face and it felt as if it belonged to someone else.

I murdered Billy, I thought.

I could have shot him in the leg and left him to Yardman, and I'd chosen to kill him myself. Choice and those cold-blooded seconds of revenge . . . they made it murder. An interesting technical point, where self-defense went over the edge into something else. Well . . . no one would ever find out; and my conscience didn't stir.

I yawned again more deeply, and thought about eating one of Patrick's bananas. A depleted bunch of them lay on the edge by the windscreen, with four blackening stalks showing where he had fended off starvation on the morning trip. But I imagined the sweet pappiness of them in my mouth, and left them alone. I wasn't hungry enough. The last thing I'd eaten had been the lasagna with Gabriella.

Gabriella. . . .

After a while I got up and went through the plane to look at Patrick. He lay relaxed and un-moving, but his eyes were open again. I knelt beside him and felt his pulse. Unchanged.

"Patrick," I said. "Can you hear?"

There was no response of any sort.

I stood up slowly and looked at Rous-Wheeler sitting on the bale of hay. He seemed to have shrunk slightly as if the gas had leaked out, and there was a defeated sag to his whole body which showed that he realized his future was unlikely to be rosy. I left him without speaking and went back to the cockpit.

Four o'clock. France had never seemed so large. I checked the fuel gauges for the hundredth time and saw that the needles on the auxiliary tanks were knocking uncomfortably near zero. The plane's four engines used a hundred and fifty gallons an hour at normal speed and even with the power reduced they seemed to be drinking the stuff. Fuel didn't flow automatically from the main tanks when the auxiliaries were empty; one had to switch over by hand. And I simply couldn't afford to use every drop in the auxiliaries, because the engines would stop without warning the second the juice dried up. My fingers hovered on the switch until I hadn't the nerve to wait any longer, and then flipped it over to the mains.

Time passed, and the sleeping country slipped by underneath. When I got to the coast, I thought wearily, I was going to have the same old problem. I wouldn't know within two hundred miles where I was, and the sky was ruthless to the lost. One couldn't stop to ask the way. One couldn't stop at all. A hundred and fifty an hour might be slow in terms of jetliners, but it was much too fast in the wrong direction.

In Patrick's brief case there would be not only a thick book of radio charts but also some topographical ground maps. They weren't needed for ordinary aerial navigation, but they had to be carried in case of radio failure. The brief case was almost certainly somewhere under or behind the four packing cases in the luggage bay. I went

335

to have a look, but I already knew. The heavy cases were jammed in tight, and even if there had been room to pull them all out into the small area behind the cockpit I hadn't enough strength to do it.

At about half-past four I went back for another check on Patrick, and found things very different. He had thrown off the blanket covering him and was plucking with lax uncoordinated hands at the bandage on his head. His eyes were open but unfocused still, and his breath came out in short regular groans.

"He's dying," Rous-Wheeler shouted unhelpfully.

Far from dying, he was up close to the threshold of consciousness, and his head was letting him know it. Without answering Rous-Wheeler I went back along the alley and fetched the morphine from the first-aid kit.

There were six glass ampoules in a flat box, each with its own built-in hypodermic needle enclosed in a glass cap. I read the instruction leaflet carefully and Rous-Wheeler shouted his unasked opinion that I had no right to give an injection; I wasn't a doctor, I should leave it for someone who knew how.

"Do you?" I said.

"Er, no."

"Then shut up."

He couldn't. "Ask the pilot, then."

I glanced at him. "I'm the pilot."

That did shut him up. His jaw dropped to allow

336

a clear view of his tonsils and he didn't say another word.

While I was rolling up his sleeve Patrick stopped groaning. I looked quickly at his face and his eyes moved slowly round to meet mine.

"Henry," he said. His voice didn't reach me, but the lip movement was clear.

I bent down and said, "Yes, Patrick. You're O.K. Just relax."

His mouth moved. I put my ear to his lips, and he said, "My bloody head hurts."

I nodded, smiling. "Not for long."

He watched me snap the glass to uncover the needle and didn't stir when I pushed it into his arm, though I'd never been on the delivering end of an injection before and I must have been clumsy. When I'd finished he was talking again. I put my head down to hear.

"Where . . . are . . . we?"

"On your way to a doctor. Go to sleep."

He lay looking vaguely at the roof for a few minutes and then gradually shut his eyes. His pulse was stronger and not so slow. I put the blanket over him again and tucked it under his legs and arms and with barely a glance for Rous-Wheeler went back to the cockpit.

A quarter to five. Time to go down. I checked all the gauges, found I was still carrying the box of ampoules, and put it up on the ledge beside the bananas and the cup of water. I switched out the cockpit lights so that I could see better outside, leaving the round dial faces illuminated only by rims of red, and finally unlocked the automatic pilot.

It was when I'd put the nose down and felt again the great weight of the plane that I really doubted that I could ever land it, even if I found an airfield. I wasn't a mile off exhaustion and my muscles were packing up, and not far beyond this point I knew the brain started missing on a cylinder or two, and haze took the place of thought. If I couldn't think in crystalline terms and at reflex speed I was going to make an ir-retrievable mistake, and for Patrick's sake, quite apart from my own, I couldn't afford it.

Four thousand feet. I leveled out and flew on, looking down through the moonlit blackness, searching for the sea. Tiredness was insidious and crept up like a tide, I thought, until it drowned you. I shouldn't have taken that codeine, it was probably making me sleepy . . . though I'd had some at other times after racing injuries, and never noticed it. But that was on the ground, with nothing to do but recover.

There. There was the sea. A charcoal change from black, the moonlight just reflecting enough to make it certain. I flew out a little way, banked the plane to the right and began to follow the shore. Compass heading, east southeast. This seemed extraordinary, but it certainly had to be the northeast coast of France somewhere, and I wasn't going to lose myself again. There were lighthouses, flashing their signals. No charts to interpret them. The biggest port along the coast,

I thought, was Le Havre. I couldn't miss that. There would be a lot of lights even at five in the morning. If I turned roughly north from there I couldn't help but reach England. Roughly was just the trouble. The map in my head couldn't be trusted. Roughly north could find me barging straight into the London Control Zone, which would be even worse than Paris.

It wouldn't be light until six at the earliest. Sunrise had been about a quarter to seven, the day before.

The lights of Le Havre were ahead and then below me before I'd decided a thing. Too slow, I thought numbly, I was already too slow. I'd never get down.

The coast swung northward, and I followed. Five-twenty A.M. The fuel gauges looked reasonable with dawn not far ahead. But I'd got to decide where I was going. I'd got to.

If I simply went on for a bit I'd reach Calais. It still wouldn't be light. Somewhere over in Kent were Lympne, Lydd and Manston airports. Somewhere. My mind felt paralyzed.

I went on and on along the French coast like an automaton until at last I knew I'd gone too far. I hadn't watched the compass heading closely enough and it had crept round from north to nearly east. That light I'd passed a while back, I thought vaguely, the light flashing at five-second intervals, that must have been Gris Nez. I'd gone past Calais. I was nearly round to Belgium. I'd simply got to decide. . . .

The sky was definitely lighter. With surprise I realized that for several minutes the coastline had been easier to see, the water beneath lightening to a flat dark gray. Soon I could look for an airport, but not in Belgium. The explanations would be too complicated. Back to Kent, perhaps. . . .

In a way, the solution when it came was simple. I would go to the place I knew best. To Fenland. In daylight I could find my way unerringly there from any direction, which meant no anxious circling around, and familiarity would cancel out a good deal of the tiredness. The flying club used grass runways which were nothing like long enough for a DC-4, but its buildings had once been part of an old Air Force base, and the concrete runways the bombers had used were still there. Grass grew through the cracks in them and they weren't maintained, but they were marked at the ends with a white cross over a white bar, air traffic signal for a safe enough landing in an emergency.

My mental fog lifted. I banked left and set off north seaward, and only after five decisive minutes remembered the fuel.

The burns were hurting again and my spirits fell to zero. Would I never get it right? I was an amateur, I thought despairingly. Still an amateur. The jockey business all over again. I had never achieved anything worthwhile and I certainly hadn't built the solid life I wanted. Simon had been quite right, I couldn't have gone on carting racehorses all my life; and now that Yard-man Transport no longer existed I wouldn't look for the same job again.

It was a measure of my exhausted state that having once decided to go to Fenland I hadn't the will to plunge back into uncertainty. The fuel margin was far too small for it to be prudent to go so far. Prudence in the air was what kept one alive. If I went to Fenland I'd be landing on a thimbleful, and if the engines stopped five miles away it would be too late to wish I hadn't.

Streaks of faint red crept into the sky and the sea turned to gray pearl. The sky wasn't so clear any more; there were layers of hazy cloud on the horizon, shading from dark gray-blue to a wisp of silver. The moment before dawn had always seemed to me as restoring as sleep, but that time when I really needed it, it had no effect. My eyes felt gritty and my limbs trembled under every strain. And the codeine had worn off.

The coast of East Anglia lay like a great gray blur ahead on my left. I would follow it round, I thought, and go in over the Wash. . . .

A swift dark shape flashed across the front of the DC-4 and my heart jumped at least two beats. A fighter, I thought incredulously. It had been a jet fighter. Another came over the top of me ridiculously close and screamed away ahead leaving me bumping horribly in turbulence he left in his wake. They both turned a long way ahead and roared back toward me, flying level together with their wing tips almost touching. Expert formation pilots, and unfriendly. They closed at something like the speed of sound and swept over the DC-4 with less than a hundred feet between. To them I must have seemed to be standing still. To me, the trail they left me was very nearly the clincher.

Yardman couldn't have found me, I thought desperately. Not after the wavering roundabout route I'd taken. They couldn't have followed me and wouldn't have guessed I'd go up the North Sea . . . It couldn't be Yardman's doing. So who?

I looked out at East Anglia away on my left, and didn't know whether to laugh or die of fear. Americans. East Anglia was stiff with American air bases. They would have picked me up on their radar, an unidentified plane flying in at dawn and not answering to radio. Superb watchdogs, they would send someone to investigate . . . and they'd found a plane without registration numbers or markings of any sort. A plane like that couldn't be up to any good . . . had to be hostile. One could almost hear them think it.

They wouldn't start shooting, not without making sure . . . not yet. If I just went straight on and could deal with the buffeting, what would they do? I wouldn't let them force me down . . . I had only to plod straight on. . . . They swept past on each side and threw the DC-4 about like a cockleshell.

I couldn't do it, I thought, not this on top of everything else. My hands were slipping on the wheel with sweat. If the fighters went on much longer the sturdy old plane would shake to bits. They came past twice more and proved me wrong. They also reduced me to a dripping wreck. But after that they vanished somewhere above me, and when I looked up I saw them still circling overhead like angry bees. They were welcome to accompany me home, I thought weakly, if that was only where they'd stay.

I could see the lightship off Cromer still flashing its group of four every fifteen seconds. The first real sign of home. Only sixty miles to go. Fifteen minutes to the lightship in the Wash, and the sun rose as I went over it. I turned the plane on to the last leg to Fenland, and up above the escorts came with me.

The fuel gauges looked horrible. I drove what was left of my mind into doing some vital checks. Pitch fully fine, brakes off, mixture rich, fuel pumps on. There must have been a list some-where, but heaven knew where. I had no business to be flying the plane at all, I didn't know its drill. . . . The Air Ministry could take away my license altogether and I was liable for a prison sentence as well. Except, I thought suddenly with a flicker of amusement, that Patrick was qualified to fly it, and he might be said to be technically in charge. Resident, anyway.

I throttled back and began to go down. If I managed it, I thought, I would be a professional. The decision was suddenly standing there full blown like a certainty that had been a long time growing. This time it wasn't too late. I would take Tom Wells' job and make him stick to it when he inevitably found out my name. I would fly his car firm executives around and earn the sort of life I wanted, and if it meant giving up racing . . . I'd do that too.

The airspeed indicator stood at a hundred and thirty knots on the slow descent, and I could see the airfield ahead. The fighters were there already, circling high. The place would be crawling with investigators before my wheels stopped rolling. Questions, when I could do with sleep.

The distant orange wind sock blew out lazily, still from the southwest. There wasn't enough fuel for frills like circuits, the gauges registered empty. I'd have to go straight in, and get down first time . . . get down. If I could.

I was close now. The club building developed windows, and there was Tom's bungalow. . . .

A wide banking turn to line up with the old concrete runway. . . . It looked so narrow, but the bombers had used it. Six hundred feet. My arms were shaking. I pushed down the lever of the undercarriage and the light went green as it locked. Five hundred . . . I put on full flap, maximum drag . . . retrimmed . . . felt the plane get slower and heavier, soft on the controls . . . I could stall and fall out of the sky . . . a shade more power . . . still some fuel left . . . the end of the runway ahead with its white cross coming up to meet me, rushing up . . . two hundred feet . . . I was doing a hundred and twenty . . . I'd never landed a plane with a cockpit

so high off the ground . . . allow for that.
. . . One hundred . . . lower . . . I seemed to
be holding the whole plane up. . . . I closed
the throttles completely and leveled out as the
white cross and the bar slid underneath, and
waited an agonized few seconds while the speed
fell down and down until there was too little
lift to the wings and the whole mass began to
sink . . .

The wheels touched and bounced, touched and
stayed down, squeaking and screeching on the
rough surface. With muscles like jelly, with only
tendons, I fought to keep her straight. I couldn't
crash now . . . I wouldn't. The big plane rock-
eted along the bumpy concrete . . . I'd never
handled anything so powerful . . . I'd misjudged
the speed and landed too fast and she'd never
stop. . . .

A touch of brake . . . agonizing to be gentle
with them and fatal if I wasn't. . . . They gripped
and tugged and the plane stayed straight . . .
more brake, heavier . . . it was making an impression . . . she wouldn't flip over onto her
back, she had a tricycle undercarriage with a nose
wheel . . . I'd have to risk it. . . . I pulled the
brakes on hard and the plane shuddered with
the strain, but the tires didn't burst and I hadn't
dipped and smashed a wing or bent the propellers
and there wasn't going to be a scratch on the
blessed old bus. . . . She slowed to taxiing speed
with a hundred yards to spare before the runway
tapered off into barbed wire and gorse bushes.

Anything would have been enough. A hundred yards was a whole future.

Trembling, feeling sick, I wheeled round in a circle and wheeled slowly back up the runway to where it ran closest to the airport buildings. There I put the brakes full on and stretched out a hand which no longer seemed part of me, and stopped the engines. The roar died to a whisper, and to nothing. I slowly pulled off the headset and listened to the cracking noises of the hot metal cooling.

It was done. And so was I. I couldn't move from my seat. I felt disembodied. Burned out. Yet in a sort of exhausted peace I found myself believing that as against all probability I had survived the night, so had Gabriella . . . that away back in Milan she would be breathing safely through her damaged lung. I had to believe it. Nothing else would do.

Through the window I saw Tom Wells come out of his bungalow, staring first up at the circling fighters and then down at the DC-4. He shrugged his arms into his old sheepskin jacket and began to run toward me over the grass.